SHATTERED HEARTS

DEVIL'S DUET (BOOK ONE)

SHATTERED HEARTS

DEVIL'S DUET (BOOK ONE)

VALERIIA MILLER

To the one I love.

In moments of solitude and disorientation, as you come back to an empty home with no one awaiting your arrival, keep in mind that I will stand by your side, steadfast and unchanging. Recall, the darkest hours precede the dawn.

IMPORTANT NOTE

ALRIGHT, I ACKNOWLEDGE THAT SOME INDIVIDUALS, MYSELF INCLUDed, prefer going into a situation without prior knowledge. However, we are all different, and this page is intended for those who prefer to be informed. I want to prevent receiving messages later about how the events in this book may have caused trauma for some readers.

The story ends on a cliffhanger. This is a dark stalker romance where one of the main characters is a serial killer. The content here gets pretty dark and includes a description of torture, murder, stalking, kidnapping, non-con, dub-con, mentions of child abuse, blood, violence, and lots of explicit sexual situations that reckon a few particular kinks involving somnophilia and knife play.

Your mental health matters.

PLAYLIST

Killer - Mareux
Eyes On Fire - Blue Foundation
Digital Bath - Deftones
Close To Heaven - Breaking Benjamin
What You Need - The Weeknd
Spectral Tease - Mareux
Never Tear Us Apart - INXS
Obey - Bring Me The Horizon, YUNGBLUD
Beauty School - Deftones
Love In The Sky - The Weeknd
Change (In The House Of Flies) – Deftones

Pinterest Board

Part 1

THE PHANTASM

CHAPTER
ONE

Lilith

H appiness was once a part of my life. Those quick nine months when I was in the depths of my tranquil haven, immersed in a pool of comforting warmth, devoid of concern—the definition of pure heaven. Until I was inevitably propelled by the forces of nature to emerge from the intimate confines of my mother's womb. It became the first but surely not the last battle I lost.

By and large, *normal* people don't remember the moment they were born, just as they don't recollect much of their early childhood. But I do. The memory of my birth continues to haunt my nightmares, jolting me awake in the dead of night as those horrifying sensations replay themselves over and over again.

Vivid in my recollection are the screams that emanated from my mother's being. Then, the blare of a car horn accompanied by a forceful jolt from her left side compelled her to succumb, collapsing onto the floor of the vehicle with me, ready to emerge at the most inopportune moment.

Oh, the miracle that after a moment, she was in the hospital, and the doctors pulled me out and said that I didn't receive any damage. Even though I felt that massive jolt that seemed to squash every normal person, especially a tiny newborn, I was healthier than any other child. But even though technically, according to all the papers, I was an okay child, I never felt that way.

The day I was born started an inescapable, suffocating cycle of torment.

My precious mother, Claire, had nobody to drive her when I started getting out. Reckless, she took her car and drove herself despite the hellish pain that I was causing her. Of course, that did have consequences. During another contraction, she lost focus right at the crossroad, and the other car crashed into hers. When I was five years old, she confessed that by the time she got into the hospital, she was hoping that I never made it. She was praying, silently begging every single god that ever existed for me not to make it.

But when she heard my squeaky screams and saw my tiny bloody body, kicking and fighting for life, she felt like she was cursed.

That's when she decided to give me such a stupid fucking name: Lilith. The demon herself. Refused to be subservient to the natural order.

Only a demon child can survive such an event.

She ensured that I felt different, as though I wasn't normal. Not like others. That I was never going to be normal because it is something that isn't in my natural code. Never will be.

The memories of my fucked-up childhood occupy my mind mostly when I need to be concentrated and calm. Those bitches.

It's not that I feel the trembling in my hands or my heartbeat becomes more frantic when I start to feel anxious, recalling the words my mother said, and replaying her actions inside my brain. It's more like an inner fight with my little demons that keep whispering shit in both my ears.

The common thing is when people joke about having an angel and a demon on their shoulders that dangle their little feet and whisper bad or good things into their ears. Except I never thought about something good. There are always two red demons on my shoulders. I lean on my left shoulder and rub my ear against it, then I do the same with the right one. Squashing them, hearing their little demonic screechy voices begging me not to do that.

I exhale loudly, as if demonstratively, although there's nobody here. It's me in the middle of nowhere—to be precise—the suburb of beloved New York City, in front of the tiny brown-wooden house surrounded by acres and acres of dark, almost ominous woods. Why almost?

Because the most ominous thing here is the future face of my mommy dearest in three... two... one.

The click of the front door forces me to tightly shut my eyes as if expecting a slap. Not that my mother beat my ass up, I mean, maybe gave me little cuffs on the nape, but nothing more.

"What?" she asks, tone unfriendly, as usual. Eyeing me from head to toe as if expecting to find something new—the thing she does every fucking year—she adds, "Okay. Come in. I don't need this cold air in my house."

Claire grabs my shoulder and pulls me inside the house. Her sharp nails dig into my skin through my sweater, and I almost hiss from the pain. I stumble on that red carpet that is always, and I mean, ALWAYS up, as if waiting for me to come, hook over it, and fall. I step on it and smooth those creases out of harm's way.

"Sorry, Mom," I begin, then awkwardly clear my throat to bring back my normal voice. "I haven't slept well. I brought—"

"I'm not blind, I see what you brought," she huffs in obvious irritation, then takes the damn cake out of my hands (finally).

I bite my already scarred tongue, looking up at the ceiling—the thing I always do whenever I feel like I'm going to snap. Claire is one of the hardest-to-communicate types of people ever, and I am lucky enough to have her as my mother. But no matter how shitty our relationship is, I never allowed myself to say anything.

I don't bite; I feel like it's pointless.

Besides, if I do, I'll immediately regret it. Because she is my mother and that alone says a lot. Yes, she is a bitch, she still thinks I'm some kind of devil and something is wrong with me, and blames me for her shitty life, but she is still my mother. As I mentioned before, she never beat my ass up, never said something too terrifying. She is just lost and alone.

Just like me.

"Happy birthday," I say in a hushed voice. She spares me a look—indecipherable as always. It's hard to tell whether she is angry or sad or doesn't give a shit. Her blank face is always a canvas as if waiting to be painted in different shades of emotions—just begging for them to take over—but never actually reaching this point.

The piercing scream from the living room distracts both of us, and Mother almost drops the cake, flying to the living room. A confused expression takes over my face. "You have visitors?"

As I step inside the living room, my jaw drops to the floor. A small baby bed with a child in it. It can't be more than two years old, dressed in pink pajamas, which tells me that it is probably a girl. I meet her gaze and she stops crying for a moment. Now we're both sharing *who the fuck are you* expressions on our faces.

"Ayla's child," Mother explains calmly. As if I have a fucking clue who Ayla is. My confusion is palpable, so she adds, never bothering to face me, "My neighbor's kid. She has a job interview today and asked me to watch her."

4

Mother takes the baby out of the bed, carefully—so fucking carefully—and wraps her arms around her little body. She walks to the closet, opens it, and takes a small shiny toy out of it. "Calm down, sweetie," she sings, placating the baby by distracting her with a toy. She wags it in front of her face, stealing all of her attention from me.

And then she smiles. My mother smiles. At her neighbor's kid. Something inside of me clicks—an emotion I can't quite pinpoint. My heart squeezes into a painful knot, and I feel deprived of oxygen. It's as though my mother took a needle and punctured both of my lungs, robbing me of every breath. I remain here, fixed in the living room doorway, without any movement. Why am I unable to move?

"Lilith." Her voice makes me flinch, and that's when I realize that she's been calling my name for the last minute. "What's wrong now?"

I don't know what kind of look is on my face right now—it feels like half of it is numb, as if I froze one side of it—but I quickly rearrange my features into a neutral, bored, unbothered, always-on expression.

"Nothing." The smile Claire had a moment ago is now no more than just a memory. A memory that no one would believe in if I told them so. Not that I have somebody to tell, but anyway.

"Why are you doing this again?" she asks with evident frustration in her voice. "Why can't you just be normal?"

Define normal. Is calling your child by the name of the female demonic figure from Jewish folklore because she survived a car accident considered normal? No? Then the same question to you, Mother.

"I'm sorry," I apologize for what I am not even sure I have to apologize for. As always. "I just—"

"I don't have time for this." An irritable hiss escapes her lips. "I'm going to put little Mia to bed and then we'll have dinner. Wait in the kitchen."

I nod, because I don't know what else I could do now. I don't even want to think about other options, to be frank. Fighting with Claire is pointless, and I don't have the energy to think about that. I don't have the energy to think about anything besides waiting for this visit to be over.

Every goddamn year is the same. I come to visit my mother only on her birthday—that's the only day in a year she allows me to. Sounds weird when you are talking about paying a visit to the woman who pushed you into this world, but that's the beauty of our fucked-up family.

The remains of it, to be precise. I never knew my father, never even intended to know him. Claire said that he was a madman, always lurking around the house looking for something to be angry about. They are the same in this case, though. She just doesn't see it.

So I was raised by a single mother who spent most of her years shitting on me, blaming me for being born and ruining her life. As if before she had a chance to do something good, find a decent job, and become rich—the thing she always wanted—but little Lilith ruined everything and took it without even knowing it.

I was wandering around all day, sometimes even at night just to not be home. Just to avoid her eyes full of contempt, along with tons of new, unspoken shit she prepared to spill on me as soon as she saw a chance. Until I got a job at the local café, scratched some money together, and moved out.

But I barely made ends meet, and I was so tired that thinking about ending this pathetic life of mine sounded like the best option. I quit, and when it seemed like the only option not to die from hypothermia while living under the bridge was moving back to my mother, I decided to try something I had never done before. I applied for a scholarship at Stellaris University—and oh miracle, I got it. As it turned out, the years that Claire spent telling me how I was not worth anything were pointlessly wasted.

Now I am studying at one of the best universities in New York, and its scholarship is enough to pay my rent and have at least some food on the table. I am trying to control my desires whenever I enter the store and see all those seductive cherry-flavored desserts because I want to save that money and buy myself something nice and shiny.

As ridiculous as it may sound, spending money on the things I want is the only thing that makes me happy nowadays. I managed to make my life bearable enough, and now I see my mother only once on her birthday, even though I still don't know why. Because as soon as she sees me, all she thinks about is how to get rid of me the sooner the better.

Well, at least it's mutual.

I wait and wait and wait, and I find myself getting a little irritated. We were supposed to be here alone. If it was like that, it would probably already be over and I would throw my ass in my truck and drive the fuck away.

But no, I'm here, sitting in the kitchen, listening to the clock that keeps ticking on the wall as if reminding me that time doesn't stand still. It flies by, and each second reminds me that I should be somewhere far away, spending it for pleasure rather than torturing myself with visits that I hate.

"You know, I keep hoping that maybe you will finally find some friends." Mother begins playing the record that has already stuck for years. "But each time I see you on my doorframe again, my hopes are reduced to zero, so now I don't even bother thinking about such fantasies."

I grind my fork against the plate, smearing the remains of the strawberry cake, trying to understand whether it really tastes like shit or if I'm just refusing to enjoy anything when I'm in this house.

"I have friends, Mother," I lie.

She chuckles. This subject was always somehow funny to her. "Keep lying, Lilith. I don't even know how you go to that school." She sticks the fork in her piece, but then puts it away as if her appetite is already gone. "The kids there are probably making fun of you. Walking around with such a name."

I unexpectedly snort. When I meet her gaze, I shift awkwardly in my chair. "But you gave me that name."

"You weren't supposed to go to school," she explains calmly. "You are just like your father, Lilith. He never went to school himself. You were supposed to follow in his footsteps."

I'm never surprised by her ability to blame me for things, even when I'm not at fault. She delivers this with an expressionless face, her voice exuding unwavering confidence in every single word. I hate it. Because everything about her makes me feel guilty without even understanding the soil of it. And I know I have nothing to worry about. Technically. I guess. But that still doesn't stop me from feeling like shit.

"Okay, Mom," I answer, accepting whatever words that are leaving her mouth because I am tired.

I always feel tired.

"I don't even understand why spending time at that school—"

"It's a university," I correct, interrupting her before I even realize it. "One of the best universities in New York, Mom. Isn't it great that I had a chance to get there?"

She mulls my response over, looking everywhere but at me. "Devil's luck. You were not supposed to end up there, Lilith, and you know that. Stop thinking of yourself as some genius."

When she stands up and comes toward me, I freeze with the piece of cake still in my mouth, looking like some sort of scared hamster. Claire cups my chin and forces me to look into her emerald eyes.

"I hate how much you look like me. Seeing you is facing my biggest failure."

"Mom."

"Every time you come here, I am forced to look in the mirror that reflects the most miserable years of my life," she continues, her nails now making their way through the skin on my chin, clawing into it.

"Mom, enough," I nearly whisper, my voice strange to my ears.

I start to feel pain—my eyes sting from upcoming tears, my chin burns from the tight grip of my mother, and my face feels half-numb again. But none of that scares me more than Claire's words. It is always like that with her—my entire childhood I was ready to take a blow, ready for her to punch me, slap me, anything.

But I never got that. Her weapon is words—bitter, heartless words that sting me better than any sharp razor. They cascade through each of my organs, mercilessly going up and down in slow, torturous movements, ending up in my lungs as if puncturing them, and I can't breathe again.

"I waited for you to change, Lilith. I gave you a chance. But you never will change," she continues, and a smirk pulls up the corner of her mouth when she watches how that tiny tear slips from my eye. "You are evil. You can't do good, Lilith. You never could."

Before more shit is going to spill on me, I break free from her grip, shaking my head so abruptly that I almost lose my glasses. I get up, nearly sending a chair flying across the kitchen, and walk out without looking back at her.

I remove my glasses and wipe away the streaming tears from my cheeks, unconcerned about smudging my mascara. I unlock my truck, hurl myself inside, and after slamming the door closed, I unleash all my emotions, feeling as if I'm breaking into a million irreparable fragments.

I can't. I just can't be in that house.

Not now, not ever again.

Ava

I can't stop crying.

Last night I went from desolate to pathetic.

When he brought me my portion of food, I dropped to my knees and started begging him to let me go. He only smiled at that. Then he shrugged me off like I was a bag full of thrash, set the food on the floor, and left, locking the door behind him.

I don't understand what is happening. I refuse to believe it. Maybe it is a sick joke?

I don't want to die. I want to see my dad. He is freaking out, looking out for me. I know he is. Unless Caleb didn't text him from my phone something about me leaving the country and starting a whole new life with my boyfriend.

Dad would not believe that. I know. But Caleb is smart. Maybe he set everything out in a way that I just got bored with my life and left to start a new chapter.

I want to beg him to check on my dad, but I am afraid he is going to get angry and kill him.

Caleb seems like a person who can do anything he wants. He has money and resources. Probably people who are going to help him to hush everything.

I bet he bribed the police. Every detective.

... a few weeks (??) after

It feels like I've cried out the decade doze of my tears. I can't cry anymore.

My whole being feels hollow. My eyes are dried out.

I just stare at the ceiling, knowing that it's pointless to beg. Everything is pointless.

I just want it to be OVER.

CHAPTER
TWO

Caleb

" T he Black Widow strikes again—Cecilia Skylark has disappeared, marking the ninth victim of the serial offender, who, as always, leaves no traces or clues behind. Despite relentless efforts, law enforcement has yet to apprehend the perpetrator, who appears to outmaneuver investigators with a level of sophistication that has confounded authorities. Residents are urged to remain watchful and report any concerning behavior to the police. Additionally, individuals are advised to take extra safety measures, including securing doors and windows and avoiding isolated areas."

I relish a sip of my whiskey sour, its bitter aftertaste lingering on my tongue. I nearly smile as the reporter displays the images of my work—the faces of the nine women who vanished without a trace over the past couple of years.

The terror among the citizens is palpable, and while I enjoy observing their bewildered, fearful expressions, it all pales in comparison to the pleasure I derive from the act of ending my victims' lives. It's in seeing them revel in their everyday joys, only to have them mercilessly ripped away, replaced by a pervasive sense of dread and anxiety, that I find true satisfaction.

Cecilia Skylark was no more than just another dumb bitch trapped in my maze. I put no effort into gaining her trust, making her fall in love with me to the point where she was ready to *die* for me. She said that herself, but when I locked her in my basement, and she realized that it was over for her, she started to fight.

They are always lying. Not that I believe any of them, no, it's just the fact that they keep singing the same song, keep looking at me with wide doe eyes, telling me about their willingness to sacrifice everything for our love. So there's no doubt that I'm making the world a better place. I'm freeing it from liars, stupid, and shallow people. Mostly girls, as you already can tell. I've killed a few men in my life, but there was not much thrill, and after it, I felt absolutely nothing. When it comes to women, things take a different turn.

The most amusing part is that I never actively seek out my victims. I don't lay traps, nor do I make any preparations.

They willingly choose me. They come across a single man whom they desire to spend time with, and how can I possibly refuse such an offer? It's all about the process—engaging with them, wining and dining, then fucking them. When I determine the right moment, I kidnap them, relocating them to my basement, all the while observing their unsuspecting friends and parents, desperately searching for their daughters—this is when I nurture emotions.

Their despair and fear.

It's always been something that grants me power and fuels my motivation. As soon as I squeezed everything I could, I killed them. I liked robbing their bodies of life, stealing every breath, every movement, and then how easy and relaxed I felt after. There's a certain allure to holding such power in your hands—feeling akin to a god.

And just to be clear, I never got hard on it. Sure, I was fucking them because I was in a relationship with every woman I killed, but that wasn't something necessary for me. I never initiated any advances, but I never declined when they sought to perch themselves in my lap.

After all, they thought I was their boyfriend. But I never felt the urge to fuck them while killing them, or after I did it, and I never got hard on that picture. It was never about getting my dick wet. It's more about power and control that keeps me satisfied not on the sexual level.

This pattern, however, becomes more and more boring. Worn out—everything is the same every fucking time. It feels like all the women I've killed were made in the same factory. From the way they talk, to the way they fuck, although Ava was the kinkiest out of all of them. She asked me to do things I never even fucking knew existed.

My phone buzzes with an incoming call, and I glance at the screen – Grayson fucking Moore. One of the fattest pains in the ass that gives me an unbearable headache. The main sponsor of my company—a venture capitalist.

One of the richest people in the whole country, although I still have no idea what he does for a living. I know he is a businessman and one of the heads of my company because of the sponsorship he's given us, but I always felt like he wasn't a simple man.

Something's telling me that his business is far from ordinary.

But I do not care what the fucker does for a living as long as he isn't tarnishing my company's name. Grayson is like a chameleon, always adapting and blending into diverse situations—a person well-versed in all matters and acquainted with everyone. Always prepared to delegate tasks for you, introduce you to his latest busi-

VALERIIA MILLER

ness connections that he makes every single week, and extend invitations to another charity event.

I won't even touch on his penchant for gossip—there's always one of his ears finely tuned to places he shouldn't concern himself with.

I take the TV remote and mute the picture that flashes some new, boring news after my minutes of radiance.

"Hey," I greet with obvious irritation in my voice. The fucker calls me on a Saturday evening.

"Caleb. Can you at least pretend you are happy to speak with me?" he poses the question with a sarcastic undertone.

I remain silent, pinching the bridge of my nose. I wasn't lying when I mentioned that this creep gives me a pounding headache.

"Lovely, as always," he pushes after I don't give him an answer. "Anyway, how is your project going?"

Honestly, I'm fed up with how he constantly inserts himself into my business. It's as if he always insists on expressing his perspective and ideas when neither I nor my associates need that. I know that he is an important figure; after all, he helped me a lot, but it doesn't mean I want to chit-chat with him.

My company's main focus is on creating a new cybersecurity solution that will protect against data breaches and other threats for now. We have been working non-fucking-stop on this project, and once a week he calls me to check in like we are some kind of friends, expecting me to report everything.

"It's going great," I cut shortly.

I hear his frustrated sigh on the other side of the phone. "That's... good. Any troubles with money?"

I chuckle. I am the CEO of one of the most successful companies in the whole country, and I could buy ten idiots like him, and I'd still have enough money till the day I die even after I quit. Having him by my side isn't even necessary, but it's more of a

14

backup plan. Plus, sometimes, he finds me people I need—other companies for collaboration and all that shit.

"Don't worry, Grayson."

"That's what I like to hear," he answers. "Anyway, I am not calling just to check on you."

"No? That's something new."

"Ha-ha. Don't be rude. I need you to do something for me."

Oh, fucking hell. I can't and I don't even want to think about what this prick could possibly want from me. If it was up to me, I'd hang up on him after that phrase. But he is useful sometimes, and I still need him as my ally.

"Have you ever heard of Stellaris University?" he asks.

Of course, I fucking heard about it. It's one of the best universities in New York.

"Why?"

"How about you and Adam give Computer Science students a little lecture and describe what your new project is about?"

I furrow my brow, processing everything he just said. "You think I have nothing to do?"

He releases another loud sigh as if he were expecting me to jump and scream at such a beautiful opportunity. Five years of working together and this idiot still doesn't know anything about me.

"Caleb. Imagine yourself in their shoes. Didn't you want to have a practice with a fucking CEO of the best human-computer augmentation company? Isn't that better than listening to the raw lectures from those old farts?" He pauses. "You are the youngest specialist I know. Hell, the youngest everyone knows in this fucking city. You'll find approaches like a shot, tell them a few things you know, and go home."

"Why me? There are plenty of young people in my company. Pick one of them. Carter, maybe. He loves chit-chatting with everyone as far as I know," I suggest.

"They don't want a regular coworker. They want a CEO."

"And why this university?"

"Because they teach better than any other university. It's one of the most expensive, hard-to-get-into places. And we have to show an example, encourage others to study and love everything they do and—"

"And blah blah fucking blah." My interruption is accompanied by a clear tone of annoyance. Grayson pisses the living shit out of me with his speech in fucking patterns. "I guess I don't have that much of a choice."

He laughs. "You're damn right."

As much as I hate this idea, I'm not a child to cause a fucking scene and scream no. I will do what he asks me to, maybe even find some sort of inspiration there.

After all, nothing bad is going to happen.

CHAPTER

THREE

Caleb

S tellaris University is fucking massive. Before today, I'd never been here, mostly because I live on the other side of New York. I only saw pictures and heard what others were saying about it—a few of my colleagues sent their offspring here to study. This building contains the most highly educated teachers from all corners of the world; it is equipped with the newest, mind-blowing technology and has the biggest library in the whole of New York.

The outside looks old and a bit ominous—constructed in the Gothic style, with pointed arches, ribbed vaults, and elaborate stone carvings. The wisdom, rich cultural heritage, and endless knowledge seem to evaporate from its very pores. At least, it creates an atmosphere like that.

Perfectly cut green bushes surround this place along with colorful flower beds that smell a hundred miles away. Or maybe I just have a sensitive flair.

The kids who are studying here are lucky bastards.

"Oh, Caleb," Grayson says, his voice pulling me back from my thoughts. "Could you wear something decent for once? We need to set an example, for fuck's sake!"

We continue to walk along the grey stone path as I catch his gaze that shifts across me from head to toe.

"I am looking pretty decent," I reply unemotionally.

Grayson has always been overdressing for every fucking event, whether it's a typical workday, a visit to his family, or other shit. He is the kind of man who will be buried in a fucking tuxedo. He even said that to me once because appearance is everything to him, and he needs people to remember him as a man who was perfect in everything, whether it was how he looked or what he said.

The fucker always made fun of me because of my clothes. Mostly because I don't give a shit about *decent* clothes. I wear hoodies and sweats for every occasion. Comfort is above all for me, and I wouldn't say that I look bad. If I don't want to fucking brag about a thousand-dollar tuxedo, it doesn't make me a person with a deprived sense of taste.

Grayson looks like an angry gnome now, and I bite my tongue to suppress an upcoming laugh in my throat. He is not the shortest man I've ever seen—5'9 to be precise—but every time we stand next to each other, he seems smaller and smaller. I have no idea whether I keep growing up or he just goes to the root.

The last time I measured my height was a year ago when I was undergoing a medical examination, and the nurse wrote *6'8* on the paper, throwing some joke about a mammoth.

"All the girls are ready to drop on their knees right here," Adam jokes—my partner in today's performance. "Some demonic powers you have, Caleb."

I give him a blank face, not even bothering to look at the side where he keeps pointing his chin. "Not interested."

"Come on, man," he pushes, some sort of lust lacing his voice. "Dozens of pretty students here."

I let out an exasperated sigh, although I'm not that surprised. He has a wife with whom he has been for five years already, and there's never been a day when he was loyal to her. Usually, I don't give a shit about other people's relationships, and I am okay as long as it doesn't affect the productivity of my people, but his stupidity and constant need to get his dick wet sometimes get on my fucking nerves.

We walk inside and exchange a handshake with the principal who's already waiting for us. The man looks like he is going to jump out of his pants—excited would be too simple a word to use here.

He guides us to the lecture room we need; inside, the place looks a bit more modern as if they wanted to trick everyone with the outside design. Minimalism—clean lines and mid-sized windows that allow natural light to flood the interior spaces. We bypass dozens of classrooms, lecture halls, laboratories, libraries, and administrative offices, feeling the intense gazes of students all the time. The kids here look more stressed than my team who's working on the hardest projects.

Maybe they're not that lucky.

Each of the students is sitting in groups—some of them large, some consisting of only two people. Somehow, this reminds me of my student years. How alone I felt during them. Each day flowed unbearably slowly, like an endless, suffocating loop.

I could never make friends. I still don't know why, though. It's not like I've never tried. People just never wanted to interact with me for reasons nobody could explain.

Because people feel that evil lurks inside of you, as my mother would say. Maybe that was the real reason.

After all, I became a serial killer.

AFTER AN HOUR AND A HALF OF CHIT-CHATTING WITH A BUNCH OF hungover nineteen-year-olds, I am free to go. I can't think about anything other than driving all the way back to work. Getting here was one hell of a journey, and going back won't be easy, that's for sure.

"That was even better than I expected," Grayson comments, clasping his hands together. The fucker had doubts? Brave enough.

"So what? I suppose we have a day off today?" Adam asks, a hint of hope in his tone.

In disagreement, I furrow my brow. "No. I expect to see you at the office in an hour."

He sighs, the little sparkle of hope extinguished without a trace. "At least I tried."

It feels like we're wandering around for hours. I have no fuck-ing clue how the students orient themselves in this labyrinth. No matter how hard they tried to modernize the university, the old architectural base is obvious. A bunch of students are getting out of a lecture room, reminding me of little ants emerging from an anthill.

"Oooh," Adam drawls, not a trace of his frustration left, his need to get laid taking over again. "Those must be writers," he says, hungrily eyeing every girl that comes out of the lecture room. "I fucking love to read."

I restrain myself from abandoning this animal behind. I hold still—professional—trying to mute Adam as if he is a video and I just need to press the button on the left side of my phone down.

After a solid minute when I think there are no more ants, *she* walks out. Left behind by the group, she bears the semblance of someone who has been rejected and deemed unwanted. Holding her books, she pauses a few steps shy of the doorframe, awkwardly adjusting her bangs and rummaging through her bag. She retrieves worn-out headphones, prompting my wonder about how they are still functional. She inserts them into her ears, unconcerned with me or Adam.

Then, she walks out in the direction we are supposed to go, and I feel like I can't move—suddenly paralyzed—able only to watch her graceful gait. My body is completely detached from my soul, but my mind seems to know exactly what I need—I begin to walk after her without even realizing it.

I even forget about that idiot with whom I came here, not bothering to explain myself to him. She bypasses a group of students, and I notice how they eye her from head to toe, demonstratively laughing after her.

And I am back again in my student years when everyone believed something was wrong with me, laughing after me just the same way.

The exact same fucking way.

I suppress the urge to slam every single person who laughs at her into the wall because today I am all about the picture with calmness and ease. But by golly, this is fucking hard.

"Meet you at the office," I blurt out to confused Adam who's been following me like an obedient puppy, ignoring his *what the fuck man where are you going*.

The October cool wind tosses her hair to the side—brown colored with honey strands in it—as it traverses across her back, pulling out of me an urge to run my hand through it. I inhale a deep breath, catching her perfume that tickles my nose with a pleasant scent—musk and sandalwood. The unique fragrance leaves my head spinning, like an intoxicating sensation.

I keep our distance so I won't arouse any suspicions from her, not even realizing how we get inside the local café and how I sit at the end of it while she sits near the window at the other side.

I watch how she orders her coffee, now able to take a better look at her features—her face so perfect that it's fucking breath-taking. I watch her mimic as she speaks to the waiter, and when she smiles, showing that little dimple on her left cheek, I almost fucking lose it.

She looks unique, unlike the typical beauty standards; she doesn't have those fucking pumped-up duck lips and strained cheekbones, or fox eyes, or whatever the fuck that is called. Her face looks natural, deprived of heavy makeup. Her awkward energy is palpable—it seems like she feels uncomfortable everywhere but at home.

I watch her thanking the waiter for her coffee, already sensing an inferno of jealousy inside me, especially the second time she gives him that little smile and her dimple forms.

Suddenly, I want to be the one and only who is going to see all her smiles.

I order myself coffee too, so it won't look suspicious. She concentrates on her book, and I concentrate on her.

God, she is beautiful. In every fucking sense.

The way she sips her coffee, tapping her forefinger above her lips as if she's afraid of getting dirty with foam.

The way she holds her book with those slender fingers brushing over printed words as if highlighting the quotes that are worth it.

The way she keeps awkwardly fixing her glasses and checking if anyone is looking at her as if afraid of sudden judgment.

The way her chest is rising and falling in a calm, steady rhythm, unaware of my presence.

I am *obsessed*. Watching her is like injecting a high dose of the most mind-fucking drug in my veins.

Something tells me that this walking beauty is going to relieve my boredom. I *won't* allow her to leave now.

Looks like I've found my tenth.

CHAPTER
FOUR

Lilith

T he blaring alarm interrupts my sleep, and I reach for the nightstand, intending to silence it. I set the most obnoxious, ear-piercing sound on my phone as the only method to rouse me in the morning. For five consecutive days, I've been waking an hour earlier just to ensure I make myself look decent. Despite my love for sleep, my appearance takes precedence.

Let's not look at the fact that I basically come to university, listen and write down my notes without a single spoken word, and then go back to my apartment. Sometimes my tongue feels like it's glued and I can't move it. One day I was silent for twelve hours and I was genuinely afraid that my mind would forget how to move my lips and talk.

When Mother said that I don't have friends, she was right. It's not like I need them anyway. I think.

I want to prove wrong those who say that humans are social animals because I don't sense an urge to talk. Ever. When I was feeling overwhelmed, I wrote it down on paper. I say *was* because I am no longer feeling that way. Not for the past couple of months anyway. To be clear – I don't feel shit. And I think it's for the best.

I don't want to talk about the situation with Claire. That, I believe, was the only time I was showing some kind of emotion. As I rise, my feet get caught in a pile of clothes, causing me to stumble and fall with my head almost colliding against the wooden closet.

"Oh fuuuuuck," I drawl, already tired. No matter that I just woke up. If I fell a little closer, I'd hit my head and probably die. Or have a fucking concussion, maybe.

Sometimes we are too close to death, and we do not even realize that.

I trudge to the bathroom, wash my face, brush my teeth, and take one last look in the mirror. I look like the walking dead without my makeup. Purple smudges beneath my eyes look like someone has been punching me nonstop the whole night. But in reality, I just have sensitive skin.

Without any desire to watch my bare face a second longer, I go back to my room and throw myself in the chair, getting all of my makeup out of my drawers.

A PUSH TO MY SHOULDER JOLTS ME FROM MY THOUGHTS, MAKING ME realize that I had been looking downward and hadn't noticed the student approaching directly in front of me.

"Watch it, idiot," he throws angrily, grimacing as if our slight touch has disgusted him, as if my skin is made of something horrifying.

"Sorry," I mumble, unclear why. It is my fault for not watching where I was going, but it's not that bad. People always make me feel like I am doing worse than I actually am.

I hear accompanying laughter behind me and don't bother looking back. I'm used to it. I pull my hood over my head, desperately hoping to hide myself from everyone.

The journey to the lecture room feels like it takes an eternity, but finally, it comes to an end. Once I step inside and settle into my seat, a stream of whispers and quiet chuckles floats from behind me. Nope. It's not over.

My savior is my phone, which suddenly buzzes with a message.

Kevin:

Morning. Are you at the Devil's Den already?

I smile to myself like an idiot. Thank God the hood covers more than half of my face. I don't need another reason for assholes to laugh.

Me:

yep. I almost had a concussion today. while enjoying those little whispers behind my back, I kinda regret that I didn't actually have it.

Meet Kevin, my best and only friend. Online friend, to be precise. We've been chatting with each other for over a year—FaceTime, night calls, or simple text messages like now. Kevin lives in Canada, and he's been planning to visit me at Christmas. He suggested visiting during previous holidays when we'd only been talking for three months, but I felt too shy and a little scared.

After all, how could I know? Maybe he is some kind of serial killer.

But time passed, and we got closer. There were days when we talked for hours non-stop, never getting bored with each other. There's nothing we wouldn't agree on. He gets me. I get him. It's more than enough. Kevin makes my days a little brighter. He is the only one who believes in my writing career besides me.

Kevin:

Don't say that, Lily. Fuck those losers.

Oh, except Kevin doesn't know my real name. I go by Lily on every social media platform, and even my only novel is going to be published under this pen name. Hell, even every time I buy coffee and the barista asks my name, I don't tell them my real one. I don't feel it's necessary to reveal my…demonic name. I am forced to share it in university, but that's where it ends. Besides my mother and me, nobody knows my real name behind these walls.

"Hey, Lilith," Diana says, placing her hand on my shoulder just as I'm about to plug in my headphones. "We're going to grab drinks tomorrow. Are you with us?"

I remain motionless, immobilized. Diana Lopez, the flawless Queen Bee of the group, engages me in conversation and even goes as far as inviting me for drinks. It feels like some kind of joke.

"Uh…okay? If I can?" I answer awkwardly. Although a question isn't exactly an answer, I suppose.

"Good. See you tomorrow at seven at our spot." Her words are kindly spoken, as if she never made fun of me with her friends, her tone calm. I'm about to ask where their favorite spot is, but she's already turning around and heading back to the rest of her friends.

I shake my head, trying to shake off the numbness. I don't rush out of the university because I have no desire to catch up with the rest of them and face their gazes. I take my time, pacing around the place and trying to think where their favorite spot could be.

I remember overhearing a conversation between Diana and her best friend Sophia at the beginning of our studies when they talked about a place called *Urban* or something like that. I Google it and quickly find all the answers.

Today started badly, just like most of my days, but it doesn't have to end that way. Right?

Me:

> guess what. I've been invited to grab drinks
> with my haters.

Kevin:

> Uh...... Wtf

Me:

> Diana just came to me and asked if I want to grab
> drinks with them tomorrow at seven. Maybe I am finally
> going to make some friends.

Kevin:

> I don't think you should go. It sounds like
> some kind of joke.

I am used to people throwing bitter words and hurtful things at me. However, this message cuts through me like a sharp blade, swiftly erasing my foolish little smile. I never realized that I was smiling until now.

Me:

> ok but you're being rude. Can't I receive an invitation to
> get some drinks for once?

An unpleasant feeling cascades through my insides as I wait for his response. Maybe I am okay with others saying shit to me. But not Kevin. He was always my support. My best friend, even if it's just online. He is the person whom I trust with everything.

Well, almost.

Kevin:

> Sorry, but they've never invited you before. You
> said yourself that this morning they were laughing at
> you. What changed?

I leave him on *Read*. My previous five-minute good mood is now no more than just a drop that dried halfway before landing in my ocean of fucking depression. But I can't deny that Kevin is right. They never bothered to even say hi to me, so what could change? It's not like I can become more popular or interesting in one day. It's naïve to even think that I could get a simple invitation to a chill evening with other people.

With normal people.

Eloise

I tried to seduce him (as much as disgusting as it sounds).
To remind him about the time we were together. To bring
back those little sweet memories.

I thought I could find the right spot, push on it, and make
him change his mind.

But he looks like a totally different person now. He is not
the Caleb I fell in love with.

I know I should think about a way to get out of here, but
the only thoughts that flood my stupid head right now are
that it was never real.

None of it.

All I can think about is how I fell in love with the person
that doesn' t fucking exist.

He is not the sweet, kind guy whom I used to know.

He is nothing but a devil.

And he left me here in this basement with my head full of
thoughts about how fucking pathetic I am, because even when
I am on the verge of death, all I think about is how he
never actually loved me.

I am left with nothing but a broken heart and soul,
uselessly waiting for my end to come.

CHAPTER

FIVE

Caleb

Lilith Leclair – twenty years old, an exemplary student at Stellaris University majoring in Creative Writing. Always wanting to be unseen – lurking in the background of photos, covering her face with her hand, pretending to adjust her glasses.

She lives in Pinewood, in a small, modest apartment where she spends most of her time. It's basic – walls painted in cheap grey that crease at the corners, a single big window overlooking a rundown neighborhood. While her peers party, she stays home, reading or writing.

The Walking Beauty has written a 600-page crime novel but never published it. Now, she starts her second book, only writing the title and chapter numbers. I've copied every file from her laptop, including her novel. I was never into reading, but fuck me, I'm intrigued by her book.

I brush my fingers across her bed, smoothing out the creases on her freshly washed sheets. I lean in and inhale, but all I smell is the velvety scent of washing powder.

It's not enough. I want to smell *her*.

The loud thud of thick books hitting the floor breaks my focus, and I realize I stumbled over a pile of her books, knocking them over with my shoulder. This apartment is so small for me, I can barely turn around.

I pick up each book, surprised to find that for someone so depressed, Lilith keeps everything surprisingly clean. Messy, but clean. Her apartment may be tiny and in a rundown neighborhood, but she's made it cozy and pleasant.

I scrutinize every corner of her room, taking my time. I've memorized her schedule like clockwork—she'll be back in two hours. Damn if I don't want to stay here and catch her off guard. If it were up to me, I'd already have kidnapped her and taken her to my place, but I can't be reckless.

Previous women were easy targets, but Lilith is different. Even when we met during the university's excitement over the CEO's visit, she never noticed me. She lives in her own little world and seems to want to stay there, avoiding anyone or anything new.

I've never been challenged like this before. It inspires me.

Excites me.

With Lilith, it's different. She doesn't share details about her life easily. But that's not a problem. The only thing I can't get is her phone. She never leaves it alone, always listening to music.

If I want it, there's only one way. I'll come back when she's asleep and get the last thing I need. I've done everything I came for, but as soon as I think, *There's nothing left, time to leave,* a strange sensation grips me.

I *don't* want to leave.

Even when this place reminds me of my childhood apartment—minimal space, cheap furniture, suffused with depression.

I fled my old home without looking back. As a kid, I had dreams of demons, dark shadows enveloping me, swallowing me into the abyss. I often felt something dark beside me and my mother—just my childish imagination, exaggerating rustling rat noises at night.

The real monster was my mother, who tormented me until I killed her. After that, I ran as far as I could. Now, I'm inexplicably drawn back here. Lilith's place doesn't feel dark, though. It feels like what my old home should have been—cheap, sad, screaming poverty, yet harmless. Many families live poorly but manage to break through, supporting each other to rise from the depths. That's why I want to stay here.

This feels like where I should have grown up, free from the horror my mother inflicted. Without violence. Without darkness.

Oh, *Lilith*. What have you gotten yourself into?

CHAPTER

SIX

Lilith

S tanding in my pretty dress, I shiver in the cold, silently berating myself for neglecting to wear my jacket.

I just wanted to look pretty.

I've been stood up. As you can probably guess. Or maybe I just confused the name of the bar. Though we both know that's a lie.

I wonder if they recorded it. I mean, nowadays it's all about recording every damn thing your eye can catch, including every single stupid prank. But I couldn't care less. I'm used to it. I even feel someone's eyes on me. Lately, it's become a regular thing, but I guess when you're the main laughingstock, it's to be expected. I doubt somebody else is going to waste their time just to watch me.

I snap, deciding to enter this goddamn bar and get some drinks myself. The feeling of being so stupid has evoked something new in me. Something brave. I'm the kind of person who would rather buy a huge bottle of red wine and drain it in one gulp at home than go to the local bar. I'm not even sure why, but I've always been a little afraid that someone could drug my drink, or that I would get so drunk that I'd lose control of the situation. The latter reason is also why I haven't been in a relationship with anyone. Yeah, I'm a twenty-year-old virgin, thank you very much.

My whole life I've lived with the thought of finding the right guy, a cliché in shining armor who will protect me from an old evil witch (Claire the dearest) and rescue me from that rotten house. I wanted him to be my first and last, my one and only. I know I should think more broadly, but I could never picture myself sleeping with someone…random.

I don't care about other girls—if you want to sleep around, go ahead. I don't care. But for myself, it was always unacceptable. I can't and I don't want to even entertain the thought of being intimate with someone I don't trust. I still believe that the guy I lose my virginity to will be my friend for at least six months. Friends first, and then maybe lovers.

I need to know the guy. I need to understand him, to be sure that he's the one, and that he isn't pretending. But as far as I know, old virgins are a huge turn-off for men. It's too much pressure, and nobody wants that. So, more likely, I'm going to die a virgin—old and dusty. Which is fine, I guess. Fine as long as nobody knows about it.

"What can I do for you tonight?" the bartender asks in a soft voice. He gives me a smile that looks almost flirtatious.

I rest my elbows on the bar table, trying to act natural. Emphasize trying. "I'll have a whiskey sour," I say.

His face shows a sudden and unexpected reaction. "On it."

For a moment, I thought he would ask some questions. Like if I was sure or something else. Thank God he didn't. I scrunch up my nose, then look around. This bar doesn't seem like the place I would spend my night. An atmosphere of intoxication and forced cheerfulness—dozens of men and women drinking non-stop, loudly talking about everything and nothing at the same time, making my headache appear and slowly spread across my forehead.

Nothing I hate more than noise. If it were up to me, I'd spend the rest of my life on a desert island with books surrounding me. And it would be good if there was a bit of electricity so I could write in peace.

"There you go," the bartender says, pulling me back from my thoughts and shoving the drink I ordered toward me.

"Thanks," I answer, flashing him a hesitant smile. I glance at the glass, observing the amber liquid that fills it. I've never tasted whiskey before. I don't want to squander this evening; it would be good to have a new experience tonight, to perhaps have a bit of fun.

I spin the glass, feeling intense stares from all sides. I know I look weird. It seems like I regret my drink choice, not even sure why I ordered it. With the thought *fuck them all*, I close my eyes, and drain the stingy liquid in one gulp. I immediately wrinkle, feeling discomfort in my mouth, down my throat, and in my stomach—it burns everywhere. "Jesus Christ," I mumble, bringing a fist to my mouth, still unable to open my eyes.

"You should go easier," the bartender says, a hint of amusement lacing his voice.

I nod, trying not to look foolish. "What's your name? I'm tired of silently addressing you as 'bartender guy,'" I say.

He chuckles softly. "Henry. Yours?"

I take a moment, though I know what my answer will be. "Lily."

I SPENT THE LAST COUPLE OF HOURS IN THAT BAR. BETWEEN chit-chatting with Henry and draining one whiskey sour after another, I was distracted by Kevin's angry messages. It sounds pathetic, but I'm actually glad he's concerned. He kept texting me about how dangerous it is to go to bars alone, and I caught myself liking his protectiveness.

Bone-tired, I step out of the bar. Now I understand why people linger in places like this as long as they can. The energy keeps you lively and vibrant, but once you step outside and breathe fresh air, weariness hits hard, and it's no longer amusing.

My phone vibrates with another, probably angry text from Kevin.

Kevin:

Can you answer your phone?

What the hell is wrong with you?

The Lily I know wouldn't be so reckless.

Oh, sweet Kevin. You don't even know my real name. How can you talk like that? Ridiculous.

I keep walking, my mind cloudy, my legs like cotton wool, realizing that maybe, just maybe, he's right again. It was foolish to spend all my money just to get drunk. I didn't even like how those drinks tasted. But I thought, well, all alcohol tastes like crap, but adults drink it anyway. Why can't I do the same? Pretend to enjoy it? Maybe that's exactly what my life lacks. I just needed to pretend to enjoy company, parties, something beyond reading and writing.

I *could have, should have*, but I didn't. And where has that led me? Here I am—a twenty-year-old untouchable woman with nothing but one online friend and a hateful mother. Pathetic.

I don't bother looking around until I bump into someone. I gasp, taking a cautious half-step back.

"Lilith? What are you doing here?"

As if my night couldn't get any worse. Meet Evan Flores—my crush since I started university. Though claiming him as *my* crush sounds wrong because he's everyone's crush. Every girl wants to be with him. I've even heard guys question their sexuality because of him.

Evan is a year younger than me, with dyed blonde hair, a square jawline, and full lips—flawless in every way, even with the emerging black roots on his head.

"Evan!" I practically shout, throwing my hands up in surprise. "So good to see you."

A tiny smirk tugs at the corner of his lips, and I almost collapse. "Good to see you too, Lilith. Had enough fun today?" His question sounds almost mocking. But maybe it's just my own stupid voice telling me others can't take me seriously.

"Yep. I was getting drinks at Urban."

An expression of surprise crosses his pretty face. "Alone?"

"No. With my close friend," I lie, surprised by the sound of my confident voice.

"What's his name?" Evan asks curiously.

Oh, fuck me. "Henry."

He narrows his blue eyes in suspicion and nods, barely detectable. "Okay."

"Do you want to go out sometime?" I blurt out, surprised at my own audacity. I swear to myself I'm done drinking—just alone at my apartment. Fuck this sudden burst of confidence.

I close my eyes, bracing for his rejection. "Sure. Someday," he answers, and I immediately try to detect any hint of insincerity in his voice, but there's none. I cautiously open one eye.

"Really?" I ask.

His deep chuckle resonates within me like the best sensation ever. "Of course. I'll text you when I'm free."

Even though Evan is the guy everyone wants, his response stings my pride. It sounds like a job interview—or any other official event—where the boss decides whether he wants to see you or not. I swallow the bitterness in my throat, the stingy aftertaste of whiskey now mixed with his words.

"Uh, yeah. I think I gotta go," I manage to say.

I think he understands from the grimace that crosses my face and the tone of my voice that I'm not satisfied. And I can tell he doesn't like my reaction.

"Uh-huh," is all he says.

If I were sober, my cheeks would be burning red, my voice shaky as if someone had just stepped on my throat, cutting off my air. I'd feel awkward and embarrassed. But thanks to the seven whiskey sours Henry served me, I don't feel a damn thing.

I think I might be the first girl who's ever shown displeasure to Evan. Everyone else dances like monkeys in front of him, ready to drop to their knees at any moment. The alcohol has surely unlocked a new and improved version of myself—one free from worry and filled with self-assurance.

As I finally reach my neighborhood, something inside me snaps. I'm sick and tired of being watched, possibly filmed.

Oh, look, we invited her and stood her up. Now she's walking home wasted and miserable—let's record this and mock her later, so she feels even more miserable!

Another burst of confidence rushes through me. Before I open the door to my building, I spin around and scream, "FUCK YOU, PEOPLE!"

It's a small relief.

I trudge to my door, silently yearning to get inside, collapse on my bed without even showering. I don't care about the glitter on my face. I can't even picture taking a shower right now.

I unzip my purse, desperate to find my keys. The lights inside the building flicker unpredictably. One day they work fine, the next they're on and off, flashing dimly, as if none of us is paying rent and the landlord can't afford to replace them. Of course, just when I need a little light to find my keys, they go off.

"You've got to be kidding me," I sigh, fumbling for my phone and turning on the flashlight. Suddenly, a loud thud from the other side of the apartment makes me flinch. I quickly turn around and point my flashlight at whatever's there.

To my relief, it's just a fat rat.

"Jesus fucking Christ," I curse, though I'm still relieved. Thank God it's not a serial killer. Finally, my drunken self finds the keys and I drag myself to my apartment.

Just when I think there'll be no more surprises, I see a sight: a man, drunk as fuck (almost like me), sitting on my freshly vacuumed doormat, back against my front door.

Releasing a frustrated sigh, I cautiously approach.

Please don't let it be Frank.

Just so you know, out of all my messed-up neighbors, Frank is the worst. He's fifty, divorced three times, and all he does is get so drunk he can't remember where he lives, confusing our doors even though he lives one floor above me. It started as soon as I moved here, and lately, it's happening more often than I'd like.

As I get closer, I confirm it's him. "Oh, Frank," I whisper, kneeling in front of him, assessing his state. He's a solid eleven on the messed-up scale. He mumbles something unintelligible as I try to lift his heavy ass.

I'm not the tiniest girl—if anything, I'm as tall as Frank, both 5'8—but much lighter. Mostly because I'm thinner and also because he refuses to move himself. "Come on, Frank," I plead, grabbing his hands and trying to drag him away from my door. "I need to get inside. Come on."

"This is my house!" he slurs angrily, throwing his hand at me, almost slapping my face. "Get the hell out of my house!"

Oh, God. I can never get used to this shit. It's one reason I stay home—dealing with Frank late at night isn't pleasant.

Somehow, after five attempts, I manage to roll him onto his stomach and push him away, like kneading dough. "Sorry, buddy," I mutter, using my leg to keep him from crawling back and blocking the door again.

I finally find the right key and insert it into the lock, but now it's stuck. I wiggle it from side to side, trying to remove it so I can try again. Meanwhile, Frank is on his knees, leaning against the wall, getting up.

"Get the hell out of my HOUSE!" he yells.

My heart races, pulse pounding in my ears. My hands shake as I carefully twist the key, and finally, with a click, the door unlocks.

Exhaling in relief, I rush inside and slam the door shut, nearly hitting Frank's nose. I ignore his swearing and name-calling, gripping the door handle as if my life depends on it. I turn the lock twice, finally able to breathe.

I collapse on the floor, lying on my back, arms and legs spread out like a starfish. I stay like that for a minute, realizing how badly I need sleep. "I can't sleep on the floor," I mumble to myself, rolling onto my stomach and crawling to my bedroom.

It feels like I'm crawling forever. When I reach the bedroom doorway, I give up. After all, I live alone. No one will question me if I fall asleep right on the floor.

CHAPTER
SEVEN

Caleb

I 'll admit it—I was wrong about Lilith. When I first saw her, I thought she was just another spoiled kid from Stellaris University, where ninety-nine percent are arrogant troublemakers. But she's different. With each new revelation about her, I'm astounded by my own ignorance.

She's unique, misunderstood, and underrated. The world doesn't appreciate those who dare to be different.

Watching her has become a daily routine. I try to focus on work and other matters, but she consumes my thoughts. It's laughable how she sees herself as dull when she's the most captivating person I've ever met. Everything about her—her gestures, her voice, her expressions—is awkward yet endearing, like a child navigating the world alone for the first time.

I stay in the shadows, keeping my distance, battling the urge to snatch her off the street and take her far away. But it has to be perfect, so I restrain myself—a challenge for my arrogant self accustomed to getting what I want instantly.

I knew Diana Lopez invited her that day. I saw how happy Lilith was, only to see that happiness vanish when she started texting someone. Whoever upset her made me want to break their neck. I followed her to the bar, where she stood alone, shivering in that *fucking* dress, realizing she'd been stood up.

The image of her in that moment reminded me of my own past as a student—a nerd ridiculed by peers, stood up by a group of guys. She mirrors my loneliness back then—no friends, no family, struggling to make ends meet.

Watching her stirs emotions I can't quite grasp. Despite her naivety, I feel protective, driven to right the wrongs she faces. Her frustration seeps under my skin, bitter and acidic. I fight the urge to comfort her, to wrap her delicate frame in my arms and shield her from the world.

These conflicting thoughts confuse me. I shouldn't be having them. I should be focused on darker impulses. But seeing her melts my resolve. In her presence, I'm not a hardened killer but a soft-hearted fool.

What fascinates me more is how she walks through Pinewood—one of New York's darkest, most dangerous neighborhoods—seemingly unfazed by its dangers. Among normal people, she's awkward and shy, but here, she exudes confidence, as if this darkness is her refuge.

I lean against my black Range Rover, watching her until she reaches her door. One of her neighbors eyes her with lust, and the sight fucking infuriates me.

I can't leave her unprotected. It's only a matter of time before he acts.

Before Lilith opens the door to her apartment complex, she spins around and screams, "FUCK YOU, PEOPLE!" Then, she slams the door shut. An idiotic grin creeps onto my face, and I can't suppress a little chuckle. She knows someone's been watching her, but she's convinced herself it's someone from her group, like that Diana girl. Part of me wants her to keep believing that—I don't want to scare her, not yet anyway. But another part of me is curious about her reaction.

What will she do when she finds out she has a stalker? Will she lock herself in, or confront me?

These thoughts are tearing me apart.

I *need* a distraction.

I step out of the shadows, unconcerned if her neighbors see me. They're always drunk, high, or indifferent. I approach the man who eye-fucked her so lecherously. With a swift move, I wrap my hand around his neck and snap it before he can react—a silent *crack* echoes through the night. He's practically weightless, another junkie who's wasted away. A threat to society, and to my Lilith.

I carry his limp body to my car, effortlessly. One hand supports his corpse, the other retrieves keys from my pocket. I press a button, the trunk opens, and I toss him inside like garbage. Closing the trunk, I lock the car and check the cameras I installed in Lilith's apartment on my phone.

She struggles to enter, her drunkenness evident as she sprawls on the floor like a starfish. Eventually, she crawls to her bedroom but fails to reach her bed, settling for the floor.

Poor thing. She's too drunk to function properly.

Once she's passed out, I trudge to her apartment. Darkness greets me inside the complex, intensifying the creepiness. It reminds me of the apartment complex from *Evil Dead Rise*—I half-expect to see deadites. I activate my phone's flashlight and ascend to her second-floor apartment, *A207* on the left.

As I scan the area with my flashlight, I freeze. It dawns on me who lies unconscious near her door—her bothersome neighbor who delayed her entry.

I'll have to deal with him if he persists in troubling her.

I pick the lock and cautiously enter her apartment. My goal is clear: retrieve her phone, transfer its data to mine, and make copies of her apartment keys. Picking locks repeatedly isn't ideal.

After closing the door behind me, I survey her half-lit apartment. Moonlight streams through a window, casting a turquoise glow on her tranquil form. Her chest rises and falls rhythmically, undisturbed by the chaos around her. She shifts uncomfortably, her face catching the moonlight, highlighting remnants of make-up and glitter on her cheeks.

Her dress hugs her curves perfectly, emphasizing her beauty she so often conceals under baggy clothes.

With each breath she takes, the fabric stretches and contracts, kindling an uncommon sensation within my chest—jealousy. I imagine my hands on her petite body, encircling her flawless waist, delicately tracing my fingertips along her pale skin. I want to rip off that dress, to feel her warmth beneath my touch, to see her surrender to me.

How did I end up here, jealous over a fucking dress?

I step toward the ottoman and take her purse, connecting her phone to mine for data transfer. It'll take some time, so I carefully set them down and focus on her keys. I've done what's necessary, yet it feels insufficient. I resist the urge to do more; it's *not* the right time.

Before I can stop myself, I lift her petite frame and carry her to the bed. This could lead to consequences—she might wake and realize someone was here, moved her. But I can't leave her curled on the floor like a kitten, even if she looks cute. Her body will ache tomorrow.

Avoiding her face and distracting myself from intrusive thoughts, I gently settle her on the bed. Our faces draw near, and I catch her scent—a mix of musk, sandalwood, and whiskey. I breathe deeply, savoring it, before backing away. My back meets the closet, and I catch a vase before it falls.

Fuck. That was close.

Realizing I've gone too far, I prepare to leave, but I allow myself one final glance at her. Even disheveled, she radiates elegance—a chaotic beauty.

My chaotic beauty.

I shut my eyes to banish the thoughts, retrieve her belongings, and secure her apartment.

As I return to my car, I'm troubled by my thoughts. None of what I did tonight was okay. I know I shouldn't think of her in any way but to end her life.

But I can't seem to stop.

CHAPTER

EIGHT

Lilith

I find myself adrift in the clouds, my body disconnected in a state of bliss. Nearby, an unpleasant noise intrudes, remote and muffled at first, but increasingly unbearable as it penetrates my sanctuary. The sound of a loud, annoying siren cuts through my tranquility, shattering the fluffy walls around me, assaulting not just my ears but my entire being. I struggle to open my heavy lids, catching a brief, painful glimpse of the bright room. Groaning, I scrub yesterday's glitter-stained hand over my face, trying to comprehend what's happening.

The relentless siren continues its assault, pushing me further from sleep. As I gaze down, I notice something odd in my bed—a small, black, and hairy object. Jumping in panic, I scramble to the other side, only to meet the unforgiving wooden floor with my back. "FUCK!" I yell, the pain shooting through me.

But it's not a spider—I realize in frustration—it's just my fake eyelash. Almost having a heart attack for nothing annoys me further. Recalling my drunken night, I try to piece together how I ended up in bed.

The blackout, Frank, and then passing out on my bedroom doorframe—it…doesn't make sense.

Did I crawl into bed myself, or did someone *move* me?

The thought sends chills down my spine, but checking the locked front door offers no clues of a break-in.

It's absurd, right? Yet, I can't shake the unease. I decide not to dwell on it; I have enough to stress about already.

Overthinking won't help; it's just another layer on my anxiety cake.

"…One of the most important aspects of creative writing is character development. Your characters are the heart and soul of your story. They need to be believable, relatable, and well-rounded. You want your readers to connect with them on a deep level and care about what happens to them—"

The iced coffee in my cup is almost gone, but I still feel dehydrated, barely halfway through. Mark my words, I'm never getting this drunk again. Hangovers are a bitch. I spent half my morning throwing up and scrubbing my skin raw, ending up missing a class for the first time ever.

"Professor Graham, what about the setting?" Kaitlyn's voice cuts through, too shrill for my hangover-addled mind. I squint and take another sip, hoping to numb the headache. The cup's nearly empty, and I'm seconds from sucking air—how embarrassing.

My attire draws no comment from the professor, surprising given I'm dressed head-to-toe in black: hoodie, sweatpants, oversized sunglasses shielding my puffy eyes. I feel like an outlier, more so now than ever.

"…It should be vivid and descriptive, allowing the readers to imagine themselves in the world you've created—"

One of my favorite professors elaborates on writing techniques, but I struggle to focus through the pounding in my head. It's not just the hangover; flashes of last night creep in after I left the bar.

How did I end up in bed? It seems implausible—I'd have remembered crawling there.

And those eyes I felt on me? What if someone followed me and moved me?

My pen jabs into the wooden desk, a near miss for making a hole. Blinking away confusion, I realize everyone's already working.

Fuck. Did Professor Graham assign something while I zoned out?

Before I can react, he's hovering over me. "Lilith, dear, what's the matter? Didn't understand the assignment?" His voice carries, sparking giggles from all sides.

Great, another moment to stand out.

"It's not that I didn't understand," I start, avoiding his eyes behind my sunglasses. "Could you repeat the assignment?"

Giggles follow. My sunglasses offer good coverage, but I can feel Professor Graham's frustration. He repeats the task, and I bury myself in the assignment, struggling to focus. Now, I need to craft a story about overcoming fear. The mere thought of constructing a sentence makes my head ache anew. I scribble something, hoping it makes sense.

Writing used to bring joy, but now it's a chore. I grasp at ideas, desperate for coherence.

The room suddenly erupts into a buzzing frenzy—every student, including Professor Graham, engrossed in their phones. Shocked faces surround me, but I'm oblivious until my own phone vibrates with a link to an anonymous profile. Clicking it, I scroll, eyes widening behind my sunglasses. If not for them, my eyes might pop out and roll onto my desk. Someone's posted Diana's photos and videos—embarrassing ones.

"Everyone, calm down! Phones away," Professor Graham commands, but no one listens. The noise grows as every student shares and discusses the content. I lift my head, expecting Diana to protest or deny it all, but she sits silently, staring at her phone, oblivious to her surroundings. This isn't her usual arrogant smile.

It's fear. *Humiliation*. Despair.

For the first time, I witness a crack in her facade. She scans the room, then abruptly bolts without taking her things. I can't help but feel a twinge of triumph.

She *deserves* this, in a way. She built herself up as flawless and untouchable, but she's just as human as the rest of us.

And for the first time in my life, I feel triumphant.

Jade

A month. Or two? But maybe less. Or more.

I lost track of time.

I tried to talk to him, but all he did was bring me food and guide me to the bathroom once a day.

Although after my little attempt to hit him between his legs and get the kitchen knife made everything ten times worse.

He is angry now.

I think I've lived without food for a whole couple of days.

My lips are so dehydrated that I practically can't feel them.

My face is swollen from all the tears I've spilled for all this time. My eyes hurt, so I prefer spending time with them closed.

The only sound in here is the growl of my stomach that desperately begs for me to take some food. But I depend on Caleb, and I can't get out of here.

I don't even want to run anymore. I just want to eat.

… a few hours (I think??) later

I found food. If you can call a skin around your fingers that way.

My cuticle has outgrown. I ripped it off and shoved it in my mouth. All ten fingers.

I don't know if it's real, but I feel less hungry. Which is good.

No one is supposed to see this note. No one but future me who lives happily, leaving this nightmare behind.

I know I can get out. I just know it.

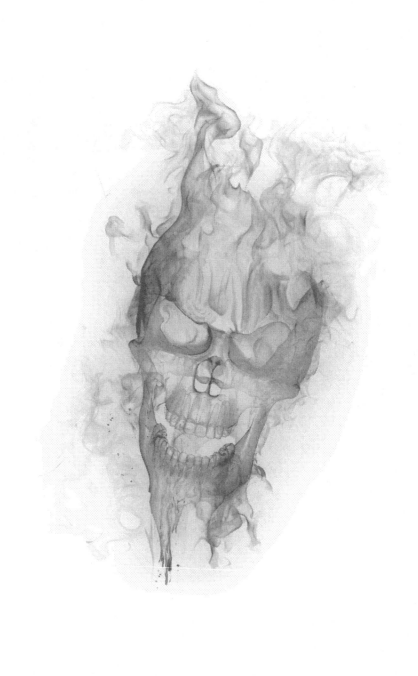

CHAPTER
NINE

Caleb

If a month ago you had told me I'd be playing vigilante-hacker games for a woman who's never even seen me, I'd have laughed in your face.

But here we fucking are. Digging into Lilith's life is one thing, but delving into the web of the internet's evil queen? It's beyond belief. It wasn't part of my plan, but Lilith's devastated expression when she realized she'd been stood up—probably not the first time for her—haunts my thoughts. Not to mention, Diana's been tormenting her long before I entered the scene, which is unbelievable in itself. How could one quiet girl attract so much negative attention, especially when she's done nothing wrong?

"You're almost finished?" Grayson's surprise tinges his tone. "Fast as hell. Though I never doubted you." He claps my back, a gesture I despise but he insists on. "What stage are you on now?"

His hand lingers, so I shoot him a look that should convey my discomfort. Ignoring it, he avoids my eyes, and I eventually shrug him off. "Two weeks, at most."

"Weren't you supposed to finish it next week?" He interrupts, making me spin in my chair to face him. "What's going on?"

"Nothing," I reply sharply. "Just a bit distracted lately."

"First time for everything," he mutters, but he's not entirely wrong. Distracted is an understatement—Lilith consumes my thoughts, unaware of her effect on me. My plan to approach her simmers, but it's too early. If I ever considered myself patient, that trait has vanished.

I'm an addict now, fixated on her.

"Yeah, here you go again," Grayson sighs in frustration.

"Why bother, Moore? I'm perfectly capable of finishing my project. The delay has nothing to do with personal reasons."

"Oh, son," he says, a term I detest. Despite being six years older, he acts like he's my elder by fucking decades. "I'm your *friend*, Caleb. I don't care about your productivity; I care about your well-being."

Jesus Christ. Grayson is like a bath sheet that sticks to my ass. Or a leech. His attempts to invade my personal space under the guise of friendship are transparent—everyone has an agenda. Trusting too much has led to betrayal too many times.

The less others know, the safer I am.

"I have no idea what you're talking about," I retort. "I'm fine."

"You remind me of myself at your age," he starts, and I roll my eyes and lean back. He persists, "I was lost and unsure too. Never seen you with a girl, though. Maybe that day will come soon, huh?"

Oh, I've had women before. Nine of them are dead. It's a part of my life I keep hidden for *good* reason.

"No, it's not about a girl, Grayson," I dismiss, ignoring his probing expression. "Just stressed about work."

56

"Yeah, yeah," he scoffs disbelievingly. "Sooner or later, if it gets serious, I'll need to know. Most guys your age are married with kids already."

"Right now, I need to finish my project," I reply dryly.

"That's for sure, because I've got another one in the pipeline."

This catches me off guard. He hasn't mentioned new projects before. "What's that?" I ask cautiously.

"The demand for home security systems is soaring," he explains. "People are afraid of the Black Widow, so they're panicking. Bad as it sounds, it's good for us."

I almost snort. Almost. "Will be done."

CHAPTER
TEN

Lilith

The morning light gently filters into the classroom, casting warm, golden rays that delicately illuminate Professor Graham's features, painting them with a soft, radiant glow. I knock on the half-open door. "Professor? Can I come in?"

He shifts his attention from the papers on his desk briefly, his expression turning blank. "Sure," he replies flatly.

It's ironic that my favorite professor, whose teaching style I admire most, seems to hate me. Well, maybe not hate, but certainly a lack of fondness. That incident last week, when I asked him to repeat the assignment, probably ruined any chance of a normal relationship.

I had worked tirelessly all week, crafting what I thought were the most impressive five chapters for my new novel. Graham always gives us optional extra work, calling it *homework for the commit-*

ted. It's not required, but it's a chance to improve our rapport with him and gain extra practice. I didn't just do it; I overdid it. I really put my all into this.

I close the distance between us and take a seat opposite him. "I wanted to apologize for my attitude last week. I've never allowed myself to be so careless." Placing my finished chapters in front of him, I cast a quick, soft glance.

"All of this is important to me. In my defense, I completed the assignment you gave us and then even more than I should've done," I say, hoping to make amends.

He stares at me for a moment before finally looking at my papers. "There's no such thing as *more than you should've done*, Lilith," Graham replies, taking my papers skeptically. "Your task doesn't end at the line between homework and free time. There's always more work to be done."

I swallow hard, feeling suddenly anxious. My hands instinctively reach for my hood, seeking a shield, but I quickly place them back on my legs. I can't hide forever, can I?

"You're right. I'm sorry," I murmur awkwardly.

"I'm not sure you know what you are apologizing for," he responds after a brief pause.

I don't know how to respond to that. I came here to fix things, but it seems I'm only making them worse.

"Okay," he says abruptly. Graham carefully folds my papers, only to tear them apart a moment later. I try to maintain a composed posture and indifferent demeanor, but from this moment on, it becomes impossible.

"What are you—"

"Consider it a favor," he interjects, handing me the torn pieces of paper. I take them back in confusion.

"As far as I know, you changed your major, right?"

I did. At first, I thought my purpose in life was to write short educational articles and news for a local magazine. But journalism felt shallower compared to creative writing, so I switched majors after a month.

"Yeah," I reply quietly, clearing my throat. "I was studying journalism."

He taps his fingers against the desk thoughtfully. "That's evident."

"What do you mean?" I ask, unsure of where this is going.

Graham lets out a frustrated sigh, as if talking to me is unbearable. "I mean, perhaps you should stick to writing short articles and news."

He leans back in his chair, picking up the papers he was working on before I interrupted. "But you never read—"

He gives me a look full of pity and disdain. "Look, Lilith. Not everyone can be a writer, and that's okay, because not everyone needs to be. Some people just *don't* fit in."

Summoning whatever strength I have left, I get up and walk out of the classroom, keeping my posture straight and my eyes dry. But as soon as I close the door behind me, it hits me—I release all the tears that have been welling up, a bitter lump in my throat depriving me of oxygen and making it hard to breathe. I can't make it to the exit; instead, I lean against the wall, sliding down as feeble sobs escape me, doubting my ability to pull myself together after this.

Graham callously crushed my sole ray of hope, obliterating the one thing that made me feel a bit happy. It's like he poured gasoline on the shards of my shattered heart and set them on fire.

"Lilith?"

I choke, slapping a hand over my mouth. This is a university, and I'm fucking crying in the middle of it. There are people around me. My eyes are closed, but I feel someone kneel in front of me, gently grabbing my hand.

"Hey, weirdo, what's wrong?" Evan asks gently.

"Sorry," I manage to chuckle, though none of this feels funny. "Just having a bad day."

Evan moves his other hand to my shoulder, giving it a slight squeeze. "It's okay. I've had my share too."

Our eyes meet briefly, and I quickly look away. I can't handle eye contact, especially with a guy I secretly like. "So, we're in the same boat, huh?" I ask.

"I don't usually hop into boats with weirdos."

I force a laugh, though his words sting. Maybe I'm just taking everything too seriously. "Fair enough," I reply awkwardly.

My glasses are streaked with tears, making my vision blurry. Evan reaches up and slides them off. "You need a little air, babe."

Heat rushes to my cheeks, turning them red. Did he just call me that? "Thanks," I mumble, feeling awkward about the endearment.

Evan smirks at me. "You look prettier without glasses."

It should be a compliment, but it only hurts. "Well, I can't see without them, so I'll stay ugly."

He helps me to my feet, and we walk toward the exit together. "If you were with me, I'd escort you everywhere," he says casually.

More blush creeps into my cheeks, and I can't help but give him a wide smile. "Really?"

"Yeah. Is that so hard to believe?" he asks, his tone light.

I shrug nonchalantly. "I don't know. You and me...it's weird, I guess."

"I like a bit of weird," he replies with a playful grin.

I swallow my frustration. It feels like he sees me as some kind of novelty, someone to date out of boredom.

But I keep quiet.

"Okay. I'm heading this way," he says, pointing to the left. "Listen, I wanted to ask you something."

"First, I need my glasses back," I object, reaching out my hand to him. He returns my glasses, and I put them on, the surroundings finally gaining clarity. "What's this about?"

"There's a party this Sunday at Murphy's place. Would you come with me, or do you have other plans?" he asks.

I furrow my brow, disbelief washing over my expression. "A party, huh?"

The little smirk Evan had a moment ago evaporates without a trace, replaced by annoyance. "Look, if you don't want to—"

"I'm in," I interrupt before he dismisses me. I've never noticed how easy it is to irritate Evan. I'll admit, it makes me a little uneasy.

He sighs, shoving his hands into his pockets. "Okay. Great. I'll text you the details."

I open my mouth to thank him, but he turns around abruptly and heads off, presumably back home. It's probably for the best that he left already. Why did I even consider thanking him? It's ridiculous.

I sling my bag over my shoulder, trying to process everything that just happened. Evan Flores just asked me to a party. I can't even remember anything about the situation with Graham.

I continue walking toward my apartment until, without realizing why, I suddenly turn around. Scanning the crowd, I try to understand the source of my sudden unease. But I can't find anything—or *anyone*. I probably look even weirder standing like a statue in the middle of the street, searching for something I'm not even sure about.

I turn back and keep walking, plugging my headphones into my ears and drowning out my surroundings with music.

I'm going to a party with Evan *fucking* Flores. What could be better?

THE WHOLE SUNDAY EVENING, I WRESTLE WITH AN UNPLEASANT FEEL-ing cascading through my insides. Something in my head tells me it's more than just anxiety. I've never been invited to parties, especially not by a guy who has the whole university at his feet. But tonight, I can choose whether to enjoy it or be miserable.

I choose the first option.

I double-check the address a couple more times before killing the engine and stepping out of my truck. The lingering fear of being stood up gnaws at me, making me more stressed than ever. But the loud music echoing down the street and the flashing color-ful lights assure me the party is indeed here.

I smooth the creases on my black dress, pulling it down in a futile attempt to make it longer. Insecurity about my body, height-ened tonight, particularly because Evan will be here. Adjusting my glasses, I jog hastily toward the house. I knock, which seems pointless amidst the blaring music inside, but the door opens to reveal a guy in a white cowboy hat with a red plastic cup in hand.

"Yeah?" he asks, leaning against the doorframe.

"Hey. This is Murphy's house, right?" I ask with a small smile.

"What?" He leans closer due to the music muffling my voice. "Murphy's house? You're Evan's *chick*?"

I bite back a sharp response. "If you say so."

"Lilith!" Evan's voice calls out, and he appears behind the guy. "Come on in, don't be shy!"

Before I can process what's happening, Evan grabs my arm and pulls me toward him. I collide into his chest with a gasp, and he chuckles softly. "Are you okay? Made it here without trouble? Goddamn, look at this dress!" He spins me around like a doll in a box, examining every inch of my body. "So pretty tonight."

A shiver runs down my spine, a strange unease settling in. His touch feels empty, devoid of genuine warmth or connection. "Yeah, I'm fine," I reply with a gentle smile.

He leans closer and plants a wet kiss on my cheek, his alcohol-laden scent overwhelming. "Come on, let me show you around," he says, already dragging me out of the living room toward the kitchen.

The place is packed with people—many already drunk or high, some openly crushing pills on the table, others downing bottles without a care. The atmosphere reeks of alcohol and a haze of various scents, dizzying my senses.

Evan grips my arm tightly, his hold almost bruising. I try to tell him he's hurting me, but he laughs, oblivious amidst the blaring music and his clouded mind.

"Okay, okay," he finally says, releasing my arm to grab a bottle of liquor and pour us both drinks. "We need to celebrate this."

"Celebrate what?" I ask, taking the red plastic cup he hands me.

He clinks our cups together. "Your ass stepping out of your comfort zone."

While Evan downs his drink in one go and pours another, I spin my cup mindlessly. I did step out of my comfort zone, but I don't share Evan's enthusiasm. The crowd feels suffocating, as if trapping me in an invisible cage. I try to shake off imagined hands from my body, realizing no one is touching me.

It's all in my head.

I hesitate to drink, suddenly unsure about everything.

"Evan, can we go somewhere more secluded?" I blurt out without considering how it sounds. He pauses midway through his drink, setting the cup down and turning to face me. Soft, kaleidoscopic lights gently caress his features, highlighting his flawless face.

"You read my mind," he says, a hint of anticipation in his voice. I realize he's misunderstood, but before I can clarify, he's already pulling me upstairs. I struggle to keep up as he practically runs, eager to find a place away from prying eyes.

In the blink of an eye, we're alone in a room and he's already undressing. "Evan—" I begin to whisper, but he pushes me onto the bed and leans over me, silencing my protest with a kiss.

I should feel excited. The heartthrob, Evan Flores, wants to fuck me. I convinced myself I wanted this, even if just a little attention from him, but now it's more than I bargained for.

Yet, I can't enjoy it. I can't force myself to.

Maybe it's because he left the door open. Or maybe it's the nagging thought that he only wants me because he's drunk. That he won't even *look* at me when he sobers up.

"Evan, stop," I mumble against his lips. "I don't want to."

But he either doesn't hear me or chooses to ignore my pleas, pressing his kisses harder against me. His bare chest against my fully clothed body makes me feel repulsed. If this is what all the fuss was about, I don't understand it. Evan's kisses make me want to gag each time his tongue invades my mouth; his touch feels cold and unpleasant, and his skin is clammy and sticky.

"Stop, stop, just STOP!" I snap as he starts pulling at my dress straps, my voice strange to my ears. I push him away with my leg. "I said I don't want to!"

His expression changes from half-asleep to angry as he rises from the floor, grabbing a small statue from the dresser and hurling it against the wall above my head. I scream, instinctively dodging away. Evan chuckles, finding amusement in his action.

"You know, Lilith, every time I look at you, I think, who the fuck does this bitch think she is?" He kneels in front of me, meeting my shocked stare. "I invited you here because Diana wasn't an option anymore. After what happened to her, I thought, well, maybe I should give you a chance. Isn't that what you wanted, weirdo?"

"No."

"No, no, no." Evan shakes his head. "Don't lie to me, Lilith. You were so desperate for my attention all the time. I thought I could do a good thing, make you less miserable, and now you're saying no?" He grips my chin, forcing me to meet his cruel gaze. "Do you think anyone will ever love you, Lilith? Or just want to fuck you? Huh? Do you think people don't see that something is wrong with you?" He laughs, the stench of alcohol from his breath overwhelming me. "Even I had to get wasted just to fuck you. No one would willingly do that."

"Fuck you, Evan," I hiss, trying and failing to keep my voice steady. I push him with all my strength, and when he loosens his grip and falls onto his ass, I get up and storm out of the room. Despite feeling trampled and humiliated, I can't bring myself to cry until I leave this house.

I storm out onto the street, trying to remember where I parked. The space is a blur of dark stains, infuriating me for some reason.

I should have slapped him. I should have said something more cutting, more humiliating. I should have stayed and enjoyed myself just to spite him, to show how little his words affected me. But instead, I chose the path that feels all too familiar at this point. I ignore everything and leave the only party I'd been invited to, ruining my chance to make something better of my night.

I tremble, not from the cold but from the overwhelming flood of emotions. Tears well up, obscuring my vision through misted glasses, leaving me unable to see a damn thing. After about five minutes of aimless wandering, I finally remember where I parked my rusty truck. I fish out my keys from my purse and try to unlock the door, but they're stuck.

Of course they fucking are. As if the night couldn't possibly get any worse.

I desperately jiggle the key, twisting and turning it until I snap and slam my fist against the car door. Pain shoots through my hand, but miraculously, the door squeaks open.

I climb inside, start the engine, and think of nothing but how I'm going to face classes tomorrow after everything Evan said to me.

CHAPTER

ELEVEN

Caleb

I wait for the fucker in his car. It is obvious that he never plans to leave earlier than morning, so I use my little hacker trick to lure him here.

The front door clicks open and Evan Flores walks to his vehicle like an obedient puppy he is. He staggers, probably high and drunk at the same time. It slows him down, and I will lie if I say that doesn't piss me off.

I can't wait to complete my plan.

He doesn't even realize that someone broke into his car—too intoxicated to think about anything. As soon as he gets inside and slams the door, I rise from the back seat and strike him in the head, steadying his body to prevent him from falling onto the steering wheel and accidentally activating the horn.

It takes me no effort to drag his bony ass on the backseat, throwing him on the floor like a garbage he is. Then, I move to the driver's seat and start the engine, feeling impatient to do what I planned to do.

IN LESS THAN FIFTEEN MINUTES, I REACH ONE OF MY SECRET SPOTS — a location with nothing but heaps of abandoned bricks, a couple of rats, and occasionally unconscious junkies scattered about. There are numerous unguarded places like this in New York, usually unfinished buildings or houses left incomplete because the owners went bankrupt.

I've rarely used these places, though. None of my victims required torture; they placed their trust in me, so there was never a need for me to extract what I wanted through force.

I don't even enjoy torture, not physical anyway. The psychological one is what empowers me — methodically breaking people down, observing as the small flame of hope diminishes each day they come to terms with the fact that it's all over for them.

But Evan fucking Flores is going to suffer tonight. I watched Lilith all the way from her home to that party, and I heard and saw everything that happened.

At one moment I thought that my plan for slowly getting inside her life would be ruined. I thought the fucker is going to rape her. If such a situation were to arise, I wouldn't permit myself to remain in the shadows and just witness it.

But thankfully she escaped, unharmed. Physically.

No matter how stupid this son of a bitch is, he knows how to make people feel worthless. He knew Lilith's weak spots, he knew exactly where to press. I should be near her apartment now, observing her as she peacefully prepares for bed — after all, my intention was simply to watch her, to study her.

But this fucker isn't going to leave without consequences. He needs to understand that he has to change his behavior. I don't care about others, though. He needs to change it toward Lilith.

"W-what the fuck?" he groans, trying to move his hands and legs. After he realizes that he is tied to the chair, the panic starts to slowly occupy his stupid head. My favorite part. "What the FUCK?!"

He hasn't even noticed me yet, and I find myself grinning foolishly as I revel in the various emotions sweeping across his ugly face — confusion, panic, and anger.

I lean against the wall, watching how he tries to untie himself, fidgeting on the place like a worm in the ground hole.

After a solid fifteen seconds, his blue eyes finally snap to mine. He grimaces in irritation, throwing his head back as the strands of his dirty blonde hair stick to his forehead, chaotically falling onto his eyes. "Who the fuck are you?"

I wear a mask, although I don't even care if he finds out who I am. Nobody is going to believe him, even after he decides to give me to the police. And especially after what I plan to do to him.

"Think of me as the arbiter of justice," I reply, approaching him with a few strides.

He flinches, still desperate to loosen the ropes. "What the fuck does this mean? Do you even know who—"

"Evan Alan Flores, a nineteen-year-old student, has chosen a Business Administration major to work as a real estate lawyer just like his daddy," I interrupt. "A typical rich prick who thinks everyone owes something to him just because he can afford shiny things on his daddy's money. You also live on a—"

I trail off as if struggling to remember his address although I remember every single detail about him like a multiplication table. "20 Lakeside Drive, right?"

There's a flicker in his eyes – pure fear. From this moment on, he no longer feels as brave as he did a moment ago. "Nice house, by the way. But the security system is pure shit. Aren't your family rich?"

He gulps down a lump in his throat. "Look, I have no idea what you want from me. I swear, if you are from that Infinity Properties company, I am not the one you need. My dad is. He was—"

I release a chuckle, thoroughly amused. "I don't give a shit about your daddy's muddy business."

His eyebrows pinch together. "Is it about the money? I could give—"

"I don't give a shit about money." I walk to the bag with all the supplies I need and take the large pliers I've prepared for him. "You know, Evan, I think I can't ever get why people like you think they are gods when in reality they are nothing but a scum." I advance toward him, deliberately taking my time. "You keep recklessly doing everything you want and don't want like it's never enough for you. You can't keep your mouth shut when it's needed which makes you no more than just another blabber who brings nothing to society. You hurt people who don't deserve it."

I stop right in front of the fucker, leaning to meet his face. I refuse to understand how the hell people find this boy attractive. He looks nothing like a man who is able to take on some responsibilities and make someone besides himself happy.

We need to talk about Lilith's taste in men.

"You hurt people who are not just better than you—you don't even deserve to breathe the same air as them. You don't deserve to walk on the same ground as them. So how can you open your mouth in their direction?" I bring the pliers to his face, forcing him to switch attention to them. "You're nothing, Evan. You were, you are, and you will be nothing for the rest of your miserable life. And now, I'm going to teach you a little lesson, with your permission."

Killing this fucker is going to be an easy punishment. I don't want to give him the satisfaction. After all, I want him to *learn* the lesson.

"What are you doing?" he asks in a trembling voice. "Hey, hey, DON'T!"

But I don't even pay attention to his pathetic attempts to stop me. I grab the hold of his jaw and grip his mouth wide open. I unclench the pliers with one hand and bring them closer to his mouth. He fidgets in his chair and even tries to jump away as if it can help him to escape. Attempts are so fucking laughable that I can't suppress a laugh.

Sweat and drool trickle down his chin as he struggles for air, while I grasp his tongue with the pliers, gradually applying pressure, disregarding his desperate pleas and futile attempts to wrest free from my grip.

With a quiet *click*, I cut away his tongue—the piece of it drops right under him. The blood sprays from his mouth non-stop and I grab the hold of his dirty hair, tilting his head so he won't choke on his saliva and blood. He coughs, cries, and lets out a sound that is more likely to be a scream, but because he lost his voice, it comes out as nothing more than just little whimpers.

I take a step back, only now realizing that he painted my clothes with his blood. And as fucked up as it will sound, I don't even want to change. I'll leave it as a small trophy, a *reminder*.

Recalling more memories about less than an hour ago, I wipe the blood from the pliers and toss them back in the bag. Then, I take the hammer and return back to the poor Evan who can't stop coughing and choking. As I close the distance between us, the unpleasant smell hits my nose.

I grimace as my eyes fall on his jeans, catching a dark stain painting the grey cloth. "You peed yourself," I state in a serious voice while I fight back an urge to laugh.

Now this is the image of the real Evan – of the scum that he really is. "Not feeling brave enough anymore, huh? Have nothing to say?" I scan his face, realizing that he may pass out from the pain shock any minute.

It's too early. I have another surprise for him.

Fueled by the picture of my Lilith when she had a mental breakdown, hitting her car door and almost breaking her knuckles, I bring the hammer to his hand.

"Bonus prize."

I swing it and then hit his knuckles, immediately hearing a loud crunch of his fragile bones. Blood sprays from his right hand—I surely remember which one my Lilith used. I take a step back, enjoying the view—watching this piece of shit suffering brings me more pleasure than it should.

I enjoy his suffering when after a solid couple of minutes, he passes out. I bring two of my fingers to his neck, and when I am sure that he is still alive, I wipe my hands from all the dirt he left and untie his bony ass from the chair.

I dial 911, and after I tell the operator all the information, I grab the bag with my supplies and walk back to my car.

CHAPTER

TWELVE

Lilith

I jolt wide awake as a familiar memory grips my consciousness—the recurring nightmare of my birth into this world. The realization that it's just the same dreadful dream that has haunted me for twenty years forces me to exhale, attempting to stifle the tremors wracking my body.

While I try to focus, another sound pierces my sensitive ears—a relentless banging on the door. I groan, rubbing the sleep from my eyes. For some reason, I slept like a baby last night, as if the shame that consumed me yesterday evening didn't almost drive me to the brink of suicide.

"Oh, God. I'm coming!" I mutter, irritation coloring my voice.

I swing the door open, surprise spreading across my face. "Hey, kiddo," Frank says casually. "You were sleeping?"

I clear my throat to rid it of its raspy note. "What time is it?"

He ducks his head, narrowing his eyes in thought. "Six in the morning."

I make a frustrated grimace. "Of course, I was sleeping."

I notice guilt flickering in his eyes as they sweep over the room. Feeling a bit like a bitch, I add, "It's fine. I was going to wake up for my classes anyway. Come in."

I turn and head for the kitchen, expecting him to follow. Inviting an old, sometimes erratic alcoholic who recently tried to break into my place might not be the wisest decision, but Frank is harmless. At least, when he's sober. Among the residents of this apartment complex, he's one of the funniest and easiest to talk to. He even helped me fix the kitchen sink once, all for free.

So, if I let his occasional drunken escapades slide, he's a pretty decent human being.

"I just wanted to apologize, sunshine," he says as I hear the door close behind us, followed by his footsteps.

I fill the kettle with water, place it on the gas stove, and ignite the burner. "Oh, so you actually remember what you've done?" I ask mockingly.

He takes a seat at the table, running a hand through his gray hair. "This time I do."

I cross my arms, settling into a comfortable position. "Go on."

He lets out a sigh. "I know I've done this countless times, and it always ends up in the same place. I just—" He trails off, searching for the right words. "I'm sorry I scared you, sunshine."

I shake my head. "That's an easy way to put it, old man."

Guilt flashes in his brown eyes at my words. "Next time, call the cops. I won't be mad."

I give a low laugh. "Whatever you say, my friend."

When the water boils, I open the cupboard where I keep my tea stash. "Green, black, herbal, mint, or mango?"

Frank gives a rare smile that warms my heart. "Herbal, please."

I nod and place tea bags in our cups, pouring hot water into them. "I know it's not my business, but seriously, Frank, you need to stop that. Getting so wasted that you're ready to break into someone's apartment isn't going to bring her back."

The main reason he drinks so heavily is the loss of his daughter from his second marriage, who died from cancer at the age of six. As much as I sympathize with him, I can't ignore his destructive coping mechanisms.

The old man needs help.

"I know," he replies in a subdued tone as I set his cup of herbal tea in front of him.

"Sometimes you remind me of her, Lilith," he says softly.

Ah, now it makes more sense. "As flattered as I am by that, I'd prefer not to find anyone blocking the only entrance to my apartment, friend."

He chuckles. "Fair enough."

An unfamiliar sensation coils through my insides the moment I step foot onto campus, unpleasantly tickling me. When I walk into the classroom, I freeze. The reason for my sudden premonition becomes clear.

"Lilith Leclair," the officer greets, taking a few steps toward me. "We've been waiting for you."

I scan the classroom, meeting concerned stares from my classmates. "What happened?"

The officer gently places his hand on my shoulder. "I would like to speak with you in private."

I hesitantly nod and follow him, trying to shake off all my negative thoughts along the way. After all, I didn't do anything wrong. But here's the thing about conversations with cops—you can be clearly innocent, but still feel like you're being accused of murder or caught with a bag of cocaine.

He opens the door for me and I step inside a smaller classroom, quietly thanking him. "Please, take a seat," he says, gesturing toward a chair.

I comply, and he sits opposite me, intertwining his fingers. "I'm not going to beat around the bush here," he begins. "Yesterday, you were at a party at Rosaline Murphy's house, is that correct?"

I'd like to erase the memory of last night, but anyway, "Yeah, I was."

"You were there with Evan Alan Flores around ten p.m.," he continues.

I bite back the unpleasant memories of Evan's advances. "Well, Evan invited me, and I was there for a while, but he got... too drunk, so I left. About twenty minutes later."

The cop studies my face intently, as if trying to catch me in a lie. "According to witnesses, you were drinking with him in the kitchen and then went upstairs."

A bitter lump rises in my throat at the thought of the lies they must have told the police. "I didn't drink anything. He offered me a cup, but I never touched it with my mouth."

"And what were you two doing upstairs?"

Jesus Christ. Can this conversation get any worse? "He misunderstood. I said no. That made him angry, so I left before things could escalate."

"Are you suggesting Mr. Flores was upset because you rejected him?"

"Upset? He threw a wooden statuette at me after I made it clear I didn't want to sleep with him, and then he insulted me," I snap, my anger leaking out unintentionally. "Why are you asking me this, anyway?"

The cop purses his lips. "Mr. Flores was found at an abandoned construction site, unconscious."

My anger evaporates instantly. "*What?*"

"An anonymous call came in to 911 shortly after you left, Lilith," he explains calmly. "We checked his phone. He received a message from an unknown number, saying someone had broken into his car. Apparently, he went to investigate and someone attacked him."

"What do you mean, *apparently*?" I ask, my voice trembling. "He didn't tell you what happened? Is he still unconscious?"

The cop pauses. "Whoever attacked him also cut off his tongue, Lilith."

A chill runs through my body, goosebumps rising on my skin as if I've been drenched in icy water.

I take back what I said. This conversation just got ten times worse.

What the hell is happening? Who could do something like that? And *why* the tongue?

"Did they...do anything else?" I ask cautiously, trying to hide the tremor in my voice.

He shakes his head. "They did break the knuckles on his right hand, possibly with a hammer."

My gaze instinctively shifts to my own right hand, where little purple bruises stain my knuckles. I tug the sleeve of my hoodie down to cover them, suddenly feeling nauseous. My chest tightens, and I struggle to take a deep breath as confusion and panic wash over me. I try to focus my eyes on a single point, to ground myself, but they keep darting uncontrollably. Frustrated, I shut them tightly, trying to make sense of the situation and figure out my next move.

Is this all just a coincidence? It has to be.

But why does it feel like it's not?

"Lilith?" The cop's voice brings me back. I realize he's been calling my name for the past minute. "Are you okay?"

I'm *not*. "Yeah, sorry. I'm fine. Can I visit him? Which hospital is he in?"

He gives me a warm, reassuring smile. "Of course. But first, I need to ask you a couple more questions."

I SUMMON THE COURAGE TO DRIVE TO THE HOSPITAL JUST A FEW DAYS after everything happened. As I approach Evan's ward, a knot tightens in my stomach, and anxiety churns within me. Each step feels like a weight bearing down on my head, making my progress slow and heavy. Despite this, I press on, determined to face whatever lies ahead.

I glance at the numbers on the doors, searching for 523b. When I finally find it, instead of knocking and entering, I cowardly sneak a peek through the small window in the door. Evan lies with his eyes closed, a noticeable purple bruise staining the right side of his head.

He looks more fragile than ever. His room is empty, and it dawns on me that his father probably rarely visits. Their relationship has always been strained. Despite the persona he portrays at university, when he truly needs someone, there's no one here to comfort or support him.

He's *alone*.

I'm unsure why I feel scared to face him. For the past few days, all I've done is think and expect the police to show up at my door, accusing me of something. It couldn't have been a coincidence. Someone must have heard what happened, seen me punching the car door.

What does this person want from me? What's their purpose?

I place my hand on the door handle, but I can't bring myself to turn it. Even after taking a deep breath, I can't do it. I'm not even sure why I came here.

What would I say? How would we even communicate? He lost his damn tongue.

The sterile white walls and fluorescent lighting seem to close in on me, suffocating me with their brightness. The smell of disinfectant and antiseptic fills my nostrils, making me feel nauseous and dizzy. I know I shouldn't be here; this was a bad idea from the start.

With a heavy heart, I turn on my heel and storm out of the hospital. My palms are slick with sweat, feeling clammy and cold as if they were made of clouds instead of skin. I hastily wipe them on my jeans as I make my way back to my truck.

As I get inside, I slam the door with a loud thud, startling myself. I run my hand through my hair as I lean forward, resting my elbows on the steering wheel, trying to make sense of why I feel so relieved despite the nerves still coursing through me.

What happened to Evan was beyond horrific. And yet, here I am, feeling this way.

It's wrong. It's so *fucking* wrong.

He's lucky to be alive, and I shouldn't feel anything but gratitude for that. But I can't ignore my true feelings.

I cover my mouth in shock at my own thoughts. Maybe people are right. Maybe there *is* something terribly wrong with me.

As my phone buzzes in my purse, I silently thank whoever it is for giving me a chance to distract myself from the messed-up thoughts swirling in my mind.

UNKNOWN:

stop tearing yourself apart, little devil. he deserved everything that happened to him.

I stare at my phone, trying to comprehend whether I'm hallucinating or if it's the truth. My hands begin to shake, and my mouth forms an "O" in sheer disbelief. I start typing a response, unsure of what or how to text.

Me:

Who the hell is this? What do you want?

81

I naively hope it's someone's prank or a mistaken number as I wait for a reply. But none comes.

Me:

> Hey?? What kind of sick game are you playing, asshole?

It's pointless, I realize.

I raise my head and scan the street, heart racing with fear, though I see no suspicious figures. I try to calm myself with deep breaths, but the shock of the text lingers.

Empowered by a sudden burst of false confidence, I send one final message to the stranger.

Me:

> Whatever you planned, I'm not fucking scared of you.

A lie. An obvious one. But maybe, the more I convince myself I'm brave, the more true it will become.

With my mind swirling with thoughts, I stash the phone back in my purse, start the engine, and speed away from this place.

PIPER

I NEVER THOUGHT I COULD HATE SOMEONE SO MUCH.

I WANT TO KILL HIM. NOT JUST TO KILL, I WANT HIM TO SUFFER. I WANT TO TORTURE HIM, TO ENJOY WATCHING HOW LIFE SLOWLY FADES AWAY FROM THOSE BLACK EYES.

I DREAM ABOUT IT BEING MY NEW ROUTINE. TO WAKE UP, WASH MY FACE, AND GO DOWN TO MY BASEMENT, PICKING A NEW TOOL TO TORTURE THIS MOTHERFUCKER.

HE DOES NOTHING BUT TOTALLY IGNORES ME AS IF I AM ALREADY A GHOST. I THINK IF HE WOULD TORTURE ME, THAT WOULD BE A LOT BETTER. BECAUSE I WOULD UNDERSTAND WHAT HE WANTS FROM ME, AND EVENTUALLY, MY BODY WOULDN'T STAND IT, AND I WOULD FINALLY FALL ASLEEP FOREVER.

BUT HE WON'T ALLOW ME TO GET AWAY THAT EASILY. HE ENJOYS SEEING ME SUFFER.

THE ONLY WAY I CAN LIVE THROUGH THIS HELL IS BY PICTURING MY TORTURE ON HIM.

TWENTY-FOUR FUCKING SEVEN.

I DESPERATELY HOPE THAT ONE DAY I WILL BE ABLE TO GET MY REVENGE.

OR IF SOMEONE FINDS THIS, HE OR SHE WOULD DO IT FOR ME.

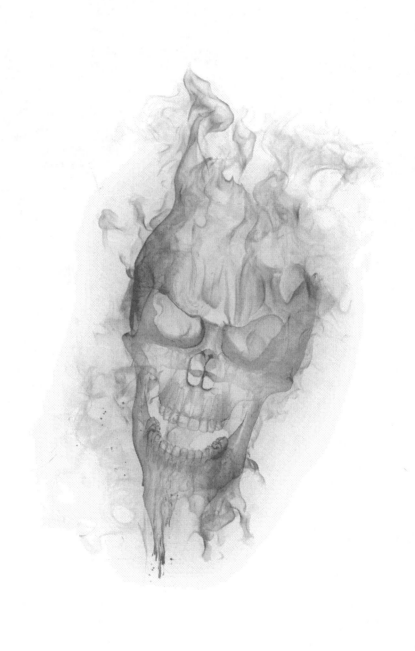

CHAPTER

THIRTEEN

Caleb

For the past few days, I've been staring at the same message, wearing the same idiotic, satisfied grin.

Lilith:

Whatever you planned, I'm not fucking scared of you.

And I believe my little devil. She's not scared. She's confused and lost, and that alone is worse than fear.

The more I watch her, the more impatient I grow. For the first time in my life, I've invented a pet name for a woman.

My little devil.

I maintain our distance, yet I can't help envisioning how small she would appear once I narrow the gap. At *5'8*, she'll not only have to raise her head to meet my gaze but stand on her tiptoes as well.

So, she's little, and well, considering how hard she is trying to hide her real name, calling her *devil* would add another layer of stress to her mind. She's aware of being monitored and someone is prepared to go to extremes for her. And she knows that whoever he is, he knows every damn thing about her life and that he is not going to stop.

Looking around, wondering when, how, and *if* I'm going to strike is going to drain her mind. But I have a new plan. And soon, I am going to meet her.

Very soon.

As usual, I am watching her through the cameras I installed in her apartment a long time ago. She put a little smiley sticker face on the front camera on her laptop—paranoid—having no clue that I occupied every corner of her place.

It amuses me.

I observe her as she goes through her evening ritual: preparing and eating dinner, heading to the bathroom and dedicating at least an hour to tending to her hair, face, and body.

Each time I watch her doing the same damn thing every day, for some reason, it feels like the first time. Lilith cares about how she looks—she keeps track of her strict schedule, tries to eat healthy food, seeks new techniques for makeup, and tips for making her skin and hair look healthier—and fuck me for admiring it.

I can't stop watching her doing it. Again, she never goes out, lives in a shithole, and has zero fucking friends except her alcoholic old neighbor and that virgin flower Kevin—an online friend who has no fucking idea what she needs and how to properly talk with her. Speaking of him, each day I check their chit-chat, I fight back an urge to fly to Canada and fucking butcher him.

I understood everything from the beginning, but I know how she cares about him, I see her face every time they speak on the phone or he sends her another pointless text about him reading another psychological book, and I can tell that she enjoys talking to him.

I can't just kill him. That would make her sad and she would break.

For now, Kevin is her one and only friend, so I can't do anything. I can just watch and wait.

So, before the virgin flower guy, I was talking about how she had not the fullest fucking life, yet she prepares for each day like it's her last. She does this one-hundred-something routine not for someone.

She does it for herself.

It's funny, watching her with her hair and makeup done, in pretty clothes as if she is going to some party while in reality she sits inside her apartment and tries to write her novel or reads something.

I've finished her first book, by the way. In one day. I drained this fucking book in one gulp, dare I say.

Recalling the memory of her talking with that professor who tore apart her chapters and said that she can't write, I am convinced that the dude is fucking blind. Stupid.

I'm bewildered by her ability to immerse me in the fictional universe she's crafted through her words, making me feel as though I inhabit the lives of every character she portrays, no matter how minor. Her attention to detail resulted in a story that feels strikingly true to life yet manages to sidestep the mundane, boring parts of reality.

Like I said, I never was a reader, but I would read every single of her book, even if she decided to switch styles from thrillers to a fucking romance.

And I am not saying this just because I am obsessed with her. The truth is, she possesses undeniable talent and intelligence. This cannot be taken away from her. Graham is worth to be killed, of course, but not now. He will willingly help me to meet my Lilith soon.

After she's done her routine, my little devil plops on the couch and puts on a movie. She likes to rewatch old classic films, mostly thrillers, dramas, and sometimes even a little action. Today she watches another 90's thriller. At some moments she pays full attention to her laptop screen as if she sees the fragments for the first time. But most of the time she scrolls something on her phone, and I check what she's been looking at, silently praying she isn't talking to the virgin flower boy.

Oh, *fuck* me.

She's been searching for the same damn thing since I've started monitoring her phone. Lilith is obsessed with a particular pajama she saw an actress wearing in her favorite movie. She's been desperately trying to find something similar because the original is too expensive.

Frankly, I don't see the appeal – it's just a cream beige silk top with thin straps and shorts with a dainty lace trim. But she wants it like her life depends on it. Each time I catch her Googling it again, my annoyance grows until I snap.

I log onto the original website and order it. In seconds, my bank balance is $300 lighter, and a notification confirms the order will arrive in two to three days. I breathe a sigh of relief, knowing soon I won't witness her endless scrolling.

Lilith has been spending more time by the window lately, especially since the situation with Evan. Another change I've noticed is her preference for more revealing clothing at home. Gone are the oversized T-shirts and sweatpants; now she flaunts mini shorts and crop tops that tease and tempt. She knows I watch her, and she enjoys it. I'm grateful she dresses modestly outside; otherwise, I'd have to kill too many admirers.

She's perfection, and she's *mine* – I can't bear the thought of anyone else seeing her this way.

After Lilith gazes out at the dimly lit street, she eventually heads to her bedroom. With a gentle descent onto the bed, a hint of trepidation crosses her face, as if she senses an unseen observer. Just when I think she's going to sleep, she surprises me, her hand slipping inside her mini shorts.

Fuck.

Lilith closes her eyes like she is ashamed of what she is doing, and then slowly begins circling her clit with two fingers.

She never pleased herself before. Not once since I've started to watch her.

She spreads her legs wider, moving her fingers with increasing urgency, her lips parting in ecstasy. My cock throbs painfully in my pants, as though I've been waiting for this moment subconsciously, longing for it.

Her eyes remain shut throughout, and I wonder what she's thinking. She's never watched porn or sought this out intentionally. What could be on her mind right now? Surely not Evan fucking Flores – she never even liked him.

I know that she never had a boyfriend. I've searched every bit of information I could possibly find. She could have one-night stands, though I highly doubt it. This little devil is too fucking shy.

Could she be a virgin? I thought about it a lot of time, and now, I'm convincing myself that she is. She never even shoves a finger inside herself, just circles her most sensitive spot.

Fuck me for finding another reason to be obsessed with her.

I never even realize how I pull down my sweatpants along with my underwear, allowing my cock long-awaited freedom.

I am so hard it feels fucking abnormal. I don't remember the last time I was so turned on by watching a woman who pleases herself.

I fist my cock, sliding my hand up and down across its length, feeling miniature flames ignite upon my skin, harmonized by her soft whimpering that evokes an intoxicating blend of pleasure inside me. My mind is already spinning with desire, the sensation heating me from within.

Here I am, jerking off right in my car, in the middle of the street. But I don't even care if someone notices.

What I *do* care is about what she thinks about. What does she imagine? Maybe the faceless man who is watching her right now? Maybe she dreams about meeting him, about letting him do whatever he wants to her?

She is telling him that she isn't scared, walking around in clothes that barely cover her little body, knowing that he watches her, provoking him.

Fuck, I want to spank her for being so reckless. But after that, I want to show her what she is worth. I want to give her the treatment she deserves, to tell her how fucking smart and beautiful she is. I want to see those little flames of shyness in her emerald eyes, watch how crimson creeps into those cheeks.

I want her to deny it, to deny me. To push me away when secretly she wants me to catch her, to devour her and unleash havoc upon her soul, forever claiming her as my own.

Everything about her is fucking gorgeous, especially the way her chest begins rising and falling faster with each second closer to her blissful climax.

As I feel my peak approaching, a sharp ache pierces between my eyes, causing my eyelashes to flutter. "Come for me, little devil," I murmur as I gaze at the image of her, absolutely convinced that I'm witnessing the most beautiful sight imaginable.

A second before pure euphoria wracks her body, she emits a resounding moan as if responding to me, forcing my stomach to tense in delight. And in perfect synchrony, I too break into a million little fragments, my sight obscuring with nothing but shimmering flashes as a cyclone of pleasure occupies my body.

"Fuck, fuck!" A moan pours from my throat, and I bow my head down, out of my breath.

As the remnants of our shared euphoria dissolve in the air and rationality begins to assert itself, a whirlwind of different thoughts engulfs my brain.

What the fuck was that? I've had countless orgasms before, with different women in different positions, but nothing like this. It's fucking laughable – how could fisting my cock in the car while watching the woman I'm obsessed with can compare to the actual feeling inside of someone's cunt or mouth?

I can't even believe it now. It pisses me the fuck off.

I started watching Lilith only because she was supposed to be my tenth. After her, I would've moved on to someone else, and so on.

What's so special about her? She's the complete opposite of everyone else I've been with before. All my previous targets were social butterflies, perfect according to societal norms, with full lives. Lilith, on the other hand, has nothing but her little hobby and dozens of interests she has no one to share with. She is quiet, humble—too damn humble and awkward.

But fuck it, when everyone tells her she's uninteresting, tedious, and boring, I find her the most fascinating person I've ever met.

There's something about her that reminds me of my past self, before I got my job as a serial killer. Back in my childhood, from my school days through my years as a student, I was incredibly shy and reserved. I never really had friends and often found myself lost in my own little world, lost in thought. I was definitely quite introverted and miserable, with messed-up parents.

Everything about her makes me question my motives toward her, revealing layers of previously unknown feelings while also evoking something familiar within me.

It's no longer just about the urge to kill her; it's about getting to know her, fantasizing about shared moments, the sensation of touching her tender skin, and inhaling her intoxicating essence.

This is a completely new experience for me. I never imagined I would feel something like this.

I fucked up.

She's too good for me. I should just forget everything, pretend it never happened, and move on to someone else to satisfy my desires. I should leave her alone because she doesn't deserve to have anything to do with me.

I'll bring about her downfall, shattering her soul into countless little fragments, leaving her unable to rebuild herself.

But it's too late now.

I can't stop.

CHAPTER
FOURTEEN

Lilith

I make an effort to attend classes as if nothing has changed. I consciously avoid the intense, probing gazes of my classmates—a skill I've grown accustomed to mastering.

But now, the pressure I once felt, the desperate urge to hide under a giant hood, has evaporated without a trace. I don't know why, but I feel more confident. It's unsettling, considering everything that's happened. I can't command my brain not to feel this sudden wave of confidence whenever I sense their eyes on me.

As for the most popular people here—Diana and Evan—they're gone as if they never existed. It's almost comical. What was the point of their popularity and adoration when now they're surrounded by emptiness?

They mocked me, feeding off my lack of confidence, but where are they now? It doesn't seem like they're having as much fun anymore.

I even had a breakthrough of inspiration. Just yesterday, I managed to write three whole chapters of my new novel in one evening. It's been a while since inspiration struck so spontaneously, but when it did, it felt refreshingly natural.

Despite how enticing it all sounds, a feeling of unease follows me everywhere. It intensified after receiving that message following my visit to Evan in the hospital. I stare at it, waiting in vain for three dots to appear.

If my suspicions are correct and the message came from the man who attacked Evan, I should go to the police. I should confess everything, connect the dots, because what happened couldn't be mere coincidence.

I can't stop thinking about the method that the asshole chose. He didn't kill him only because he wanted this humiliation to haunt him for the rest of his life. And if he really called 911 himself, making sure that the medics were able to save him, that confirms it.

Discovering his identity may not leave me unscathed. Yet, my morbid curiosity overrides common sense. I know he watches me, keeping his distance to torment and fuel my reckless fascination. I understand it's a trap, yet I find myself falling into it, unable to resist.

He initiated this game, and I play by my rules, though I never quite understood what they were until I saw myself in the mirror, barely clothed, and felt a sudden urge I hadn't had in months.

Evan's note to the police described a masked figure with piercing obsidian eyes, tall, and commanding. It disturbs me how twisted my response is—pleasing myself with thoughts of a psychopath who tortured someone I knew.

The idea that he did it for me, now watching over me, evokes… *conflicting* emotions. I don't dare consider what comes next. He's not the type for park walks and ice cream; he's devoid of boundaries and morals.

Maybe my mother was right. There's *something* wrong with me, fantasizing about facing a maniac, inviting his gaze.

Yet amid the storm of emotions, fear finds no place—just an incredibly foolish curiosity that promises dire consequences.

JUST AS ANOTHER BURST OF INSPIRATION BEGINS TO TAKE HOLD, THE sound of the doorbell interrupts my thoughts. I close my laptop and carefully set it down on the couch before heading to the door. The only person who uses that half-dead doorbell button on the right side of the wall is Randall Reed, my landlord. He visits at the end of each month to collect rent, despite my insistence that I can come to him on time.

I open the door, my toes curling from the cold air outside. Note to self: start wearing socks under my fluffy slippers.

"Hey, Randall," I greet, my tone friendly despite my discomfort. I've never liked him; he always makes me uneasy. He's single, around thirty, and gives me those weird glances whenever we meet. I often catch him coincidentally bumping into me at my favorite spots. But I try to dismiss my negative thoughts, telling myself I might be overreacting.

"Good evening, Lilith," he replies softly, bypassing me and entering my apartment without invitation. He does this often, irritating me, but he's the landlord, so I can't exactly kick him out.

"I thought I'd pay for the rent tomorrow morning by myself," I say.

I close the door, leaning against it as I watch him settle on my couch.

Fucker.

"Come on," he says, patting the seat beside him as if I'm expected to join him. "Can't I visit my friend without reason?"

His incessant patting makes me uncomfortable, so I ignore it and choose a chair across from him. "I'm flattered, but cut the bullshit, Randall," I retort, trying to hide my irritation. He gives me an exaggerated look of innocence, but when I don't buy it, he sighs loudly.

"I just came to check if you're okay. Heard about what happened to your boyfriend," he remarks.

Disgust creeps into my expression. "He's not my boyfriend. We barely spoke."

He studies my face as if searching for a lie. "No? Okay. So, do I have a chance?" Randall often makes absurd jokes like this. I force a faint smile, hoping he'll take the hint and stop. I clearly don't enjoy it, but he seems to relish my discomfort.

"I'm not looking for a relationship, Randall. Can you please get to the point? I need to study."

He lowers his head, strands of light hair falling on his forehead. "Am I distracting you?"

I feel an urge to punch him but restrain myself. "Obviously," I reply sharply. He chuckles, enjoying getting under my skin, knowing I can't afford to alienate my landlord.

"Fine, I'll leave you alone if that's what you want." He stands, heading for the door. Pausing in the doorway, he glances back at me. "Just so you know, I'm here for you, *dolly*."

I nod tightly, forcing a smile while suppressing a wave of nausea. I hate it when he calls me that. He sounds like a creep every time he says it. As soon as the door closes, I rush to it, locking all three locks.

But then I remember he has spare keys and can enter whenever he pleases. He's done it before, checking if I follow his rules: no kids or pets, no music after 10 PM, and limit hot water usage. It wouldn't be so bad if he didn't come late at night, waking me up once and nearly getting hit with a lamp when I mistook him for a burglar.

But now he's gone, and I can get back to what I was doing.

I head to the kitchen and start the kettle. As I ponder which tea to brew, my phone rings. Seeing Kevin's name on the screen, I feel a pang of disappointment for reasons I can't quite grasp. "Hey, Kev," I greet, my tone dry, finally deciding on a tea.

"You sound a bit disappointed," he observes. "Am I interrupting?"

Talking to Kevin has become...dull. I don't know when or why the spark faded, but it's gone, and conversing with him now feels almost unbearable. Maybe because I can't tell him about everything happening in my life. I don't want to. He'd insist I go to the police, move out, and all that. He wouldn't approve of me keeping those messages from that man. So, as far as he's concerned, my life remains unchanged.

"I was writing." It's not an answer, more of a roundabout evasion.

I sense his frustration. "I think you're avoiding me."

"I don't know what you're talking about, Kevin."

"I think you know exactly what I'm talking about, Lily." His voice takes on a note of aggression. Kevin rarely gets angry, which means I must be really messing this up.

"Look, Kev, I'm sorry," I start, trying to inject sincerity into my mechanical response. "I'm just tired. I have a lot of homework, and I don't have time for...communication."

There's a long pause, tension thickening between us. "Why are you lying to me, *Lily*?"

I almost scald myself pouring boiling water into my cup. I hate when he uses my name like this—an old psychological trick to guilt or open up someone. What annoys me more is that he doesn't even know my real name. As much as I hate it, I hate his pointed *Lily* even more.

"I'm not lying. Stop interrogating me, Kevin. If I say I'm fine and tired, that's how it is. Stop pushing my buttons," I snap, surprised at my own rudeness. I've never been this curt with Kevin. Hell, with anyone. I didn't realize I had it in me.

"Sorry," I start before he can respond. "I'm so sorry. I didn't mean to." I cover my eyes with my hands, suddenly ashamed of my outburst. "I'll call you back later, I promise." I hang up before he can protest, feeling like a coward.

Leaning against the wall, I tap the back of my head against it, hoping to banish the demons prompting me to lash out at the only person I communicate with.

I resist the urge to dwell on my thoughts as a knock at the front door interrupts me. Despite not wanting any visitors, I welcome the distraction. There's no benefit in stewing alone with my thoughts.

Unlocking the door, I find...no one. Despite the cold, I peek outside, scanning both sides for signs of presence.

Have pranksters moved in? Are there new people I don't know about?

I'm about to close the door when I spot something at my feet—a box, white with a ribbon and a large red bow, accompanied by a small card. I hesitate, weighing my options.

What if it's a...I don't know. A bomb? Or maybe it's poisoned? People shouldn't accept items left by strangers, just as they shouldn't enter unfamiliar vehicles.

But given everything happening in my life, I take the box inside, locking the door behind me. Placing it on the kitchen table, I reach for the mysterious card first.

For my little devil.

My eyes widen in shock, repeatedly scanning the sentence, hoping for a different outcome. I turn it over—nothing. A memory flashes—morning after the party, the cop's face when he described what the maniac did to Evan, his disbelief clear. Placing the card beside the box, I cautiously run my fingers over its surface.

Just as my phone vibrates, I startle, fixating on it. Face down, it gives me a moment to gather myself. I wipe clammy palms off my thighs and flip it over, seeing a new message.

UNKNOWN:

Don't be afraid, little devil. His tongue isn't there.

This is fucked up. Who does he think he is? I decide not to lock my phone, leaving it on the table. Undoing the bow, I let the ribbon fall.

Now or never, I lift the box lid, eyes shut tight. Opening one cautiously, I see no red and catch a familiar scent. Opening the other eye, I frown in disbelief. A pajama set—exactly what I've wanted for six months—and my favorite perfume.

Feeling assured, I handle the contents, fingers gliding over smooth fabric. It's beautiful, worth the months of anticipation. Holding the top to my chest, I realize the fucker knew my size.

Another buzz interrupts, drawing my attention back to the screen.

UNKNOWN:

There you go. I want to see that dimple more often from now on.

Heat washes over me, cheeks turning red. I hadn't realized I'd been smiling.

This is insane. *He's* insane.

He watches me, but I didn't know he was this interested in my browser history. How did he know about the perfume? Did he guess or see it in my house? Probably both.

Carefully replacing everything, I close the box. Grabbing my phone, I text him.

Me:

You're sick, you know that?

UNKNOWN:

I thought you liked it.

What's his self-assurance?

Me:

I don't know your game, but I'm not interested.

Show yourself or leave me alone.

UNKNOWN:

Do you know what you're asking for, baby girl?

I start an aggressive reply, but delete it halfway. Talking to him seems futile. Bending, I grab the ribbon, ready to return it when the screen lights up.

UNKNOWN:

Don't even think about it. I'll use it to tie those
little hands, baby.

My mouth forms an *O* as I read this. He's so sure, expecting me to comply silently.

Me:

Why did you send this?

Expecting me to wear it so you can satisfy
your sick desires?

UNKNOWN:

You don't like it?

Me:

I don't like anything from you.

A feeling twists inside me, suggesting I'm lying. Why can't I be normal? Why haven't I blocked him?

UNKNOWN:

Slide your hand into those mini-shorts and say you
don't like anything from me.

I slam my hand over my mouth, shocked by his blunt words. How can he even...write something like that?

I toss the ribbon onto the box and prepare to toss it into the trash. But as I start to move, shame washes over me.

He's right. I'm aroused.

I don't understand how this happened, how I could feel something for a man I've never seen or heard, just a forbidden and dangerous fantasy. And that's enough to turn me on. I squeeze my thighs, silently cursing myself for these feelings.

I make my way to the bedroom, tucking the box into a corner with no idea what to do with his gift. All I know is I need a shower. Now.

Before heading to the bathroom, I check my phone one last time.

UNKNOWN:

You're going to wear this set like the good, grateful girl you are.

I want to watch how it suits you.

Me:

Fuck you.

UNKNOWN:

Soon, little devil. Very soon.

I leave his message unanswered, trudging to the bathroom with a head full of conflicting thoughts.

Part of me feels like I'm already tearing myself apart, slowly giving pieces to a man who's going to destroy me, leaving nothing but my shattered soul behind.

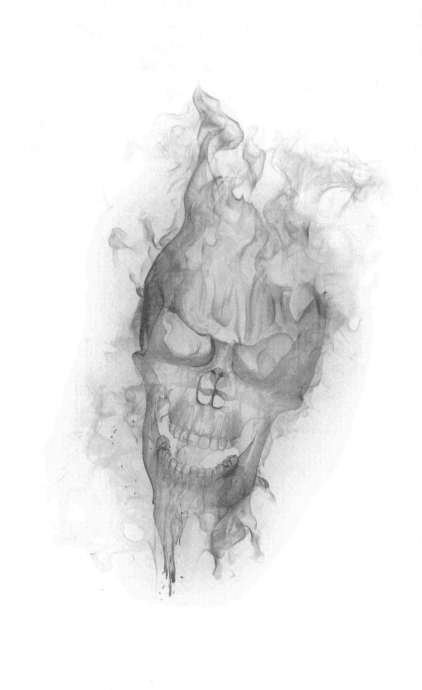

CHAPTER

FIFTEEN

Caleb

I'm meeting my little devil in just one day. A part of me screams that it's a terrible idea, that I'll regret it. But I refuse to wait; patience isn't my virtue when it comes to Lilith. Despite my recklessness, a nagging consciousness surfaces. Lilith is smart. When we meet, she won't figure everything out immediately, but suspicions will grow like seeds. I can't stomp out every doubt, so I need a plan B.

As much as I hate to consider it, I can't naively assume she won't try to escape once she learns the truth about me. My previous victims met their end in a cold, raw basement—where hope dwindled to nothing in a mid-sized box, a peculiar prison. Each discovered their fate on my terms, my preparation.

But with Lilith, I have no post-meeting plan. I have no desire to throw her into a cold basement upon discovery, yet I can't let her escape. She's the only one who evokes anything positive in me.

No matter how brave she is, her instincts might lead her to do the sensible thing. So, I'm transforming my basement into more than just a place to survive—connecting a bathroom, kitchen, and small bedroom. I've even planned shelves by the bed for her favorite books. I'm determined to make it a space surpassing the finest apartments, focusing on every tiny, crucial detail.

If I must lock her in, I want her to feel comfortable.

"ARE YOU READY FOR YOUR TRIP?" GRAYSON ASKS, TAKING A SIP OF his drink—whatever the hell he bought himself today. I shift my gaze back to the papers on my desk, irritated by the sight of him sipping it. His face somehow manages to look uglier when he does that, if that's even possible.

"I am. And I don't want to hear anything about a possible assistant."

I'm headed for a trip to the neighboring city to collaborate with another company that has the expertise to advance my new project. I've been engrossed in developing smart security systems for people who fear intrusions into their lives—though some seem more like subjects of a social experiment than actual human beings to me. Why would the Black Widow, the maniac who makes women disappear without a trace, take an interest in men or rich families?

These people have inflated self-esteem.

"I trust you, but I'll admit, this time I'm worried you might mess up. Lately, you've been off your game," Grayson persists.

When I remain silent, he adds, "Gloria is eager to assist you with everything. The look on her face when she realized you'd need a writer—priceless."

Yes, I do need a writer. Just not Gloria. Not any other girl he suggests, hoping desperately I'll give another opportunity to a friend's daughter or a friend of a friend. These girls know nothing about their craft. I've fired so many writers since reaching this position, I've lost count.

I *need* Lilith.

Not just because I'm obsessed with her—though that's the main reason—but because of her talent. Before she turned to novels, she wrote dozens of articles on every conceivable subject. She excels at everything, and I'm not exaggerating.

It's unbelievable how sharp this little devil is.

"I already have a writer," I cut in abruptly.

I never wanted Grayson to find out about Lilith. Not about her in general, and definitely not that I'm taking her with me. But he's our biggest sponsor, and no matter how much I hate it, I have to report to him at least on some matters.

"Who is she?" he asks, curiosity piqued.

I run a hand through my hair, making it even messier. "A friend. Very talented."

I sense a wide smile spreading across his face from the corner of my eye. "A friend, huh?"

I roll my eyes. "Yes. Do you have any more pertinent questions? Or can I get back to work?"

"I'll find out one way or another, son," he replies, his voice tinged with excitement. "Can't wait to meet her."

Tomorrow, I head straight to Graham—a key figure on my to-do list. More than a professor, he holds sway over student participation and event approvals.

After our chat, I finally get to meet my little devil.

CHAPTER
SIXTEEN

Lilith

"Yeah, I know. I have no idea what he wants from me. Do you think he's going to apologize?" I ask Kevin as I briskly make my way toward Graham's office. The professor had called me during my literary class, insisting I come to see him immediately.

Kevin lets out a dreamy sigh on the other end of the phone. "I don't know. Maybe his bipolar ass changed his mind? Hurry up before he gets angry again."

I've made amends with Kevin after feeling like a bitch for lashing out at him, though his forgiveness doesn't ease my guilt. "Okay, I'll call you after everything. I'm almost at his office," I blurt out, orienting myself in the right direction and closing the distance between myself and the room that holds unpleasant memories for me.

"Okay. *Love* you," he answers, and before I can process his words, he hangs up. Kevin has been saying *I love you* to me often, even though I've never said it back.

I have no clue what that's supposed to mean. I love him as a friend, but romantically? No way. We've never even met in person.

I unzip my purse and slide my phone inside, the voices growing louder the closer I get to Graham's office. One is Graham's—squeaky and a bit annoying—but the other is unfamiliar. I slow my pace, making sure my sneakers don't squeak on the floor, desperate to figure out who he might be talking to.

"I can't understand. There are plenty of capable students specializing in writing on that subject. But Lilith?" Graham's frustrated sigh echoes from the office. "She's a creative writer. I teach them poetry, literature, everything. She doesn't even—"

"How many times do I have to say I don't need other students?" the other man interrupts, making me flinch involuntarily. His voice is deep, resonant, and unwavering—commanding attention even before I see him.

I rap on the partially open door and cautiously step inside. "Come in, Lilith," Graham says, his voice grating on my nerves. As I enter, my gaze shifts to the owner of that illegally perfect voice, and a profound numbness washes over me, nearly paralyzing me in place.

He isn't just tall. He is fucking enormous. I have to crane my neck and stand on tiptoes to meet his eyes. I take him in from head to toe like a child staring at a candy store display. I'm fully aware of the impropriety of my gaze, but I can't seem to help myself.

He's dressed casually in a dark green hoodie and charcoal gray sweatpants, effortlessly exuding an air of confidence. I catch myself imagining what it would feel like to wear his oversized hoodie, enveloped completely in its vastness, like being wrapped in an ocean of fabric.

When I finally muster the courage to meet his gaze, his eyes captivate me entirely—deep and unreal, like artificial lenses rather than natural eyes. Their darkness defies mortal existence, his pupils blending into his irises. His tousled chocolate-brown waves look as though he hasn't bothered to brush them, adding to his effortless charm.

He doesn't seek attention, yet I'm irresistibly drawn to him. It feels as though some demonic force has ensnared me in an invisible web, compelling me to stare at him, unable to look away. I've never been so overwhelmed by anyone else.

And it's not in a regular *wow, he looks hot* kind of way, but in a manner I can't quite define.

Somehow, he seems familiar, though I'm certain I've never seen him before. His gaze holds an intensity that borders on possessive, a sensation that simultaneously excites and alarms me.

Why does a part of me scream that this is a bad idea? Despite the faint warnings in my mind, I find myself choosing to ignore them.

"Caleb Walker," the stunning man introduces himself, extending his hand to me. His hands are fucking large, almost unbelievably so. Is it possible for a normal human to have hands like his?

Or is he even human?

I bite my lip, trying to suppress the storm of emotions inside me. "Lilith Leclair," I respond softly, and the instant our hands touch, we're shocked—sharp pain jolts through my fingertips, and I instinctively shake my hand.

Caleb simply smiles, and as I wonder how he manages to be so perfect, he seizes the moment, taking my hand again and giving it a subtle squeeze. "It's nice to meet you, *Lilith*."

Only now do I realize that I've just told him my real name. Well, Graham did it before me, but the fact that I willingly pronounced my name to him without disgust feels...*normal*. It came out naturally.

"So, Caleb," Graham interrupts, redirecting our attention to him. "If this is what you really want, then I give my permission."

I furrow my brow, recalling that there was a reason I was called here, still a mystery to me. "What were you talking about?"

I meet Caleb's piercing stare, and he asks, "Does TechMind Solutions ring any bells to you?"

I've heard of it, though I was never interested. "Yeah," I say hesitantly, still clueless as to what this has to do with me.

He nods. "I'm the CEO of this company. I need to make a trip to another city for a collaboration with a company that has the expertise to advance my new project."

He keeps his eyes on me the whole time, making the rosy crimson hue spread across my cheeks. "I need a writer who can help me document all the upcoming events and occurrences there. Can you do that, Lilith?"

I swallow, shifting my attention to Graham, who just shrugs his shoulders. I let out a sudden little chuckle. "Why me, exactly?"

Caleb's mouth curls into a smirk that almost makes my knees buckle. "Why not?"

My stomach churns with a warm sensation, butterflies fluttering in a cyclone within me as he releases them from their cage. A gentle, pleasant euphoria tingles beneath my skin as we share a silent moment, just gazing at each other.

Then, Caleb takes a step closer, making the room feel smaller, if that's even possible. His presence shields me from everything else in the room, including annoying Graham. "I know you studied journalism before. I saw the articles you posted. And I am impressed, Lilith," he says, his tone now lower, flowing into my ears melodically like a poem.

"I also know you are the only student with a scholarship among your classmates, am I correct?"

I adjust my glasses, desperately hoping they hide my eyes, which flood with all emotions at once. I've never been so...*noticed* by anybody. I've lived with the thought that what I do is nothing out of the ordinary, and further, it still isn't enough.

But just these few minutes of Caleb speaking facts aloud make me feel worthy. It's as if for the first time in my life, someone acknowledged my small achievements and made me proud of them.

"Yeah...that's correct," I answer, my voice nearly a whisper.

"That is more than enough to consider taking you among everybody else."

"*Oh.*" I feel like he's devouring me with his gaze. "Okay."

What kind of spell has he put on me? I don't usually react like this when someone isn't even saying much.

"You remind me of myself," he begins softly, his voice tinged with nostalgia. "As a child, I never even envisioned attending university, believing it was beyond my reach." He lowers his head. "But I took a risk and eventually got in, even earning a scholarship, the only one among my classmates. Just like you."

Everything about this situation is surreal. I think I'm unable to process it sensibly. This unnaturally beautiful man blurs my consciousness—the way he talks about me, and the way he looks at me like I am the only star in his sky—forces my common sense to melt like butter on a heated pan. I enjoy how he ignores Graham's presence as if he doesn't exist. The mischievous part of me feels satisfied, especially as I recall a memory of Graham tearing apart my work and making me feel worthless.

"Do we have a deal, Lilith?" he asks, already knowing the answer. It's impossible to refuse a man like him, especially after hearing the way he speaks about me.

"Of course," I manage, attempting a genuine smile, though my cheekbones quiver in the effort. I can't remember the last time I felt this nervous.

I have no idea how much Caleb knows about me, but judging by his facial expressions during this conversation, the way he spoke the facts aloud makes me think he knows enough to take me with him and trust me to complete the job he gives me.

I WAS GRANTED A BREAK FROM CLASSES TO PREPARE FOR MY UPCOMING trip. Caleb mentioned I should be fully prepared in two days to spend five days in Jersey City. I packed my suitcase without even thinking about how fast and surreal everything was happening right now. I checked the weather and picked out appropriate clothes, gathered my makeup, hair tools, and everything I thought I might need or not need.

Time has been crawling by, fueled by my incredible excitement about this trip. I've never participated in a practice session in another city, nor have I ever been selected by someone else. But Caleb Walker is not just anybody. He is the CEO of one of the most successful human-computer augmentation companies, and I admit, I felt deeply ashamed that I hadn't recognized him earlier.

TechMind Solutions isn't a company I've followed closely, mainly because I'm not interested in new technologies, science, and those subjects. I heard about it, and I still remember a couple of years ago, everyone buzzing about the youngest CEO of all time—a remarkably talented and unbelievably intelligent man.

With one day left before the trip, I'm desperate to find a way to make time pass more quickly. So, I decided to thoroughly re-search everything about him and his company.

I open my laptop and Google his name, feeling a bit...I don't even know how to describe it. *Interest* seems too mild; it's something much more intense. Besides being crazy happy about the upcoming trip and the opportunity to practice, more than half of my mind has been preoccupied with him.

There's something about Caleb that makes me feel like he is more than just a smart, rich man. But I can't understand whether it's something good or bad. He carries a strange aura around himself, and just the memory of his eyes—so dark, so captivating—causes a flood of different emotions inside me.

He looks intimidating, yet I'm not scared of him. Part of me wishes to hide, not out of fear, but to escape his intense gaze that delves unapologetically into the depths of my soul and exposes my secrets. It's as if his stare strips away every layer, baring my soul completely, inside out.

I scroll through one article after another, reading about how successful his company has become practically from nothing, how he built it brick by brick all by himself. I come across a lot of information about their latest accomplishments—smart prosthetics, devices that monitor and analyze physiological data, predictive analytics tools—so many things that honestly leave me feeling dumber with every scroll. It fascinates me how smart people can actually be. But if someday I need to work on a project like that, I might end up having a mental breakdown.

The latest article details their new project—a cybersecurity solution. That's why we are going to another city, and that's where my main focus should be. At least the name of it sounds understandable enough for my little brain. Despite finding a lot of information, it still feels like it's not enough for me.

Unconsciously, my hands drift back to the keyboard, typing the name of the only man who has ever consumed my thoughts so intensely.

I adjust my glasses as I read a few articles about him. There's a photo with him and his crew—the only picture that includes him, surprisingly sparse for a public figure.

I tap on an interview with him, which unfortunately is text-only, no video. The interviewer asks him about basic stuff—his family, friends, life before opening the company, his private life. Caleb gives half-answers, leaving me even more curious than before. I keep rereading his responses, hoping to catch something more, but no matter how hard I try, I can't find anything.

The man is a walking mystery.

And fuck me for craving more information. For wanting to spend more time with *him*.

I zoom in on the only photo he's in—standing in the middle of dozens of people, the tallest among them. I could write a book just about how tall he is. He looks out of place in his hoodie and sweats amidst everyone else in suits and blazers.

When we first met, I was perplexed and disoriented. I tried to focus on his face to understand what he wanted and give him a proper answer to avoid seeming stupid.

Now, I find myself wanting to take a better look at his body. He is lean yet packed with muscles, capable of catching me with ease and effortlessly breaking me in half. Glancing at his hands, I marvel at their perfection—large, one hand the size of my entire face, with prominent blue veins that are irresistibly captivating. His fingers are elegantly slender, and I can only imagine the fortune of those who've had the privilege of his touch.

Fuck. Lilith. Why are you even thinking about this?

I shake my head, trying to banish these thoughts. It's wrong. Inappropriate. The man gave me an opportunity, noticed my small achievements, and saw potential. I can't think about what his fingers could do or how skilled he might be in bed.

I should be fucking ashamed.

I close every tab and turn my laptop off. I think I need a distraction. Because if I keep thinking about…such things, seeing him tomorrow will make everything very awkward for me.

Reese

I try to strain my brain and guess the date. At least approximate.

But it's too hard.

I am drained physically and mentally after being held in a fucking squared cage for weeks.

I was cautious when he came in here to bring me some food. Caleb is a psychopath, and I needed to find an approach to him.

I thought I could make him a little...I don't know. Softer?

But he chose to ignore my little attempts as if I didn't exist.

After the last trace of hope was trampled, I realized that it was pointless. I got angry. So I started to mock him and throw hurtful words anytime he came in here.

I knew I was risking everything. Well, by everything I mean getting at least a little piece of food.

But I was starting to feel better. It was a little victory of mine - forcing him to hear my anger. I spilled it on him like a bucket of shit.

He just kept smirking at me, but I hope deep down I pushed the right spot and made him feel fucking worthless.

Just the way he made me feel.

I feel like I am writing it on my last day. I woke up with a dreadful feeling inside me. Like today he is going to kill me. I have no idea how.

But I know this is the day.

Fuck, I think he's coming. I hear the footsteps. Or it's my hallucination?

There's only one way to find o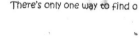

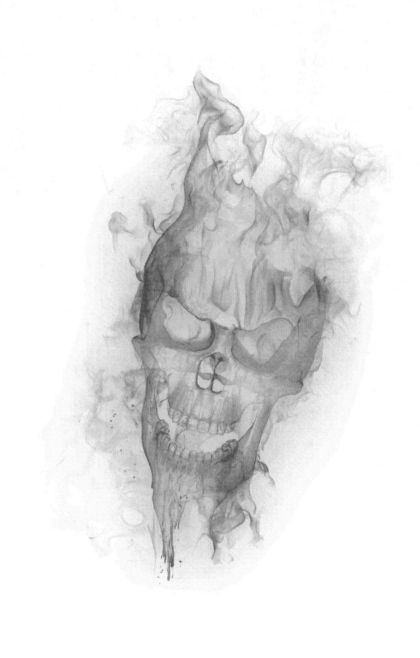

CHAPTER
SEVENTEEN

Caleb

My little devil has shown interest in me. You have no idea how amused I felt watching her a few hours ago, scrolling through every single article about me and my business, desperately searching for more. If only she knew. There's no need for her to scour the internet—I'd willingly tell her everything she wants to know. Well, almost everything.

A few minutes ago, I received a call from one of the men I trusted to remodel my basement. They're working round the clock, understanding the importance of every detail and the urgency of completing it.

The right people will do whatever it takes for the right amount of money, smart enough not to ask unnecessary questions. I'd prefer to do everything myself, but time is not on my side. Plan B's basement is in the house far from here, about an hour's drive from my apartment, nestled on a hill surrounded by acres of private woods.

I should be resting to prepare for our morning trip, but sleep eludes me. As usual, I find myself parked near her apartment complex, watching her. Seeing the emotions play across her face earlier as she struggled to comprehend why and how I chose her was immensely satisfying.

Everything about her is addictive, even her awkwardness. It took immense effort not to seize her right there in front of her damn professor.

From the moment I wake until I sleep, she consumes my thoughts. Even in my dreams, her presence lingers. Once, I wanted to end her life, reveling in the sight of life fading from those green eyes, tasting her hatred and disgust toward me. Now, I would gladly kneel before her, like a man before his goddess.

Her power over me is inexplicable, unlike anything I've ever experienced. No woman has ever held me in her grasp as she does.

I savor every second watching her peacefully sleep through the cameras. A satisfied grin never leaves my face—she obeyed my instructions. Lilith sleeps in the nightwear I bought her, not even bothering to cover herself with the blanket, almost as if inviting my gaze.

I don't realize how I find myself storming into her apartment. It's reckless, greedy—a sharp departure from my usual restraint. Before, I held back, biding my time. Now, on the eve of our departure, I act on a sudden urge to watch her up close.

Frozen in the doorway of her bedroom, I watch her shift in her sleep, turning her pretty face toward me, yet she remains unaware.

Too close.

I should retreat to my car, but I can't. When this woman consumes my thoughts, retreat is impossible. With measured steps, I approach her, shielding her from stray moonlight with my body. She shifts again, finding a more comfortable position.

Is she dreaming now? If so, what—or *who*—is she dreaming about?

Boldly, I let my eyes roam over her flawless form. In this light, her beauty intensifies, if that's even possible. Her shorts accentuate her thighs, offering a glimpse of her round ass. The V-neck top hints at her breasts—ample enough for my hands.

When she shifts, the strap falls from her shoulder like art. I swallow hard, trying to stay composed. But before I realize it, I'm kneeling beside her, my breath caressing her face. I trail kisses along her hand, each one drawing a soft whimper from her lips before she leans toward me.

Fuck. Her vulnerability blurs my morals, leaving me uncertain how much restraint I can muster. With her, self-control eludes me. As I kiss her neck and inhale deeply, her scent intoxicates, clouding my mind. She's wearing the nightwear I bought her, soaked in the perfume I chose.

I know where this is heading—fucking tragedy.

Yet I'm *selfish.*

Greedy.

Tactless.

Fuck me for denying Lilith the chance to be with someone normal. The mere thought of her with another enrages me, clouding my judgment.

Despite my desire to crawl into bed with her, to offer her warmth and comfort she craves, I resist. She deserves a peaceful night before everything changes in five days.

CHAPTER
EIGHTEEN

Lilith

W hen I open my eyes, a pleasant warmth envelops my body. My gaze falls immediately upon the figure standing in the shadows of my room—a tall, dark presence exuding an intimidating aura. Yet, despite this imposing presence, his true energy is palpable—calm and untroubled.

Safe.

Warmth envelops me from a distance. I shift in my bed, pulling the blanket over me though I'm not naked. But I feel exposed. The mysterious man moves slowly toward my bed, his steps weightless on the ground. His effortless grace is almost unbelievable. In the darkness, I can't make out his face, but strangely, that feels safer to me.

Faceless. Faceless is safer.

"Do you live here all alone, baby girl?" he murmurs, gradually settling onto my bed, causing the mattress to yield under his weight. I've only experienced sleep paralysis once before, back in my childhood, and as I strain to re-call that nightmarish memory, I'm gripped by the same sensation—completely paralyzed. Yet, I'm not afraid.

"Yes," I manage to whisper, my voice barely audible. As he positions himself over me, I draw in a breath, feeling the weight of his body upon mine. His sheer mass is such that if he were to collapse upon me, he might effortlessly crush my body. The man's hands descend on my quivering legs, his fingers grazing my skin and provoking goosebumps to emerge. A quiet whimper escapes me—an inappropriate reaction, yet the sensation is undeniably pleasurable. So, I press my eyes shut, pretending to be asleep.

"Are you sure about that?" I'm struck by the realization, feeling it resonate all the way down to my toes. He's been observing me from afar. His hand glides through my hair in an unexpectedly tender gesture, which feels out of character for someone who doesn't exude sweetness or tenderness.

"What are you going to do to me?"

He continues to stroke my hair before drawing closer to my face—so close that I can feel his warm breath drifting across my features. As I open my eyes to gaze at him, I'm nearly taken aback. Caleb.

"I'm going to consume you," he whispers, pressing a kiss to my forehead. Then, his lips journey downward. "Claim you." He kisses my collarbone, then the small area between my breasts. "Shatter you." His lips trail lower. "Love you."

Unaware, I instinctively arch my back, meeting his mouth as he reaches my core, kissing and nibbling my skin without giving me a chance to compre-hend. His hands clasp my thighs as he consumes me, bestowing a pleasure that causes my eyes to roll back. I moan, surrendering to the present, yielding to what he brings forth, even if it feels completely wrong.

"Caleb—" I whimper weakly, my hand diving into his soft hair. "Oh, Caleb."

THE BLASTED ALARM DISRUPTS MY DREAM, RUDELY YANKING ME OUT of slumber. With a frustrated groan and my body still half-numb from sleepiness, I reach for my phone and silence it. I think I just had the best night's sleep of my entire life. I slept like a baby despite the swirling emotions within me, experiencing the finest dream imaginable.

But this delicious aftertaste evaporates without a trace when I realize I have to face Caleb in forty minutes—after dreaming about him doing things to me. I shield my eyes with my hands, as if they could protect me. After blinking a couple of times, I reach for my glasses and slip them onto the bridge of my nose.

I've had such a vivid, pleasant dream once before—on the night after I moved out from my mother's place. Despite the headache that greeted me when my neighbors decided to start drilling at seven in the morning, it was the first time I felt truly free from judgment, like my life had taken a brighter path. That was the only good dream I've ever had.

But this one isn't just pleasant; it's vivid as hell.

It felt almost as if he were here, in my bedroom.

I can't afford to dwell on it. I rise from my bed and wearily make my way to the bathroom. Suppressing the temptation to crawl back under the warm blanket and let the dream continue, I splash cold water on my forehead in an attempt to clear my mind.

Caleb and I are going on a work trip.

Nothing more.

I'm already outside my apartment building when I nearly collide with Randall, stumbling as I almost bump into his chest.

"Woah, easy," he says, grabbing both of my shoulders. "Where are you going in such a hurry?"

I cautiously shrug him off, uncomfortable with his touch. "Hey, Randall. I'm heading...to study."

His eyes scan the suitcase behind me. "With a whole suitcase, huh, *dolly*?"

I bite my tongue, trying to suppress a wave of rage. "It's for a few days of practice in a neighboring city. Nothing special."

"A few days? I'm going to miss you, you know," Randall says, throwing his arms up in defeat.

Behind him, a silhouette appears, towering over him. "You got a problem?"

Reed slowly turns around, meeting Caleb's intense stare. He ducks his head. "What's the CEO of the smart-ass company doing here at nine in the morning?" He laughs scornfully.

"Randall, we're in a hurry," I interject, walking past him to stand beside Caleb, hoping to defuse the tension.

"I'm just going to miss my friend," Randall says, flashing us an arrogant smirk.

"Touch her like that again and I'll chop off your hand, Reed," Caleb responds in an unbelievably calm voice. My eyes widen in shock at his words.

If some other man had said that, I would have laughed in his face. But coming from Caleb, it sounds different—confident, sincere.

Randall takes a step back, smirking. "Noted."

I inhale sharply, acknowledging that Caleb's words should have been a red flag. But I remain composed, as if this were a daily occurrence. I'm unsure how to react—the situation is just too strange.

Caleb gently touches my shoulder, forcing my eyes to meet his. "Come on," he murmurs, his voice tender despite his earlier threat. "We gotta hit the road."

I acknowledge him with a nod. "Yeah. Okay."

He takes my suitcase and loads it into the trunk of his car. Glancing back at where Randall stood moments ago, I ponder his strange behavior. I've always excused it, but now it seems worse.

What does he want from me?

Caleb holds the door for me as I slip into his car, and I silently mouth a thank you. He responds with a barely detectable nod, closing the door and settling into the driver's seat.

"So, how was your night? Did you sleep well?" he asks.

I immediately turn my eyes away, afraid he might read my mind about that dream. "Uh…yeah. I had a pleasant dream."

"What was that about?"

Shit. Fuck. Fuck me. Why couldn't I keep my mouth shut? Damn it.

A surge of heat thunders through me. "Uh…it was about my dog." Jesus. That was the worst lie I've ever told.

He smirks, buckling his seatbelt. "You have a dog, huh?"

"I don't. I had one when I was a kid." I fumble with my seatbelt, hands shaking inexplicably. Suddenly, his shadow falls across my face, and he gently takes my hand to buckle me up like a child. My cheeks burn.

Numbness overtakes me as I find myself paralyzed by his intense gaze, unable to breathe.

How will I survive five days with him?

"Relax," he says calmly. "I don't bite, Lilith."

His eyes hold mine, his jaw tight with the memory of Randall. He presses down on the gas pedal, as if trying to leave the memory behind.

"I meant what I said to him," he adds, his eyes fixed on the road ahead. "But you have *nothing* to worry about, Lilith."

"I have to thank you for standing up for me," I say, nervously twirling my fingers. "Randall is my landlord, but sometimes he forgets that and crosses the line."

"You don't have to thank me, Lilith. I did nothing…yet."

I smile to myself, realizing only after a moment that I took satisfaction in imagining Caleb's threat becoming reality.

Something is definitely wrong with me.

"I CAN TAKE IT," I SAY, WATCHING CALEB EFFORTLESSLY UNLOCK THE trunk and hoist my heavy suitcase with just one hand. He gives me a quick warning look, and I nod, feeling a little awkward about letting him carry my baggage.

My heart sinks to my toes the moment I lay eyes on the five-star hotel we'll be staying at. Even the road leading up to it screams luxury. I had grabbed money from my stash, but I would prefer spending it on something delicious or even a small souvenir rather than giving everything to a hotel.

"Caleb—"

"Don't even think about it," he interrupts.

I blink up at him in confusion. "About what?"

"I'm paying for it," he insists, his tone strict as if he were my parent. "I don't want to hear anything, Lilith."

I'm still getting used to someone calling me by my real name so often. It feels a little weird. Mindful of not testing his patience, we make our way to the reception to book rooms. I keep my mouth shut, focusing on my plan—to perform my job duties to the best of my ability and exceed his expectations.

Caleb assists me in carrying my belongings to my room and provides a thorough explanation of our upcoming plans. Today, we are only meeting with executives from the collaborating company to discuss the project and their expertise. Despite the storm of emotions swirling inside my head, I'm confident I can handle the task at hand without much difficulty.

"So," I begin, "are you going to pick me up after three and a half hours?"

Caleb leans his shoulder against the doorframe. "I was actually thinking about inviting you to grab some lunch with me."

Before I realize it, a foolish grin spreads across my face. "That sounds good."

"Twenty minutes. Is that enough for you to get ready?"

I take a moment to think. "Fifteen, even. Just going to make everything," I circle my finger around my room, "decent. If I'm going to come back bone-tired, the last thing I want to do is unpack my suitcase and search for a toothbrush."

He bestows upon me a little smirk that awakens all kinds of feelings inside my stomach. "Sure. I get it."

As Caleb moves away from the doorframe, he reaches for the handle, his hand poised to close the door behind him. "I'll knock."

I nod, and after he leaves, I catch myself feeling hollow. He evokes various emotions in me, but once he's gone, my life returns to its usual state.

It's so weird, especially when I remember that I barely know him.

IN JUST TEN MINUTES, I TRANSFORM MY BLANK SPACE INTO AN ORGA-nized oasis. As I survey my room, a sense of accomplishment washes over me. Not only does it look presentable, but it also exudes a warm and inviting ambiance. With my belongings all around, this room truly feels like home. I'm scared to think about how much Caleb has paid for this, though I could definitely spend the rest of my life in an apartment like this.

The room is expansive and flooded with natural light, boasting large windows that provide breathtaking views of the surrounding area. The décor is sleek and refined, marked by clean lines and a minimalist aesthetic. The bathroom is so generously proportioned that I feel a bit dwarfed standing within it—equipped with marble countertops, a deep soaking tub, and a separate walk-in shower.

My favorite part, however, has to be the bed—it serves as the focal point of the room—adorned with high-quality linens and plush pillows. I can hardly wait to sink into it and experience the most comfortable sleep I've ever had.

The knock on the door demands my immediate attention. "Come in."

Caleb doesn't walk inside—he remains at the doorframe just as before. "I hope you're hungry."

I seize my purse and the room card, closing the distance between us. "I'm starving."

THE MINI CAFÉ IS SITUATED INSIDE THE HOTEL ON THE FIRST FLOOR. As I glance at the glass case displaying pastries and sweets, their delightful smell wafts toward me, causing my stomach to coax a quiet growl.

"Don't even look at that," Caleb says in a soft voice. "Those are for dessert. We need to give you something appropriate first."

I smile at his concern. It's cute that he worries about what food I should have, and ironic how a man whom I barely know cares for me more than my own mother. We take a seat near the window and place our orders. A memory flashes in my mind— how my mother never cared about *what* or *how* I ate triggers me momentarily.

After a solid five minutes of analyzing the menu, I squeak out that I want only an omelet. But Caleb orders more food for me, ignoring my shaking head and wide eyes.

"Caleb, you're being too kind. But I'm not that hungry," I say, trying to get his attention.

"Can you do me a favor, Lilith?" After I give him a hesitant nod, he continues, "Would you mind just enjoying the time we're spending here and not worrying about a damn thing?"

A crimson blush engulfs my cheeks. "I'm sorry—"

"Stop apologizing," he interrupts. "Stop worrying. And stop thinking about your past."

A frown takes over my heated face. "How do you know I am thinking about my past?"

He runs a hand through his hair, making it even messier. An urge wakes up inside me—I want to touch his hair and check if it's as soft as it looks. "I see it in your face," he explains. "I want to know you better, Lilith. But I'm not going to force you to confess anything you're not sure about."

I take a moment to digest everything he just said. How can he read me so accurately? Am I *that* obvious?

"But I'll admit, if it's about a high school boyfriend who made you feel insecure, I'm going to be disappointed," he adds, sarcasm lacing his tone.

I touch the tip of my glasses. "Not a boyfriend. My mother."

He purses his lips in a thin line. "Mother."

"That's why I ran away when I was seventeen. I couldn't stand her. Couldn't stand the way she kept making me feel worthless," I confess—the truth spills before I can even understand that I am talking about a painful topic.

"I know I should forget, and most of the time I don't remember anything about it, but sometimes triggers bring it back," I continue.

"Did she tell you that you needed to eat less?" he asks.

"Yeah. She always told me I was fat."

"And do you think you were actually fat?"

I shake my head in confusion. "I don't think so. I sure was skinnier than I am now."

"You are gorgeous."

"What?" When he doesn't answer, I raise my head and meet his eyes, trapped in the intensity of his gaze without a chance to escape.

"You are gorgeous, Lilith. Isn't that obvious?"

I blink several times non-stop, trying to find a way out of his gaze. "I don't think so."

"You need to realize that yourself," he says, his voice now softer. "It's a long path. Requires a lot of patience and time."

Caleb pauses for a moment. "But fuck that. Sometimes people need someone else to help them."

"What do you mean?"

He licks his lips, never breaking eye contact. "I think you know exactly what I mean, Lilith."

My stomach reacts again, unleashing a swarm of butterflies within. I feel a sudden urge to crisscross my legs, feeling the pulse between my thighs. As my leg rises and inadvertently brushes against him, a surge of electricity courses through me. I close my eyes, now sensing flames not only across my face but my whole body.

Jesus Christ. What is this reaction? What am I doing? There's no comparison to how my body responds to this man—a sensation so palpable that I feel it down to my toes.

Caleb refrains from making any inappropriate remarks, advances, or hinting at his desires for me. We're just having a simple conversation, but I feel like I am naked in front of him. If I'm responding like this when he hasn't made any moves, what would happen if he chooses to touch me elsewhere?

Fuck. No.

I can't think about it.

I just want to enjoy my lunch with him, and then do my work, which is exactly why I came here.

Lia

My dear Derek. If you find this letter it means that I am already dead. But I don't want you to be sad about it. Just let me go.

I know I was doing things I shouldn't. I cheated on you. I betrayed your trust. And I know I'll have no redemption. I don't even ask about one.

There was a time when we were happy. Do you remember it? Do you remember the first year of our relationship?

I should've tried better.

You were broken after your father's death, and I know I hadn't been a great support. If I could just change everything. If I could just take the time back.

I would give everything just to try again. Just to see your face. To touch you.

Even just for a second.

I just want you to know that I love you.

Please forgive me for everything I've done.

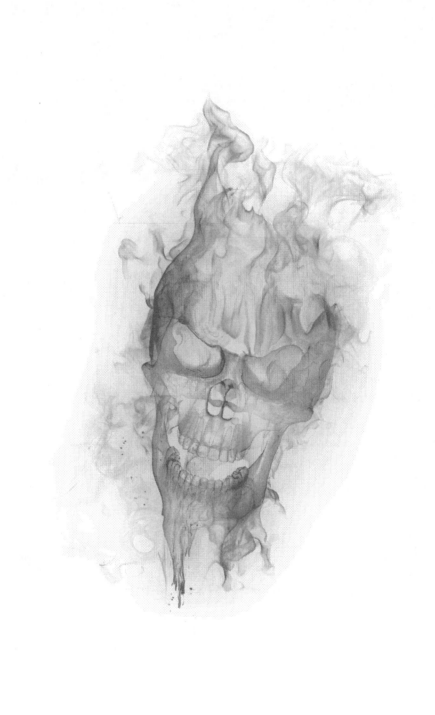

CHAPTER

NINETEEN

Caleb

This project is the main reason I can spend time with Lilith without raising suspicions. I doubt she would listen if I approached her on the street, and showing up at her door would only annoy her, likely prompting her to tell me to fuck off. So, I should be grateful for this opportunity. But with each passing second, I grow to resent this project and the damn work it entails. Lilith is closer to me now—closer than ever before—but work distracts both of us, leaving me unable to think of anything but her.

I can't stay away.

We've been here for three days already, and I've been cautious around her, engaging in small conversations. I thought I could stick to this plan without problems. But it's no longer an option for me. That's why I'm doing something I'll probably regret later.

I unlock the door and enter her room. She's asleep; it's three in the morning. For a moment, I just watch her. I'm fascinated by the tranquility she exudes, seemingly undisturbed as she enjoys a well-deserved rest. She's sleeping on her back, one arm under the pillow, the other resting on her stomach, without a blanket. In the set I bought her. Deep down, she knows it's been me haunting her all this time. She just can't prove it.

I climb onto her bed, the mattress sinking under my weight. I move my head toward her neck, inhaling her intoxicating scent once again. She wears her perfume every day, but I just can't seem to get enough.

I will *never* get enough.

As my lips graze the tender skin of her neck, the urge to bite her overwhelms me. But I can't be this reckless. I need to take it slow. I place one kiss after another, slowly making my way to her collarbones, descending along her stomach, and further downward.

With each passing second, my impatience swells. I trace every inch of her with my lips, leaving moist trails with my tongue after each kiss. Lilith instinctively arches her back toward me in her sleep, prompting me to move my attention toward her inner thighs. I release a muffled groan into the fabric of her shorts, then carefully remove them, earning a soft, almost inaudible moan that escapes her lips.

"Caleb—"

I don't stop showering her tender skin with kisses. "Yes, baby?"

Lilith runs a hand through my hair. In a sleepy voice, she murmurs a question, "Is this a dream?"

My hands hug her thighs as I adjust my face between them. "Yes."

She pushes her legs wider apart, allowing me to bury my whole face in her pussy. "It's a good dream," she breathes, her hand pushing me further between her legs.

I'll admit, I am a little taken aback by her participation, which only intensifies my desire. My cock twitches painfully in my pants, hungry for her. Without thinking twice, I push my tongue inside her, met by a rush that envelopes me immediately. She tastes even better than I imagined—sweet and warm, the most delicious thing I've ever tried.

Lilith releases breathless moans as I alternate between her hole and clit, teasingly moving my tongue from one point to another. "Oh, God—Caleb—"

I gently raise her legs, throwing them over my shoulders as I continue to pleasure her. "Are you the man of my dreams?" she whispers, her hand caressing my hair in slow, gentle movements while her feet crisscross behind my neck.

"Yes, little devil," I answer between licks. "I am the man of your dreams."

She arches her back, tightening her legs around my neck. "I knew that."

I'm restraining myself from devouring her mouth and thrusting my cock inside her, craving not just moans but her screams. The way she welcomes my pleasure makes me want to fuck her until she blacks out from the orgasms. But tonight, I'm crossing only one boundary. My desires are my problem; I need her to want this, to crave me as I crave her.

Deep down, I know that's what she wants too. But my little devil is too shy to admit it. That's why I have to give her a little push, like I am doing now.

She arches her back one last time, suffocating my neck with her legs as she climaxes with a loud moan. I bury my face deeper, desperate not to miss a drop, my tongue continuing its work even after her body trembles as though electrocuted. I feel her juices flow down to my chin, but even now, it's not enough for me.

Breathless, Lilith's eyes remain closed when I finally raise my head and look at her. It's easier for my little girl to think this is just a dream, avoiding any embarrassment. On one hand, her shyness and awkwardness are endearing, as if she's the type to cover her ears at any mention of sex. But a part of me yearns to unleash her inner devil, to make her less inhibited. There's nothing more alluring than a woman who pursues her desires openly, especially when that woman is Lilith.

Adjusting her into a more comfortable position, I watch as she relaxes, a soft whimper escaping her lips. "Caleb—"

"Shh," I whisper, covering her with a blanket. "Sleep, little devil."

When I'm sure she's comfortable, I quietly leave her room, my mind filled with thoughts about what will happen tomorrow.

CHAPTER
TWENTY

Lilith

S omething fucking happened last night. I realized it after waking up from the most vivid dream of my life, wrapped snugly in a warm blanket.

Except, it wasn't a dream. I distinctly remember falling asleep uncovered.

Caleb was in my room. I know what he did.

I grab my glasses from the nightstand and take a moment to gather my thoughts. We have a meeting with a potential investor in an hour, so I need to get moving and prepare for the day. But I simply can't focus when all I can think about is what happened last night. A naive part of me wants to believe it was just an exceptionally vivid dream—I've had colorful dreams before, though not sexual ones, more like prophetic or recreations of traumatic events. Sometimes I've questioned my sanity because they felt so real. But the other part of me knows that's bullshit.

My head is buzzing with thoughts—I anticipate a looming headache—but my body feels strangely good, better than ever. As I get up and start moving, I notice a slight soreness. I try to ignore it while I brush my teeth, style my hair, apply makeup, and select an outfit. But my mind keeps drifting back to last night, and at some point, I can almost feel his touch again. My body still hums with the echoes of his embrace. I wonder if I'll ever be able to break free from his hold.

Or if I even want to.

The question answers itself when my hand instinctively slips into my shorts and I realize I'm wet.

Fuck.

I hurry back to the bathroom to clean up, trying to shake off the unsettling feeling that if this was all a dream, then maybe I'm more messed up than I thought. It's hard to reconcile dreaming about a faceless man all my life, then having a near-death stalker and now a vivid dream about my practically unknown boss on a work trip. How could my life go from boring monotony to this whirlwind without a chance to catch my breath?

But I have no time to dwell. A knock on the door startles me. It could be housekeeping. Or Caleb himself. I freeze as the sensations from last night flood back. The person knocks again, louder this time. "Breakfast!"

I exhale in relief. I just need a little more time before facing Caleb.

That's all.

I jog to the door and meet the staff member with a bounty of food. My stomach growls at the sight, and I retreat to my room, plop on the bed, and turn on the TV.

It dawns on me that neither Caleb nor I mentioned breakfast delivery. We planned to go straight to the café. He must have ordered it for me. Could it be a form of apology for intruding into my room and giving me the best orgasm of my life?

Jesus, even thinking that sounds absurd. But he did cross a line. We're not dating, barely know each other. Certainly not well enough for orgasms. Maybe I need to start taking things more...easy.

I've always held out for the right man, but where has that gotten me? Perhaps it's time to be more open.

OUR MEETING WITH A POTENTIAL INVESTOR IS IN A GRAND OFFICE ON the twenty-ninth floor, which means we have to use the damn elevator. The thing is, I've had a phobia of elevators since I was six. It all started when Claire took me to the mall that day.

Everything was going smoothly until we entered the elevator to go up. She realized she had dropped her phone and dashed out, leaving me alone as the doors closed. The lights went off, and the elevator abruptly stopped ascending. I was too small to reach the buttons to call for help. I screamed for my mother, but she couldn't hear me.

I vividly remember the fear and panic as I stumbled backward and hit the mirror, leaving a small hole in the glass. For what felt like an eternity, I lay on the floor, hyperventilating and crying until we were rescued twenty minutes later.

After that incident, I couldn't speak for days, which infuriated my mother. It's a stupid memory I know I need to overcome to be a normal person, but whenever I see an elevator, I freeze like a rabbit caught in a trap.

"Are you okay?" Caleb's deep voice snaps me out of my thoughts. He's been surprisingly quiet after...whatever happened last night.

I want to ask him directly, but how do I even formulate the question?

Hey, did you break into my apartment last night and eat me out, Caleb?

Jesus Christ, I'd die of embarrassment before finishing that sentence.

"Scared of elevators, huh?" he presses when I don't answer.

I nod hesitantly. "I got stuck alone for twenty minutes when I was six. I prefer taking the stairs. Can we do that?"

"On the twenty-ninth floor?" His eyes soften, and I hide my trembling hands in my jeans pocket.

"Yeah, sorry. I'll go alone and meet you there."

Before I can react, Caleb steps closer, taking both my hands in his. I watch as his slender fingers brush softly over my knuckles, almost afraid to scare me away. Then, he brings my hands to his lips and kisses each one. I'm transported back to my room, feeling his sensual kisses all over my body.

That definitely happened.

Caleb *was* in my room last night. The realization doesn't surprise me as much as it should. At least I'm not crazy.

I blink up at him, silently asking questions I can't voice.

Why me? What do you want from me? What happens *next?*

"I'll be right beside you, okay?"

A tear slips down my cheek. "What if we get stuck?"

"We won't. The chance is one in a million," he reassures, wiping away my tears. "But even if we do, we'll press the button and be out in ten minutes. *You won't be alone anymore.*"

Caleb's warmth envelops me as he wraps an arm around my shoulders. I close my eyes as we step into the elevator, focusing on the sound of the button being pressed.

For a moment, I feel okay. I think I can do this without embarrassing myself. But as the elevator starts to ascend, I snap, burying myself in Caleb's chest to escape the trauma that follows me everywhere.

He holds me closer, and I relax into his embrace, cocooned in warmth that shields me from fear. "You're safe," he whispers, running a hand through my hair. "Everything's okay."

I choke out a sob, realizing how not okay I can be sometimes. I've lived thinking nothing bad happens and I don't need anyone, but moments like this, or coming home to a dusty apartment, remind me how lonely I truly am. The feeling has haunted me all my life, muffled by time but never truly gone. But everything changed with the strange occurrences in my life lately. As strange as it sounds, having a stalker somehow made it better.

He made me feel seen.

Heard.

For the past month, I've lived with the sense that he's always watching over me, caring about me. It made me feel valuable.

Wrapped in Caleb's arms, I finally feel like what I've been waiting for has arrived. Everything feels like it's falling into place. He's intruded into my life in an audacious way, but somehow, I find myself embracing it.

For the first time in twenty years, I feel *secure*.

"Caleb, I—" The elevator door opens suddenly, and I realize we've arrived.

He gently lifts my chin, turning my face toward him. "What?"

A man in an expensive suit interrupts the moment, waving at us impatiently. "Finally here! And why are you standing like statues? Come on, we're waiting!"

I pull away from Caleb's arms, feeling the emptiness wash over me instantly. Awkwardly clearing my throat, I step out of the elevator, Caleb following close behind.

"You must be Lilith Leclair, right?" The man grabs my hand and shakes it vigorously. "Caleb's been eager to have you on this trip."

"What the fuck are you doing here?" Caleb's voice is sharp, anything but friendly, as he stands beside me, his presence almost looming over the man. "You were supposed to be in New York," he adds.

A wicked smile spreads across the man's face. "Oh, Caleb. Always so direct. Don't you want to introduce me to your lovely companion?"

His jaw clenches, tension thickening between them. I can practically taste it in the air.

"Lilith, this is Grayson Moore," he introduces, voice stern. "A venture capitalist and a key supporter of my company. But he was supposed to stay in New York. He's not the investor we're meeting today."

Grayson's smile doesn't falter. "I know this investor. He's a friend of a friend. Thought I could help. Isn't that what friends do, Caleb?"

I sense the rage simmering beneath Caleb's surface. My fingers brush his lightly, a silent reminder of my presence, hoping to ease his tension. He looks at me, and in that moment, the anger that was directed at Grayson dissipates. His obsidian eyes, flickering with hate just moments ago, soften as he focuses on me—the person who *needs* him right now.

And he looks at me like I'm the center of his universe.

THIS IS OUR FINAL DAY HERE. WE'VE COMPLETED EVERYTHING ON OUR agenda, even the unnecessary tasks, and severed all possible connections. I've gathered and organized all the information I had, and despite my initial doubts about writing such articles, I believe I've done more than just well.

But right now, I can't focus on anything. It's mainly because I haven't mustered the courage to ask Caleb for what I want. Since the meeting with Grayson, he's become...more distant. It feels like a stab in the stomach, and all the butterflies are dead now. I don't know what changed, maybe it was like this from the beginning.

Perhaps I created something, made myself believe in it, and nothing more.

This time, the knock on the door doesn't distract me—I keep my eyes closed. It must be the cleaning service. "Go away!" I shout.

I could never keep maids in my house if I were rich. Too much distraction, even from just one person. But whoever it is behind the door unlocks it with their spare card, entering as if it's routine. It feels strangely personal, considering I just told them to leave.

I get up from bed and head toward the living room. I freeze when I see Caleb. "How did you—"

"You should have asked that two nights ago, Lilith," he interrupts, his voice calm and steady, as if nothing is amiss. He begins to approach me, and I remain motionless, unable to move.

"What you're doing is inappropriate, you know?" His small laugh escapes, resonating pleasantly in my chest. Even his laughter is perfect.

"But it doesn't seem to stop you from enjoying it," he adds, closing the distance between us, enveloping me with his presence.

His face inches closer to mine, his warm breath grazing my lips. "Caleb—"

His hand intercepts me as I reach for my neck, encircling it like a collar. "*Are you scared, little devil?*" He calls me this, and I should be upset or disgusted, but I feel aroused instead.

"No," I whisper with closed eyes.

He squeezes my neck slightly, and a quiet whimper escapes before I can stop it. "You should be." His other hand moves to my face, brushing his fingers across my lips. "You should have been scared when I cut off the man's tongue for you."

He pushes his thumb between my lips, and before I can protest, he shoves it into my mouth, sending my pulse skyrocketing. "You should have called the police and told them you were being haunted by a very bad man."

I open my eyes, ignoring the heat on my cheeks. I take his finger to the end, sucking and twirling my tongue over it, feeling the warmth between my legs grow thicker. "But you decided to be a good, grateful girl and let me watch you, Lilith." His half-opened eyes show hunger, his thumb leaving my mouth, smearing saliva across my lips and chin.

"So tell me," he licks his lips, "why aren't you scared of what I plan to do to you?" Caleb tightens his grip around my neck, making it impossible to move, and it already hurts from staring up at him for so long.

"I know you won't hurt me," I answer softly, placing my hand on top of the collar around my neck, pressing down and making him squeeze me harder. "Not until I want you to."

I have no idea what's happening to me right now, where that shy, awkward version of me went. But the words flow from my mouth as if they've always been on the tip of my tongue, my actions dictated automatically by my brain, as if all I needed was a little push.

But bits of my consciousness are still trying to make their way through the surface of arousal I'm experiencing right now because my legs are trembling and I can feel how red my face is, not even to mention my heart that is going to jump out of my ribcage at any minute.

Caleb offers me a smirk, fully aware of its effect, evoking a sense of vulnerability within me. "That's right, little devil."

While his one hand is still on my neck, his other hand travels from my face down to my stomach, causing a rush of goosebumps to occupy my weak body. He feels my reaction and teases me on purpose, slowly tapping his fingers on my sensitive spots, but after a moment, he finally buries his hand inside my shorts, diving into a pool of wetness he caused.

"Look at you," he gathers my juices on his fingers and smears them across my clit, "you're soaked for me."

I release a quiet moan as an answer, my hips rolling to meet his hand. If he wasn't holding me by my neck, I would've collapsed already.

"Eyes on me," he demands as he begins to rub my most sensitive spot.

"I—I can't—" My voice breaks and my eyes roll as I succumb to the pleasure this man gives me.

"Don't make me repeat myself," he growls, his voice now a shade rougher than a moment ago. When I comply and our eyes meet again, he asks, "Does this feel good?"

Another moan escapes me, this time a little louder. "Yes," I breathe, my eyes rolling at his slow, steady pace.

I don't even realize how Caleb closes the distance between our faces and clings his lips to mine. He never stops rubbing my clit as his tongue enters my mouth boldly, without a chance for me to escape.

I whimper, trying to keep pace with him, but it feels like he's eating me alive. When he pulls back, my head almost falls on his chest. He releases my neck, now running his hand through my hair and slightly grabbing it.

"Stick out your tongue." I comply, surprised by how easily I obey every single demand he gives me. "Now, when I press mine to yours, don't just freeze, Lilith. Relax and try to circle it."

I blink up at him, embarrassed by my lack of experience. "I'm sorry."

"Don't fucking apologize for it."

As soon as I feel Caleb's tongue on mine—I do as he asked, relaxing a bit and starting to circle it in slow movements. He groans from pleasure, and that gives me more confidence—my hand grabs him by the back of his neck and I begin to roll my hips faster, riding his hand like it's something I do every fucking day.

This is what all the fuss was about. This is how it is supposed to be. Not those lizard-sticky touches and disgusting kisses like with Evan.

"That's a good girl," he says in between our kisses, his fingers accelerating. "There you go."

I break the kiss and my head kicks back as I feel an upcoming orgasm, but he doesn't stop—his lips moving to my neck. "I can't, Caleb," I cry out. "I'm going to—"

"That's right, Lilith." He tightens his grip on my hair. "Come for me."

And I do—pure euphoria courses through my body as I let out a loud scream, disregarding the fact that our neighbors might hear me. I am blinded by how intensely it overwhelms me, feeling tears welling at the corners of my eyes. Caleb holds me tight as I ride the waves, my hands reach for the collar of his hoodie as I clench the fabric in my fists, holding on for dear life.

Even after a solid minute, I'm still shaking violently, my breathing is erratic and I can't open my eyes. My chest is pressed into him so tight that I feel his bulging abs through the cloth, and that alone sends another zing of electricity through my body as if all the pleasure I've just experienced wasn't enough for me.

As if I want more.

"Open your eyes," he orders, his voice again with a tint of roughness, but the rock in his pants that presses between my thighs tells me that he is seconds from breaking apart. "I want you to face the man who has claimed you, Lilith."

Despite all the sweet feelings that coursing through my veins right now, the aftermath comes pretty fast—I start to feel ashamed for what we've done.

But it's already done, and I comply, my eyes catching his obsidian beads. "What are you going to do to me?"

His mouth forms a tiny devilish smirk. "What do you want me to do to you?"

That's a good question. I know I shouldn't fall for my stalker. If you would ask me a year ago *what* would I do in a situation like this, I would say run. I would go to the police and move out of my apartment, maybe even move back in with my mother. Anything to keep me safe.

I have no idea what changed. When Caleb appeared in my life, it seemed like he erased all possible borders I had without even trying much. He made me realize that there's something more in me—demons that lurk inside my soul are finally slowly releasing.

And that should scare me, that should push me to go to the fucking therapy to understand what's wrong with me. What has been wrong with me for all these years that I've tried to deny it.

I guess, everyone was right. My mother, my peers. I was feeling offended when they all told me that I was weird, that something within me made me different from the others.

But when the truth is exposed, and I am finally facing every single demon, I don't want to deny it. For the first time in my life, I feel like all this—whatever Caleb has started—isn't ugly and scary.

It's as if I've woken up for the first time in two decades. It's like I'm getting the opportunity to be myself—my genuine self—without any shame.

"I want you to *stay*," I whisper.

Caleb withdraws his hand from under my shorts, and I steal a quick glance at it—his fingers glistening with my juices. Oh, God.

"Even if it means risking everything?" he questions, brushing his moistened fingers across my lips, leaving a slick trail behind. "Even if you're not entirely sure what you're getting into?"

He studies my expression, perhaps searching for hesitation. Maybe he's giving me a chance to back out, knowing I might not fully comprehend the consequences. Or maybe it's a challenge. Either way, I'm tired of letting fear hold me back, tired of staying within the safe confines of my apartment.

"Yes," I murmur, feeling a surge of determination. His reaction is fleeting, a flicker in his eyes as he licks his lips, inhaling deeply. "I want *you*."

He leans to my ear, and whispers, "From now on, you're mine, little devil."

CHAPTER
TWENTY—ONE

Caleb

B y the time we arrive in New York, my phone is tearing apart.

After five days of working, talking to dozens of different people and discussing our plans, when I arrived back, thinking that everything had finally come to an end and me and Lilith could spend some time together, it started to get even worse.

Those couple of busy days in Jersey City felt like a vacation compared to what is happening now. The project needs to be done ASAP because more and more rich asses are trying to protect themselves, afraid to be robbed or become Black Widow's tenth.

They think that it's calm before the storm and as soon as everybody relaxes, he is going to strike and another poor girl will disappear without a trace.

And while busy with this shit, I catch myself thinking about my past. I've earned a reputation as the most uncatchable, intelligent serial killer who has been terrorizing the city for the past couple of years, and I can't just disappear from the scene.

Right?

But then I remember about Lilith. I imagine her finding out about what I actually am, what I have done, and how much blood is on my hands.

I can't allow her to know the truth. She isn't scared of me, but if she finds out the truth, she will be. She won't even try to listen to me. She just will run away like a scared little rabbit, thinking that I've lied to her and that it was my evil plan all along.

Well, it was. Until I started to learn more about her.

All of my previous victims that I murdered were different—I didn't have a certain type. Some of them were too naïve and stupid, and some of them were smarter and more mature. And as I said before, I've never picked up who and how I am going to kill. I could sit in the random bar on Saturday night and without doing anything, a girl would approach me and strike up a conversation about something trivial.

I've become bored after my seventh. I even refused a couple of girls, telling them that I was not interested. I had no clue if I wanted to keep doing it, it stopped bringing me pleasure at all.

But then Blake happened. She accidentally—or not—spilled a cup of coffee on me when she was running for work in the morning, and no matter how much I placated her that it was okay, she kept apologizing and offering her help.

The conversation happened not intentionally, and boom—she left her number and the next day we were going out on a date.

As usual, she began to insist on telling her father about me, citing her difficult relationship with her mother, kept insisting on inviting me to her family home, and then I got rid of her. Kidnapped, locked in a basement, and visited once a day, then after some time I killed her and got rid of her body in the swamp near my murder house.

Cecilia, on the contrary, wasn't an accident. I met her at the café when I was grabbing my lunch, and I was the one who insisted on getting her number, simply because I was curious if I could light that sparkle for killing inside of me again.

But the whole plan was irritating me more than it should; I'm not even talking about the possible pleasure of doing it. I was relieved when I killed her not because I was enjoying doing it again, but just because it was finally over and I could live unbothered again.

After Cecilia was gone and I met Lilith, I felt something inside of me. At first, I thought that was that usual spark—an urge to kill, to force her to suffer.

But it was something more. Lilith isn't like women I've met before, I already told you that. And the fact she never even noticed me when I came to her university, never even bothered to look at my side, made me feel thrilled.

Fun fact—I was never a stalker. Like I said, they all came to me because of their own desire. But Lilith challenged me.

I can't imagine myself fixating on anyone else. It wouldn't bring me the same satisfaction as it does with my little devil.

She opened my eyes to feelings I had previously believed were impossible to experience. I take pleasure in observing her and getting to know her. And my feelings are beyond simple obsession.

Now I understand what was that little flame that ignited when I first saw her. It was an immediate attraction and interest. I don't want to blabber about love at first sight because it's too fucking corny.

I've never even experienced love. I never loved my parents. I never loved any woman in my life. And nobody ever loved me. All those women that I've killed, I knew they weren't loving me. They were attracted to me—because of the way I look, or because of my achievements. Every single one of them said it.

Those feelings aren't what love is. Attraction, fixation, interest, obsession—maybe. But not love.

With Lilith, it's different. Each of us is attracted to each other, of course, but there's more behind a simple attraction. It's about sensing each other—feeling the demons that lurk in the depths of our souls and letting them break free and intertwine with one another.

As I got to know Lilith better, I realized how similar we are. I am just like her—surrounded by nothing but squared walls, devoid of friends and family. We both grew up in a fucked-up environment, although her situation thankfully is a shade lighter, without her mother beating her up and locking her in a basement for days because her little ass did something wrong. My family had a lot more violence going on. Her parents just don't give a fuck.

As she revealed why she was afraid of elevators, I experienced a sensation I never felt before. In a flash, I pictured a vulnerable Lilith trapped in a dark box, frightened and alone. It makes me want to protect and care for her until we are buried six feet underground, and even after, haunting her soul in another world, robbing her of a chance to meet someone else.

A flashback of my own surfaced—each time my mother locked me in the basement and I sat in the darkness, witnessing unsettling sights. Formless shadows with claws and red eyes mingled on the walls, ceaselessly whispering unsettling thoughts, prompting me to wish for an end, simply to escape the overwhelming fear.

And I was just as old as her when that happened for the first time.

Learning about her during the stalking process is one thing, but learning something new and personal from her mouth is different. Her story leads me to consider that we are not merely similar, but rather a reflection of each other, intertwined in our experiences.

However, no matter how satisfied I am because she is finally right here, in my hands, a part of me starts to feel genuine fear for our future.

I find myself overwhelmed by the thought of her discovering the truth about me. She occupies my mind as powerfully as a potent drug, and I am feeling anxiety due to the fear of revealing something so horrible to her.

Because I *never* want to lose her.

After a few days, I've completed all my work, finishing everything required for the project. The hired workers have exceeded my expectations, completing their tasks swiftly.

As I descend into the basement, each step creaks in the dimly lit stairwell. With a twist of the key and a flick of the switch, the room is bathed in light. I am momentarily frozen in place.

It resembles an entire underground apartment, akin to those seen in movies prepared for a zombie apocalypse or alien invasion. Thoughtfully designed with warm color schemes, soft textures, and carefully curated decor, the space feels inviting and cozy. The open layout includes a bathroom, bedroom, and compact kitchen, all furnished for comfort. It's a place where one could imagine living without worry.

I breathe a sigh of relief, reassured that this doesn't resemble the location where something terrible happened in the past.

Though unsettling to think of it as a backup plan, having this roof over my head is undeniably wise.

CHAPTER
TWENTY-TWO

Lilith

As the power of the thunder vibrates through my apartment, heavy raindrops cascade across the one and only window in here, seemingly painting an amateur masterpiece. I nearly flinch as another bolt of lightning strikes in the distance, briefly illuminating the city streets.

Experiencing such a powerful storm in New York for the first time, I can't help but feel a touch of worry for my window, pondering how much shaking it can endure. It has remained unrepaired since the building's construction in *1987*, as Randall mentioned.

This shit is thirty-five years old. If by some miracle it survives the night, I am asking Reed to replace it.

However, the piece of shabby glass isn't my main concern. Caleb is.

I've been struggling to resist the urge to reach out to him for the past couple of days. What can I possibly say? What if he feels overwhelmed by me?

When you discover a man who makes you feel heard and seen, the last thing you want to do is frighten him away.

So I've been waiting. Thinking.

When the sound of the front door clicking open reaches my ears, followed by the weighty rhythm of his footsteps as he secures the lock behind him, advancing toward my bedroom, at first, I don't believe it.

But as a towering figure materializes at the doorframe of my bedroom—his form blending with the shadows, the moon's gentle glow casts a sliver of light on the contours of his face, contouring his sharp features—I am convinced.

He is finally here.

Anxiety builds in my stomach as I can only observe him closing the gap between us, unable to move.

"I waited for you," I whisper under my breath.

Caleb sits on the bed, the mattress sinking beneath his weight. "I know, little devil," he answers as he covers my hand with his own, the touch damp and chilly from the rain. "I had to finish my work."

I affirm with a nod. "Yeah. I know."

"But I'm here now," as he leans in closer, my nose catches the scent of fresh rain, "and I'm not going anywhere."

Caleb clings to my lips and gives me a sensual, soft little kiss as if a few nights ago he wasn't forcing his tongue deep into my throat when I almost choked on it.

Those kisses felt like claiming, avowing ones. But this feels like a safe promise.

I assert my control by wrapping my hand around his neck. He effortlessly lifts me up, and when I find myself in his lap, I feel the bulge in his pants. Pressed closer to him, I moan, sensing his heartbeat - faster than it should be.

Caleb continues to peck my lips, his hands traveling to my face as he firmly grasps me, reclaiming his power. He controls my movements as his tongue slides between my lips and confidently enters my mouth. He doesn't allow himself to go further, keeping a slow pace despite how hard it is for him to restrain. I can feel it.

Without even realizing it, I grind myself against his cock, the fabric still separating us, but it doesn't restrain both of us from feeling a zing of electricity across our bodies.

"Fuck," he moans as he breaks the kiss.

Caleb moves me further onto the bed and gets on top within a second, hovering over me like a dark storm cloud. Every fiber of my body is ablaze as I anticipate his next action; my heart is pounding in my chest with more intensity than usual as if desperate to escape from its ribcage.

Maintaining eye contact, he reaches his hand inside my shorts. "Tell me," he begins as his fingers reach out to my clit, "have you ever been fucked, Lilith?"

I bite my bottom lip, shaking my head. "No."

His fingers acquire a slow pace, circling my clit in torturous movements that force my back to arch. "Not even fingered?" Echoing with depths akin to the demonic, his voice takes on a gravelly quality.

"No," I whimper. "Not even my own."

He bumps his forehead into mine, reaching out to my slit. "Do you want me to fuck you, my little devil?"

I tense when he pushes the tip of one of his fingers inside me, immediately feeling a little uncomfortable. He allows me a moment to get used to it before shoving it further.

"Do you want me to claim you whole?" My body reacts to his touch more swiftly than my mind, ignoring the countless subconscious warnings about him.

About us.

"Yes," I answer, my voice barely audible as he adds the second finger and starts to fuck me, slowly, but pushing his long fingers till the end. "Yes, I want it."

"Say it," he growls, leisurely quickening the pace. "Say what you want me to do to you, Lilith."

I get used to his presence, feeling how he already stretches my walls as he adds the third finger while his thumb circles my clit, balancing a slight pain with pleasure. "I want you to fuck me," I moan, gripping the bed sheets, and my head kicks back, succumbing to the waves of pleasure washing over me. "Fuck me, Caleb."

When he gets his fingers out of me, I immediately feel hollow, but I'm not quick enough to react as he crushes his lips to mine. I barely can keep pace with him as he kisses me like a man starving, our tongues circling like a pair of intertwined serpents. He breaks the kiss for a brief moment to take his hoodie off, and as soon as I am allowed to face his bare chest, my breathing stops for a moment.

As Caleb takes my hand and places it on his chest, allowing me to touch him, I shamelessly scan his perfect body - broad shoulders, six-pack abs, and the enticing V that tempts me to remove his sweatpants and explore the perfection hidden underneath. My hand travels up and down across his flawless chest, savoring the sensation of his smooth skin under my touch, and I ponder over the realization that I never knew anyone could be this perfect.

I reach out to the edge of his pants and glance at him from under my lashes as if asking permission to go further. He brushes his fingers across my cheek. "Take them off."

My pulse throbs between my legs at his demand as I comply, placing my other hand on his sweatpants and slowly sliding them off along with his underwear. When I'm done, I raise my head and my eyes pop out from shock.

"No," I squeak out, immediately scooting away. "No, no, no."

A deep, mischievous chuckle vibrates through his chest. "What's that, little devil? Scared?" He leans to me, once again trapping me into an invisible cage of his presence. "Taking your words back, huh?"

"Caleb, I can't. Feeling your fingers was already painful enough for me. You are going to rip me in half with this."

His cock isn't just big. It's fucking huge. I don't even understand how he walks around with it without feeling uncomfortable. He's hard and hungry, with thick veins all over his flesh and pre-cum dripping from his tip.

I suspected that it wasn't…normal, just the way the rest of his body is, but I had no clue that he was going to be this enormous.

He bares his teeth. "You sound like a scared little mouse right now." Caleb takes me by my calves and adjusts me back into the position where I was in the beginning. "Aren't you agreed to be mine, baby?"

I move my face away from him. "I can't—" He grabs me by my cheeks and turns my face back to his.

"You can. And you are going to be a good girl and take the whole thing, do you hear me?"

My body automatically reacts to his rough tone as I sense the waterfall that thickens between my legs. "Yes."

"I'm going to try to be gentle," he says, adjusting me in a comfortable position and taking my shorts off. After he hears my quiet laugh in response, he asks, "What's funny?"

"The way you are being scary and gentle and the same time," I respond while he strips me off completely.

Caleb takes a look at me when I lay completely naked in front of him. His intense stare makes my cheeks go red and I wrap my hands around my breasts to cover myself up but he immediately grabs them and pins them above my head. "You can't interrupt me when I'm enjoying you, Lilith. Don't you dare do that again."

He tilts his head toward mine, kissing and nibbling my lips. His hands depart from mine and move toward my breasts, pressing and kneading them, coaxing a moan from me.

"You are so fucking gorgeous," he rasps, his hands giving me the massage I never knew I needed, turning me into a jelly with its steady, torturous pace. "I am the luckiest man on the Earth."

His words flutter through my clouded mind like a tender caress. I surrender completely as he leaves me engulfed in a sensation of warm pleasure that makes my head swim, momentarily leaving me dizzy.

But when I feel him shoving the tip of his cock inside me, I gasp—both from unexpectedness and pain. "Fuck, it hurts," I cry out as I feel a blinding pain shoot across my body as if thousands of needles piercing through me.

Caleb stops, allowing me to get used to his presence, although I doubt I can do it. He's too much.

"It's okay," he reassures, kissing my temple. "You can take it."

I let out a loud cry as he shoves himself further, feeling with every single inch of my body how he stretches me, afraid that he's going to rip me in half. "Oh, God, Caleb," I whimper, my nails digging into his back as I try to keep still. "Oh my God—"

"I love the way you pray me, little devil," he says, groaning from pleasure as he continues to shove himself further, and I feel like it's never going to end. "So fucking tight." After another pathetic cry slips past my lips along with a few hot tears across my cheeks, his smooth voice swirls around me once again, "Open up for me, Lilith."

I push my legs wider apart, hoping it will ease the pain. "You're killing me."

Another chuckle escapes him as he leaves a little kiss on my collarbone. "You're taking me so good, my girl. Just try not to black out."

My hand moves to his cheeks as I grab him just the way he grabbed me a few moments ago, and dig my nails into his skin while he keeps shoving his endless cock inside me. "Fuck you."

His obsidian eyes flicker with something unfamiliar as in one rigid movement he grabs my hands, pins them above my head and slams his dick with a loud slap inside me. My eyes bulge from all the sensations I'm feeling, but the pain mixes with pleasure when he hits that spot and starts to roll his hips back and forth, fucking me.

"I need to make better use of that pretty little mouth of yours, don't I?" he asks, his tone rough and cold, devoid of even a hint of its previous softness, as if it had never existed.

"Caleb, fuck!" I scream as he quickens his pace, slamming into me with indescribable force. It feels as though I am on the verge of overflowing as my body feels too full.

I can't move my hands—not when his grip is so fucking right on them—I'm sure marks will be visible in the morning. It seems as though he has lost all the patience he once possessed, fervently giving in to the sensations, seemingly intent on pushing me into a state of overwhelming bliss.

However, I feel like it isn't enough for me, so I throw my legs on his shoulders and crisscross them behind his neck, pulling him closer and crushing my lips to his. This time I am the one who forces my tongue into his mouth, kissing him so insatiably—just the way he is fucking me.

We both gasp for breath, exchanging only whimpers and moans of pleasure as we kiss, the sounds filling my room along with the rhythmic slapping of our bodies as if it is our last time together.

As he unglues from me to catch some breath, a trail of saliva—mine or his, or maybe both of us—hangs down from his lips, dripping on mine, and I lick them dry, realizing what I've done only after I meet his little satisfied smirk.

"I love witnessing the extent of your corruption," he rasps, and my body grows warmer still, arousal coursing within me in response to his guttural voice.

I don't even feel ashamed for what I did. Probably because my mind is cloudy while I am aroused and I can't think of anything rather this man that keeps fucking me into oblivion.

I want to answer him, to say something more than just let out raspy moans and screams, but I can't—the wave of an upcoming orgasm washes over me, slowly enveloping my weak body with its force as my eyes are rolling painfully.

"Are you going to come, little devil?" he asks, slowing his pace on purpose, thrusting into me slower but harder, making everything for me ten times worse as I feel like at any moment I am going to break apart. "Are you going to come right on my cock?"

"Yes," I cry out, rolling my hips intact with his movements. "Oh, Caleb—"

The next moment he hits that spot, I explode. An orgasm so vivid that its painful waves wash over me, causing me to clench around his cock. My back arches as I release a loud scream, so loud that probably every neighbor in my apartment complex hears me.

"Fuck, Lilith, fuck!" Euphoria follows Caleb closely—he groans, giving one final thrust as I feel the warmth of him inside me, seeping and trickling out of my core.

None of this feels normal. A person can't experience *this* much pleasure.

It's only when Caleb slides out of me that I realize I not only allowed him to enter me but also let him take control and completely dominate me, shoving his endless cock till the end.

My body trembles uncontrollably, rendering me immobile, as I struggle to regain control of my breathing and calm myself. I feel our mixed juices dripping down my thighs, as I remain unmoving even after a few minutes, needing to consciously remember to breathe.

Caleb reaches my hand and takes it so gently as if he wasn't just griping me so hard that my hands went numb. "You okay, baby?"

I take a moment to answer. "I don't think so."

"Get used to it," he answers casually, squeezing my hand a little.

Can I even get used to something like this? "Do you realize that this isn't normal?"

"How do you know? You're saying you had a *normal* experience before and I have just been fooled?"

I heave a sigh. "No. I never had any."

Caleb takes both of my hands, pulling me closer to him. I rest my head against his chest, my fingers brushing over his abs. I feel his heartbeat, quickly returning to normal, a stark contrast to my own racing pulse.

"I'm your first, huh?" he asks, running his hand through my hair as he begins to caress it.

"Yes, Caleb."

His fingers sift through my locks, revealing the golden highlights woven among the brown strands. "First and last," he adds with a note of pride in his voice.

"It sounds creepy. But okay," I snicker mockingly.

"I thought you were aware that I'm a creep. Don't you love it?"

I almost snort. "I think I do." After a pause, I ask, "Can I ask you a question?"

"Do I have a choice?"

I raise my head and meet the playful gleam in his eyes. "You don't. What's your favorite color?"

His eyes roll immediately. "Lilith, that's so lame."

"Answer right now."

He covers his eyes with his hand. "Pink."

I giggle softly. "You're an asshole."

"It's true because it's the color of your lips. Up and down."

It takes me a few seconds to realize what he is talking about. "Gross. You are unbelievably gross."

"And my favorite meal is your—"

I shut him up by pressing my hand on his mouth. "I'm starting to dislike you."

"It's going to make things ten times worse for you if you don't enjoy it," he mumbles and then licks my palm.

I immediately pull my hand back and he pushes me on my back, hovering over me. "Do you have more questions?"

"Your birthday. I know your age but I couldn't find a date," I confess.

He puts on a haughty smirk. "So you did stalk me online, huh?"

I quirk a brow at him, unimpressed. "You aren't the one who should be surprised by that. "

"Fair enough. October 23th. We are the perfect match, if you're wondering."

I try to remember if Scorpio's match with Virgo's or if he's just being a smartass, and he gives me a judgmental look. "You don't believe me?"

"I'm trying to remember the table of compatibility," I answer honestly, biting back a laugh. "You could be lying."

"I'm not. Couldn't you feel our bond tonight?"

"Why me?" I ask unexpectedly.

"What?"

"Why me, Caleb?" I parrot, keeping eye contact with him. "There are so many girls around. I am not even close to perfect. Why did you choose me?"

He scans my face, taking the strand of my hair and tucking it behind my ear. "I don't give a fuck about others, Lilith. You are the only woman who for some incomprehensible reason has occupied my thoughts. It hurts me to witness how you don't realize how fucking perfect you are."

"Stop saying that."

"It's the truth. I'm weary of you seeing yourself as nothing but a flaw. I could say that you deserve the entire planet, but I refuse to do so because who cares about the rest of the world? We'll set everything ablaze and revel together in the ashes, my little devil."

As Caleb's features become nothing but a blurry mess, I realize that I'm crying. I don't even need to mention that nobody said something like this to me before. Not even fucking close. Even now, as we lie in the same bed and I soak in the comfort he provides me, a part of me doubts the reality of this.

When surrounded by people who overlook me, it feels like I've finally met the one who truly perceives me.

Rowan

I want to laugh. Which is pretty weird in the situation I am in right now.

It's just the absurdity of it.

I thought I was dating a regular guy, a little weird, but we all have our weirdness, right?

But our quirks don't include kidnapping and locking people who trust us in the basement.

And I was wondering why he never told anyone about me. Not his colleagues. Not his friends. He insisted that he didn't want anyone to know about me, and I thought he was a little possessive, but that's what I liked about him. A little control never hurt anybody.

I was so fucking stupid. I basically told my family to fuck off because they kept warning me, telling me that he is odd and the fact that he never shows me to anybody and never lets me show him is a huge red flag.

But I fell in love. Can you blame me for that? It's fucking Caleb Walker - the man is a definition of perfection.

Though I had no idea he was a psychopath. A kidnapper. A killer, probably.

I say probably because part of me still can't believe that he eventually is going to cut my throat. Or choke me. Or fucking drug me, I don't know. I have no idea what he planned to do.

My overthinking along with feelings of uselessness and despair are driving me crazy.

I want it just to be over already.

Mom. Dad. You were right.

I'm sorry.

CHAPTER
TWENTY—THREE

Caleb

I hastily make my way to the front door, which seems on the verge of collapsing under the relentless pounding of an unseen force. I can't fathom how Lilith managed with this flimsy excuse for a door. As I swing it open, I'm greeted not by anyone but Randall Reed himself.

"Is there a particular reason you're bothering us at nine in the morning?" I ask, my frustration clear in my voice. He looks annoyed, as if I'm the one who disturbed him.

"Yes, Caleb," he replies, nodding toward the door down the hall. "There have been complaints from her neighbors about the noise last night."

I let out a chuckle. "From whom exactly?"

He gives me a resentful once-over. "From everyone who lives here. Thin walls, what did you expect?"

I try to stay calm, mindful that Lilith is still asleep nearby. But my patience wears thin as Randall continues to push.

"If your life is boring, that's not our problem, Randall," I retort, my tone icy. "Find someone else to bother, and spread the word."

Pure jealousy and anger flash over his ugly face as he prepares to say something he'll regret later, but he quickly rearranges his features in a neutral expression when his eyes dart behind my back.

"Is everything okay?" Lilith asks, rubbing her eyes with her hands before reaching out to hug me.

My blood stops boiling up for a moment, and I relax, the thoughts of murdering this motherfucker are just background noise. For now.

I give her a warm look. "Nothing, baby. Your landlord just came in to tell you great news about how he is going to reduce the cost of your rent." I switch my gaze back to the fucker. "Right, Randall? "

A muscle twitches beneath his eye but he only smiles. "Right. Ten percent discount on your price."

I feel her intense stare, but my eyes remain fixated on Reed. "That's wonderful. Now, if you'll excuse us, we'd like to return to our *duties*. Have a nice day, Randall."

I slam the door shut before he can even process everything, then turn the lock. "God, Caleb. You've almost hit his nose," Lilith murmurs, her voice still hoarse from sleep.

I turn to her and take a full look at her appearance. Her hair is messy, and her face is swollen with a slight trace of the pillow imprinted on her right cheek. I also notice that she's wearing my hoodie, which is so big on her that she could easily get tangled up in it.

Fucking gorgeous.

"Why aren't you in bed, huh?" I lift her up, her legs circling my waist as I carry her back to the bedroom. "It's early."

I place her on the bed and scoot right beside her. "I'm a morning person. It's the time I am usually already at my classes." The next moment, her eyes round in shock and she slaps a hand over her forehead. "Fuck. My classes."

Without warning, she jumps to her feet, appearing poised for flight, but I swiftly catch her with one hand and draw her into my embrace. "Fuck your classes."

She resists, trying to break free from my tight grip. "No, Caleb. I can't miss."

"You swear you can't do certain things, but somehow you manage to do them." Nestling my face in her hair, a strong urge to sneeze comes over me. "I want to prove how wrong you are again."

"I worked too hard to just throw it away. They're going to expel me if I am not going to visit the classes."

"I'll solve the problem."

She keeps trying to get out of my embrace. "No—"

"Yes. Stop fidgeting like a worm, Lilith. I am not restricting you to go there. You will, but later. I need you here, with me."

"That's cute." She finally gives up, wrapping her arms around my neck. "So now I'm going to hide behind my big boyfriend's back?"

"Big boyfriend I am?"

"How do you prefer?"

"I like it. I'll expect you to call me Daddy, actually."

She lets out an exasperated sigh. "No. You won't use my daddy issues against me. That's rude."

"It's fine," I answer, lifting my head to meet her emerald eyes. "I have daddy issues, too."

A surprised look takes over her features. "What about your mother?"

"Worse than yours. Beat my ass up my whole childhood and locked me in the basement when I did something wrong." I stop momentarily to think. "Sometimes even without a reason."

She freezes, obviously stunned by my sudden honesty. "Shit. I'm sorry, I didn't mean to...I didn't know it was so dark."

I shake my head. "It's fine. I know it's not what I used to tell everyone about my parents during interviews. But don't worry about it, I moved on a long time ago."

She wets her lips before asking, "Where are they now?"

"Dead."

Her eyebrows pinch together, but she quickly rearranges her features into a neutral expression. "I'm sorry for what you were forced to go through, Caleb."

I don't mention that the reason for the death of my parents is me. I killed them. With my bare hands.

She doesn't ask because she feels like she already dug too much. And it's good because I don't want to lie to her.

But I don't want to tell the truth either.

I flinch as her little hands move toward my face, halting them halfway there. "What are you doing?"

I never allowed anyone to touch my face. I know it may seem absurd, but even I try to avoid touching my face as much as possible. The reason behind this may sound ridiculous, but it's a result of my tumultuous childhood. My mother would often hit me in the face, and now I can't bear even the sensation of fingers brushing against my facial skin.

The moment when Lilith dug her sharp nails into my cheeks, I lost it. I glance at her wrists—the marks that my hands left are not that visible, but I still recall the memory of gripping her so hard that I was seconds from breaking her little hands.

"Did she hit your face?" A tender voice brings me back from my ugly thoughts. "Is this happened because of her?"

She barely touches the little scar at the right sight on my jawline.

Nobody noticed it before.

"Yes," I cut shortly. "An exposed wire. Sometimes hands weren't enough for her."

Lilith's worried eyes fixate on me—a brief moment before she moves her lips to my scar and kisses the spot so gently that it feels more like a whisper than a kiss, but for some reason, I feel it down my toes. "Lilith—"

"It's okay," she murmurs softly. "You can close your eyes if that is going to make it easier for you."

A little laugh almost escapes my chest. Not her using my techniques on me. But I do close my eyes. She takes it slowly—her soft fingertips touch the outlining of my jawline, moving across it like a brush on a canvas. Then, she travels up to my cheeks, and I fight back an urge to shrug her hands off, telling myself that she is not my mother.

Because my mother is dead. I killed her. Next to me is no one else but the first woman I fell in love with.

My skin vibrates with discomfort from under it, but I keep repeating to myself that nothing bad is going to happen now. Not with Lilith by my side.

"Everything is fine, Caleb." Her hands travel up to my nose, eyes, and forehead—she keeps brushing her fingers across my skin back and forth at a slow, steady pace. "Do you like it?"

I lean to her hands like a cat, now brave enough to feel them whole on my face. "Yes. Keep going."

Lilith pulls me closer, bumping my nose into hers. "Now open your eyes."

A part of me is ridiculously scared to do that—afraid to see the face of the woman I hated the most. But suppressing it, I slowly open my eyes, and when I see nothing but the pretty face of my little devil, I relax. "Baby—"

She silences me with a kiss—a slow and gentle one. But instead of stopping there, her lips trail across my cheeks, nose, and even my eyes. She showers every inch of my skin with her affection, leaving no millimeter untouched.

God, it feels good. Better than everything I've ever experienced in my life.

It probably sounds fucking laughable—a man like me isn't supposed to need anything like this—but now, with Lilith by my side, it feels like I've finally found a missing piece to my soul. And I know that nobody could make me feel the way she makes me feel.

It wouldn't work if it weren't for her.

She moves the falling strand of hair from my forehead and kisses it.

"Your hair looks curlier today."

I let out a quiet laugh. "Yeah. Sometimes it looks like a nest. Well, most of the time."

Her smile brings forth a little dimple on her left cheek. "Do you feel safe with me?" she asks quietly.

"Yes, Lilith."

"Me too." She takes a brief pause. "I feel safe with you, too. I think I'm going to keep you."

This time my laugh is louder. "You think you're going to keep me, huh?"

Lilith wraps her hands around my shoulders and slowly moves them lower. A frown touches her face. "Wait. Turn around." She never lets me even process anything, just turns me around. "Oh my God."

"What?"

"Your back. I didn't—" I try to look at the reason why she sounds so shocked, noticing little red dots across both sides of my back.

"Oh, come on. I wouldn't even notice them if you never it pointed out."

Lilith's cheeks immediately acquire a crimson color as she fixes her glasses, looking everywhere but me. I made her scream so loud that the whole apartment building complained, but now her face gets all pinky when she realizes how passionate she got.

"I'm sorry," she says awkwardly.

"If I ever going to hear you apologizing for anything again, I will spank you so hard that you're not going to be able to sit for weeks."

Her shyness takes over again, but she keeps her face blank. Tries to. "Then you are going to be the one who needs to apologize."

I open my mouth to answer, but suddenly, she gets up and wraps herself around me—legs around my torso, and her hands slowly brushing across the little marks her nails left on my back. Enjoying the feeling of her touch on my skin, I close my eyes and let myself be carried away.

"Careful, little devil. At this rate, it's possible that you'll fall in love with me."

A comforting cascade of her warm breath flows across my back. "I won't mind it."

CHAPTER
TWENTY–FOUR

Lilith

C aleb stayed with me for a few days. I never imagined I could literally do nothing for days on end without feeling guilty. I usually studied, read, or attempted to write something. Every time I took a break, whether for tea or anything else, guilt would creep in. It was my way of warding off loneliness. Staying busy always kept my mind occupied.

But with Caleb, everything feels right. Every minute we spent cuddling, talking, and eating delivery food was filled with comfort. It just feels okay with him. However, both of us had responsibilities to attend to, so he returned to work and I resumed writing my second book. True to his word, he called my university and they granted me a temporary break from classes, allowing me to focus fully on the book.

Despite feeling embarrassed before, as if I didn't want to hide behind Caleb and let him solve my problems, now it feels more than okay. After leaving the apartment, I headed to the nearest café, feeling I deserved to treat myself to something delicious before diving into work.

In Pinewood, there's only one decent café, and despite the neighborhood's bad reputation, this place feels like a pleasant oasis in a desert. It's a typical, minimalistic modern café with the delightful aroma of coffee beans and freshly baked pastries, which always makes me hungry, even if I've just eaten. What I appreciate most is its quietness and lack of crowds, providing me with a space to think and enjoy my own company. It's no secret I'm not a fan of large groups, and there aren't many places like this in New York.

There are a few advantages to living in the worst part of town.

I'm halfway through writing the fifteenth chapter, fully immersed, when I notice someone taking a seat directly opposite me from the corner of my eye. I grasp the edge of my laptop cover and slowly lower it to see who's there. Grayson Moore. Caleb's primary sponsor.

"Lilith?" he asks, surprise evident on his face. "Our new writer, huh?"

I adjust my glasses and force a tight smile. "Oh, it was just practice. Temporary."

Grayson shakes his head. "*Darling*, I don't think so. Your article exceeded all expectations. I think we'll hire you as the head of our writer's department."

I should feel flattered and pleased, but I can't. An odd sensation washes over me; it seems Grayson isn't sincere. When Caleb compliments me, I feel it deep inside. I blush, and butterflies stir in my stomach, giving me confidence. From Grayson, it feels like empty words. And that's probably fine because he has nothing to do with me, just as I have nothing to do with him. He's simply being polite, and I should respond respectfully.

"You're too kind," I reply modestly.

He sets his hands on the table, and for a moment, I think he might touch me. I place my hands on my thighs under the table, just in case.

"I'm just being honest. I can see why Caleb is all over you, darling."

His choice of words feels like a stab in my stomach—probably nothing serious, but I feel a ball of impending nausea rise in my throat.

"What brings you here, if I may ask?" I soften my tone so he won't think I'm being rude. He annoys me, but I don't want trouble for Caleb. After all, Grayson is an important figure.

"I came for a coffee before an important meeting," he explains calmly. "Then I saw you," he gestures toward me, "and decided to say hi."

I glance at him quickly, a sudden alarm shooting through my brain—he's lying. Grabbing coffee in a Pinewood café? In an Armani suit?

But *why* lie? Maybe he does have a nearby meeting, maybe the client is a cheapskate, and he wanted to save money by renting an office in a lousy neighborhood. Maybe I'm just overreacting. Grayson seems like the kind of person I wouldn't trust, even if he were the last human on Earth. But that's just my impression, and I could be wrong. Perhaps he's a good guy who donates to charity and helps sick children, and I might just be in a negative mood.

"I like the coffee here," I say after a brief pause.

Something flickers across his face—an emotion I can't quite place. He knows I don't believe him, but he only smiles—a wicked, untrustworthy smile.

"Me too, Lilith."

When he says my name, a wave of goosebumps washes over me, causing me to fidget in my seat, suddenly feeling uncomfortably uneasy. I can't understand why this man elicits such a strong reaction from me. Wrapped in an expensive perfume—a mix of leather and tobacco—but to me, he smells as if he's decaying from the inside out.

His appearance exudes authority and wealth, even his dark hair, impeccably styled, seems too perfectly arranged—as if he's trying too hard. It's as if his appearance is nothing more than a brilliant facade for a man hiding something beneath the surface.

The devil in disguise.

"I'm sorry, I need to get back to work," I say, then immediately clear my throat because my voice sounds strange to my ears. Almost scared.

As he rises slowly, the scent of his cologne hits my nose even stronger, causing a dizzying sensation in my head.

"Of course, Lilith. It was a pleasure seeing you," he says in the most repulsive voice imaginable. "Would you mind saying hi to Caleb for me?"

I swallow the messy ball of emotions again, and although forcing a smile becomes harder, I try my best.

"Of course. Have a nice day, Mr. Moore."

I pretend to focus on my book, but in truth, I keep my eyes fixed on Grayson until he disappears around the street corner. Without a coffee in hand.

This makes me feel even more uneasy, if that's possible. I don't know this man, but my gut is screaming a warning—do not engage with him. I felt it when we first met, and now I'm feeling it again. Each time he looks at me, says my name, or flashes that smile, it's as if he's extending invisible claws that reach deep inside me, uncomfortably tickling my insides and leaving a sense of revulsion, like an internal bleeding that seeps downwards.

I try to return to my writing, but I'm too overwhelmed. I shut my laptop, pack it into my bag, and leave the café, pondering whether I should tell Caleb about this encounter. The demon on my right shoulder continues whispering in my ear, reassuring me this isn't normal and I should trust my gut. Meanwhile, the one on my left shoulder tries to drown out the other voice, insisting I'm overreacting and my gut instinct is merely nerves.

As always, I silence my inner demons with determination, indifferent to the people on the street. It might look strange, but I don't care. I've started to notice a newfound confidence in myself. I'm not sure if it's real or if I'm just imagining it, but I no longer feel the need to constantly adjust my glasses or avoid eye contact. The latter isn't entirely comfortable, but at least it's bearable.

Maybe being normal isn't such a far-fetched idea after all.

CHAPTER
TWENTY-FIVE

Lilith

As the cold wind envelops my body, causing a shiver, Caleb immediately wraps his arm around my shoulders, providing the comfort and warmth I need. When I close my eyes for a moment, his pleasant scent fills my nose—a blend of smoky aroma and amber that blankets around my body. I want to sink into his scent, letting it cover my own perfume.

"I'm scared. Maybe we should go somewhere else," I blurt out impulsively, glancing at him from under my lashes although I don't mean what I say. I'm just curious about his answer.

"Scared of what? Of roller coasters?" he ridicules scornfully.

I breathe out a heavy sigh. "Yes. Of roller coasters. Not everyone is fearless like you, Caleb."

"You are on a date with your stalker and the only thing you are afraid of are roller coasters, little devil?"

I cough out a small laugh. The way he reminds me that our relationship isn't…ordinary, makes me want to fall into hysterical laughter sometimes.

"So it's a date?"

"Of course it is. How else can you call this?"

Caleb took me out into the *world* tonight, as he called it. See, my small apartment filled with books and my constant back-and-forth to the university wasn't the real world for him. At first, I rolled my eyes in response, but as I started to think about it, I couldn't help but agree with him.

As we enter the park, the dark sky is illuminated by bursts of colorful smoke. My eyes widen in amazement at the sight before me. Roller coasters of every kind stretch out before us, each one adorned with vibrant LED lights and glowing orbs.

The air is filled with the sounds of screams and laughter, creating a symphony of excitement that echoes throughout the seemingly endless park. The aroma of sweet treats fills my nostrils—a delightful blend of popcorn and candies.

I can't help but feel a rush of adrenaline as I take in the thrilling atmosphere of the amusement park. To be frank, I was completely unaware that places like this even existed. Sure, I had seen similar locations in movies and shows or stumbled upon them online, but to me, they were nothing more than a childhood fantasy tucked away in the depths of my mind. I feel a burst of joy that reaches deep into my soul, causing my inner child to scream with delight. I take a deep breath and let the happiness wash over me.

"Do you like it?" My senses are ignited by the soft touch of Caleb's voice.

I turn my head to him, meeting a playful gleam in his eyes, and can't help but break into a wide smile. "Do I like it? Jesus, Caleb."

As he chuckles, I feel a warmth spread through my chest. I've been paying more attention since the day he told me about what his mother did to him. It's hard to fathom what he's been through. I just picture little Caleb in the dark basement, being punished for nothing. It somehow reminds me of the day when I got stuck in the elevator, although I wasn't there for long.

But he has endured years of suffering, and the trauma he's experienced must have had a lasting impact on him. And the way he told me about that...he said that he moved on, but I don't believe a person can completely move on from something like that. The damage had left a huge stain, and it's going to be with him till his last days.

Although I cannot erase his memory, I am determined to create as many joyful moments as possible to drown out the painful memories. The mental and physical scars that remain are a testament to his strength and bravery, not a haunting reminder of a soul that has been destroyed.

"So," he begins, taking my hand in his, "which one do you want to try first?"

As I survey the park, my mind races with thoughts of which ride to choose. However, a nagging feeling deep inside me warns against choosing something too daunting, as I fear I may lose my nerve for a second go. Thus, I must make a wise decision.

My attention is drawn to the colossal roller coaster located a short distance away. "I want that one," I blurt out, pointing my finger at it.

Caleb scans the coaster I picked and I notice the little devilish smirk across his face just before he squashes it. "Whatever you like, baby."

I stop, trying to force him to do the same, but his grip on my hand is tight as he drags me after him. "No. Stop. What was that?"

"What was what?"

"Don't play dumb, Caleb."

"I'm not."

I hate myself for my inability to keep my laugh inside me because he thinks I'm playful about this. Well, I am, but a part of me doesn't like this little sinister smirk. "Whatever you planned, forget about it. Because if I sense something wrong, I will jump off the roller coaster immediately."

"I have no doubts you will."

I just...I can't with him. I hate that he is so confident about everything he is doing. As we wait for the previous ride to end, Caleb holds onto my hand tightly, and I can't help but watch the people on the seats with intense curiosity. I try to make sense of their screams, some of which sound like pure terror while others are accompanied by hysterical laughter, indicating a sense of enjoyment.

"Oh, God," I begin as the ride comes to an end, and people start slowly getting out of their seats. "Maybe it is a bad idea."

Suddenly, a woman beside us rushes to a man and hands him an empty popcorn bag. He staggers as he grabs it, bringing the bag right to his mouth. The next moment I blink—he vomits right inside it. The woman claps his back, trying to reassure him, but he doesn't react. For a second, I think he might die because his face is paler than a white lily.

"Fucking hell."

Caleb snorts out a laugh at that, and I turn my face to him. "Did you just...snorted?"

He quickly rearranges his features back to neutral. "No."

I let out a frustrated sigh. "You did. The man could've died, Caleb. Have some compassion."

"Why? I don't give a single fuck about the rest of the people, Lilith," he answers. "I only care about one woman who stands right in front of me with a judgmental look on her pretty face."

A deep crimson flush suffuses my cheeks. "You are unbelievable."

"And you are playing for time. Come on, it's our turn." As Caleb drags me behind him, I struggle to keep pace with his long strides. I swear, standing next to him makes me feel like the shortest woman in the world.

When I settle into the plush leather of our seats, a sense of ease washes over me. However, the moment the attendant responsible for our tickets signals the commencement of the ride, my knees buckle. I shut my eyes in an attempt to compose myself, and an unsettling dread grips my insides, slowly sifting through my being with torturous persistence.

Caleb places his hand on my thigh, slightly pulling me closer to him. "Relax, little devil. Or you are going to die before it even starts."

"God damn, Caleb. I don't want to embarrass myself like that poor man. I don't want to pick up my insides at the end." I glance toward the side where that man still stands, watching how he tries to collect himself. "I don't want—"

He swoops in, capturing my lips in a bruising, shameless kiss, his hand firmly gripping my face, leaving me no room to inch away. "Shut your pretty mouth up and just enjoy the moment, my Lilith," he says in a flavorful voice.

Caleb delicately divides and tucks a golden strand of my hair behind my ear—a gesture I've come to realize he loves to do. "And when are you going to finally understand that I won't ever let anything hurt you?"

My teeth click shut. This man knows what and how to say. Damn him for always having the last word after him.

As the roller coaster begins to move, a jolt runs through my body. I try to swallow the ball of fear that has formed in my throat and force myself to relax. I close my eyes and focus on my breathing, trying to push out any thoughts that might make me panic.

Caleb is right. He is with me, and he won't let anything bad happen to me.

I *can* trust him.

His hand remains on my thigh in a possessive and claiming gesture. It stays there even as we ascend higher and higher at a steady speed. Then, his touch becomes a gentle caress, sending hundreds of butterflies fluttering in my stomach and causing goosebumps to rise across my skin.

I keep myself focused on his movements, and the forming of a little ball of panic starts to slowly deflate.

As the coaster glides up along the level track at a constant speed, my body remains relaxed. However, as it gradually decelerates, I instinctively tighten up, tearing my gaze away from Caleb's hand and fixing my eyes on the track ahead. It comes to a halt before the descent, prompting my eyes to automatically drop as I realize the breathtaking distance from the top.

I never thought I had acrophobia, but now when my head feels dizzy and the fear stings my guts, I tense all over again, calculating how long it is going to take to fall and how I am going to look with my brains smeared across the ground.

But Caleb's grip tightens as if a little warning to stop thinking about that. To stop thinking about everything. "Focus on my touch, little devil," he reassures, his calm and steady voice belies any sign of fear.

I had no doubts. I am sure there isn't a thing in the world that can scare Caleb.

"Close your eyes."

I don't want to have a stroke because of overthinking, so I comply. Then, his hand slowly makes its way under my dress as I feel the coaster starts to slide down. "No, Caleb—"

"Don't open your eyes," he warns. "Just feel."

I've never encountered someone who speaks to me quite like Caleb does. His tone carries an alluring, authoritative command, directing me to do things I'm unaccustomed to. Each time, it grips my heart and envelops my body, prompting compliance without the need for more words.

It should be frightening, how readily I bend in front of him, yet it evokes nothing but a sense of security as I entrust my entire being to his care, unafraid of shattering. He doesn't anticipate my breaking; rather, he embraces and delves into the darkest, most concealed corners of my soul that no one has ever encountered before.

As we begin to slowly slide down, his hand dives into my panties so casually as if we are home and no one can see us. Unconsciously, a moan escapes me as the coaster accelerates, hurtling downward, and a sensation flutters in my lower stomach when his fingers reach for my clit, beginning to circle it.

While I tilt my head back, feeling its weight, I press my thighs together and embrace the engulfing waves of pleasure, akin to gentle whispers caressing my body. In tandem with ascending once more, Caleb increases the pressure, this time his fingers move much swifter, and a sense of height rushes over me, akin to the sensation during the descent.

I settle into a more comfortable position, seeking shelter by burying my face in his neck. The pleasure is too overwhelming to resist, yet, simultaneously, I feel too vulnerable to sit nonchalantly, too exposed.

"What's that, little devil?" Caleb teases in a luscious voice. "Too shy?"

My lips are parted, while his fingers persist in their agonizingly slow torment, I sense my nipples growing harder, pressing through the fabric of my dress. "We shouldn't do this."

"Yeah. We shouldn't," he answers. "But you look even more gorgeous while enjoying something forbidden."

I moisten my lips, sensing the impending orgasm. It's steadily and sweetly building while my stomach echoes with a mixture of nagging pain and pleasure.

Caleb cups my chin with his other hand, forcing me to look him right in the eyes. "Are you going to come soon, little devil? Right here, when people can watch us?"

Just when my breath quickens and my body slightly tenses, he lowers the pace, robbing my body of awaited euphoria. "Yes. Please."

As we go down, the wind nips at my face and that sensation fills my stomach once more - it's as if an invisible hand is gripping my core and pulling me downwards. "Yes please what?"

"Please, let me—please," I cry out, ready to die because of overstimulation. What this man does should be fucking illegal. I can't feel anything below my shoulders each time he lowers the pace.

"I don't understand what you want, baby." He brushes his thumb across my upper lip, which on top of everything, turns my body into complete jelly.

"Please make me come, Caleb," I beg, my voice so unbeliev-ably desperate that it's almost laughable. Almost. Because I don't feel anything funny right now. "*God*, I'm begging you."

A deep chuckle escapes him. "I don't understand. Are you begging Him or me?"

"You are my God, Caleb," I murmur, my eyes rolling. "Make me come."

My head nearly drops down, but he quickly leans closer, steal-ing my last breath with a kiss. He quickens his pace and I grind against his hand, feeling my hot juices spreading down my legs, staining my dress.

If I am going to get out of here with a huge stain, people may think that I've pissed myself. I guess, that's better than allowing them to know the actual reason.

"You're so fucking gorgeous when you beg me, little devil," he whispers, bringing me to the long-awaited euphoria, blackness al-ready slowly rimming my vision. "Come all over my hand, baby."

His words along with the last ride down hit me, forcing me to release a loud scream that blends with dozens of others all across the park as I break apart—the force of my orgasm so colorful that I could fall off the damn coaster if it wasn't for Caleb's tight grip.

"Oh, fuck," I cry out, my body trembling so intensely that I have to clench the fabric of his hoodie to steady myself. "Oh my God."

When he takes his hand out of my dress, it's up and down covered in my juices. Inhaling deeply to calm my nerves, I disregard the flush of emotions surging within me. "I…I think I have wet wipes with me," I stumble over the words in my answer, reaching into my purse.

Just as I'm about to hand him the wipes, he unexpectedly plunges his fingers into his mouth and savors the remnants of me, emitting a pleasurable groan that reignites a pure desire within me as if everything that just happened wasn't enough for me.

Fuck. I don't think I'll handle another orgasm tonight. My eyes crinkle with a smile. "That was your evil plan all along?"

As the coaster gradually slows to a stop, and we begin to exit our seats, Caleb reaches for my hand. "No. It was spontaneous."

I offer him a nod, although I don't believe him. "You are very…creative when it comes to things like this."

He breathes out a laugh. "*Things like this?*"

As we begin to walk away from the roller coaster, I notice a slight tremble in my legs. "You know what I mean."

"I don't."

My eyes roll in a slight exasperation. Sometimes he is too annoying. "Whatever you say."

"Just say it."

I stop walking. "I'm tired. Can you carry me?"

"No," he cuts shortly. When I am not moving, he waits a few seconds, but eventually gives up, rushing toward me.

VALERIIA MILLER

"Can I get on your back like a koala?" I ask when he tries to decide how he should carry me.

Now Caleb is the one who rolls his eyes. "Jesus. Okay. Get up." He turns away, and I leap onto him, entwining myself around his frame. He supports me, his hands securing my calves as we keep moving forward.

In an instant, a playful mood overtakes me, and I lean in toward his ear, whispering, "You are very creative when it comes to devising new ways of providing me unforgettable orgasms."

He guffaws. "That was very pretty." He partially inclines his face toward me. "Maybe I can fuck that little shyness out of you completely."

Stunned by his casual use of dirty language, I cover his mouth with my hand. "This was so inappropriate." I let out a frustrated sigh. "Just take me home."

"So we can work on getting rid of your shyness?"

"Oh my God. Do you ever plan to stop?"

I wait for an answer, but he doesn't give me one. Well, I guess I could count that silence as a peculiar answer, too.

"How many girls did you have before me?" I ask without even thinking how the question sounds. Admittedly, I've been thinking about it, albeit in a somewhat childish manner, but regardless, I want to know. Even if his response will make me upset.

"Does it really matter?"

I grimace, already having a hunch of his number. "Yes. For me, it does. Do tell."

Caleb takes a moment. "I don't remember precisely. But I think around twenty."

I am stunned by the number, although I always knew that a man like him would have many women. It was foolish to entertain the naïve notion that perhaps he remained chaste, saving himself for the right person, as it seems implausible. Not with his attractive appearance, sharp intellect, and evident proficiency.

190

I bite back my frustration. "Were they better than me?"

I can't fathom why I asked that. Naturally, they were better. They possessed greater expertise and experience, whereas I am... just myself. It's a bit disheartening, but I try to push those feelings aside because there's no use in feeling disappointed.

I can't see his face but I feel how he is grinning. "No, they weren't."

I chortle. "No shit."

"I am serious," he says, confidence lacing his tone. "I never felt the connection I feel with you."

I can't restrain myself from breaking into a wide smile. "So corny. I can't believe you're saying this."

"Think whatever you want. I am telling the truth. I have never met a woman like you, Lilith, nor have I ever experienced anything even remotely similar to what I feel for you."

Despite the foolish grin persisting on my face, his words carry a tinge of bitterness in comparison to all the women who came before me. It leads me to wonder how many hearts he has shattered and how many tears the other women have spilled because of him. However, I am convinced that he feels just as deeply toward me as I do toward him.

This realization ignites a small flame of pride within me, as I understand that I am the one who sees him in this light, who pushes him and evokes the emotion that, as he claimed, he had never felt before. It's captivating to discover that I have such an effect on a man like Caleb.

The way he treats me as if I am the sole thing of value in his life surpasses every *uneasy* feeling I had before.

"I DON'T KNOW WHAT YOU EXPECT TO SEE, CALEB." I STRIDE TOWARD the weathered, cracked wooden closet and grasp the small handle of its door. With a muted thud, the door falls off, leaving me standing motionless, holding nothing but a door handle in my hand. "Nice."

"Fucking Christ," Caleb groans, quickly rushing to me. He takes my hand, forcing me to let go of the handle. "An easy way to get a splinter."

I shake my head. "Believe me, splinters are the least of my worries while living here."

He gently brushes his fingers across my hand, double-checking for splinters. "I think I'll need to kidnap you eventually, because you are not staying here. Not anymore."

Caleb has been suggesting I move in with him. I'm open to the idea, but not at this moment. Despite my crappy apartment, there's still some attachment to it. I've grown accustomed to it, and besides, I've already paid the rent through the end of this month.

I grab the photos he asked me about and nod toward the couch. "Sit. Let's do what we planned and then maybe have a little fight because I am not moving out. Not now anyway."

He lets out an annoyed sigh. "Stubborn ass."

I ignore his remark, though I want to laugh. It's always amusing to hear him say something like that with his deep, solemn voice. As Caleb returns to the couch, he accidentally bumps into the edge of the shelf next to my dilapidated closet. Reacting swiftly, he pushes back, only to collide his head with the top of the doorframe.

"Fucking Jesus Christ."

As he rubs his head, I struggle to contain a hearty laugh that causes my whole body to tremble. "See? I am not built for an apartment like this. I can't even fit in here without hitting against everything."

That's true. He's been spending more time at my place lately, and not a day goes by without him accidentally bumping into something in my apartment. Just a few days back, he nearly ripped off a chandelier in my bedroom.

As he settles onto the couch, I arrange the old photos on the coffee table before us. "It's everything I have. I doubt she has more of these."

I wrinkle my nose. "Actually, I doubt she has *any* of these. I am the biggest disappointment, after all."

Caleb grabs one of the photos—the picture where I am six, wearing my Mickey Mouse pajamas with two little braids entangled with a pink bow, smiling. "You are not a disappointment," he answers, casting a gentle glance in my direction before switching his attention to the picture. "She couldn't make something of her life, and she blames you for it just because it makes it easier for her. When people shift the blame onto others, causing them pain, they rarely consider how they've actually messed up."

I look at the side of his face while he sorts through my childhood photos, wondering if he wanted to have something like this. Caleb told me that his parents didn't take a single photo of him when he was a little boy, and deep down he always wanted to have some, just to remember how he looked as a child. Going through these isn't exactly my idea of fun, but I can manage that. If he wants it, then I want it, too.

"Oh, I took that one," I say when he picks up the Polaroid photo of thirteen-year-old me in a basketball uniform.

A frown takes over his face. "You were on a basketball team?"

I snort, bowing my head down. "Yeah. I was. But at my first training, I fell, embarrassed myself, and almost broke my knee. I never came back after that."

His frown rearranges into pure amusement. "If you didn't show me the photo, I wouldn't believe you."

"I know."

"For a moment, I thought I missed something."

"What do you mean?"

"I went through your school information a dozen times, and there haven't been any records about you playing on a basketball team," he says casually, stunning me.

I don't even know what to say. "Creep."

He flashes me a superior smirk. "I know."

As he continues sorting through the photos and asking questions about their locations and times, I kneel behind him and lean my chest against his broad back, my hands gently embracing his neck.

"You were a painter?" He holds up the photo where my nine-year-old self has drawn a huge, ugly black flower on my right hand. I am sitting at a table, focused just on the middle of drawing it, my tongue poking out in concentration.

"I couldn't wash off that ugly-ass flower for a week," I confess. "Claire then told me that I should hand in my drawings at the painting class separate from others so I would not embarrass myself."

"I'm sorry, but Claire should've gone fuck herself," he answers.

I laugh, though it feels a little wrong. "Yeah."

"You wanted a tattoo?"

"I still want. I just don't know what."

Caleb gets up, forcing me to ease my grip on his shoulders. "Stand up."

I comply, straightening up and reaching half of his height. "What?"

He clasps my face in his hands before planting a tender kiss on my nose. "We're going to get a tattoo, little devil."

My eyes are practically popping out from the shock. He can't be serious. "What? But—"

Caleb squeezes my cheeks just a little. "Trust me. Can you do that, baby?"

"Oh. Do I even have a choice?"

As Caleb parks near a tattoo salon, the expected feelings of unease, anxiety, and doubt are surprisingly absent. I am as calm as a monk in meditation. I have no idea what my next steps will be, but I don't let it bother me.

When I glance at Caleb, meeting his dark eyes, I notice that whereas before they seemed like a warning or precaution, now I sense nothing but warmth in his gaze.

He is the first person with whom I allow myself to be so reckless, so carefree, so happy. I let his gaze delve into the depths of my soul, allowing him to see every part of my being. It's as if, were I to ask him to set the world ablaze for me, tearing it apart, he would do so and offer me the burning fragments, just as he promised.

For the first time in my life, after much contemplation, I made a groundbreaking choice—I chose to surrender, to abandon my habit of overthinking about the future. I gave myself the freedom to ignore the possible outcomes, taking a leap of faith and giving myself to this man.

And I feel like it was the best decision of my life.

"Give me at least a hint about what we're going to do," I say, casting him a puppy-dog glance. "If you're going to get us the *love* word or me the *Caleb Walker's property* phrase, I am going to strangle you with a pillow."

His deep chuckle reverberates in my bones. "No, baby. It's going to be much worse than that."

I pierce him with my stare, silently demanding an explanation. But the asshole stays silent. Of course, he does.

As we enter the tattoo salon, we are welcomed by a pleasant administrator who asks us what we want. Caleb speaks for me—he tells her everything so fast and answers all her questions as if he came prepared for everything. While the decision is totally spontaneous, he acts so confidently as if it's the opposite of that word.

Then, after I give him a nod in agreement, he leaves me in the corridor, disappearing into the studio with the tattoo artist to explain the design he wants.

In an attempt to distract myself, I scan the surroundings. The place is decorated in neutral tones, adorned with numerous decorations: skulls, spider webs, bold logos, and inscriptions. They even have their own merchandise—T-shirts and hoodies crafted in dark colors and adorned with explicit art, hanging on display. I am taken aback and my eyes widen in surprise. I quickly avert my gaze, feeling a twinge of embarrassment.

As I glance around the room, my attention is drawn to the price list on the administrator's desk. I find myself intrigued and begin to scan it, my curiosity piqued by the range of services offered. The idea of tattoos and piercings on every part of your body to suit your taste is intriguing.

It's something I've never really considered before.

As I contemplate the possibilities, I realize that this is a whole new world that I had never considered. It's not just about drawings and holes in my body, but about exploring new experiences and pushing myself out of my comfort zone. I picture myself with a piercing in my nose or brow, realizing that it could actually look pretty on me. Maybe I'll return here someday and get myself one.

After a moment, the tattoo artist returns to the corridor and waves me over. "We're ready."

Ready for what? I tear myself apart with questions about which tattoo Caleb could possibly want. He isn't the type of guy who would like to get our names, corny phrases, or simple drawings like hearts or birds. My curiosity sets my whole body ablaze, and I catch myself shaking a little from excitement.

As I see Caleb, he is already without his shirt, his perfect abs pleasing my sight. He looks at me with a glint of mirth in his eyes, surely enjoying my palpable, child-like amusement. Another artist appears and points me to the tattoo bed that stands behind Caleb's, with only a black curtain separating them.

"Take off your sweatshirt and lie down."

I glance at Caleb, who is already lying on his stomach, and he just shrugs his shoulders. "There's no fun if you see what we're doing."

I sigh in defeat, trying to look a little annoyed, although I feel only trepidation and pleasant worry. "I guess we're doing it."

I comply, taking my sweatshirt off and lying on the bed on my stomach. I close my eyes, feeling how the artist tosses my hair to the side, lowers my bra straps, and places a sketch on my upper shoulders. I think I am okay with this placement. I just hope it's not going to hurt too much.

And I have a feeling that I am going to love it.

"There you go," the artist—Courtney—says. We had plenty of time to talk, and I found out a couple of interesting details about her life. One of them is that she started drawing when she was six years old, almost just like me.

"Are we like…done-done?" I ask, part of me refusing to believe it's finished. Realizing the intrigue will be destroyed any minute makes me a little sad. I can't lie, I loved the idea of going in blind with this. And it wasn't painful at all. A little uncomfortable, yes. But not painful.

"Done-done," she parrots, placing the needle away and stretching her hand to me. "Get up."

I push myself up, struggling a bit because I've been lying on my stomach for a couple of hours without moving, and my bones are numb. As I rise, I groan, stretching, and hearing my muscles crack. And only now do I realize how badly I want to pee.

"Are you ready to look at it?" Courtney asks, her voice brimming with excitement. This woman truly exudes passion for her work.

I glance at her, reciprocating her slight smile with one of my own. "I don't know. I guess I am. Is it good?"

"I don't like to brag, but I would add it to my *best- works-ever* list."

I nod, pointing my chin at the portable mirror on her desk. "Show me."

She hands me the mirror, and as I lift it to catch a glimpse of her work, I can't believe what I see. If I weren't seated, I'd have collapsed.

Black as night angel wings stretch across my shoulders. They extend slightly beyond where the straps of my bra typically lie. The perfect length. They look so realistic that it seems as if I touch them, I would feel their softness, the smoothness of the feathers.

Strangely, it seemed to be just what I needed. It's as if it completes my look like I've finally found the missing piece of my body.

"Do you like it?" Courtney's voice pulls me back from my reverie as she lowers her head to catch my eye. "You look paler. Are you okay?"

"Yeah, I'm fine," I answer. "I'm just shocked. It's fucking beautiful, Courtney. I have no words to describe how much I love it."

"Caleb's is done, too," she informs, tilting her head toward his bed. "You ready to see him?"

I nearly flinch at the sound of his name. I believe I've transitioned to the next stage—from slight fear and confusion to sheer happiness. I feel an overwhelming desire to kiss the living shit out of him for doing this.

As I rise from my seat and head toward Caleb's bed, I nod my head vigorously, as if I'm being jolted with electricity.

When Courtney draws back the curtain, a scene unfolds before me—he sits with his back turned, giving me an unobstructed view of the fresh tattoo. Although the concept is the same for both of us, Caleb's wings appear considerably larger and more imposing, casting a massive and domineering impression because his shoulders are ten times broader and bigger than mine. While my wings emanate sophistication, appearing thinner with a slightly less pronounced black tint at their edges, his, in contrast, exudes an air of intimidation, with the black tint more prominently expressed.

If before I thought that paired tattoos were lame, I don't even dare to suggest that anymore.

As Caleb shifts his shoulders, his muscles flex, causing the tattoo to move and envelop his skin, creating the illusion of it being his real wings.

Fuck, it truly appears as though we were born for this, and at this moment, we're simply accentuating and contouring this part of our bodies that was always a part of our nature.

Fallen angels, exposing their true essence.

He turns his face to me, probably feeling my intense stare. A smirk pulls up the corner of his lips as he looks at me. "Give us a moment," he commands, and our artists disappear the next time I blink.

Caleb pats his knee. "Come here."

Unaware, I wear this foolish grin for so long that my cheekbones begin to ache. As I move closer to him, he doesn't even wait for me to sit on my own—he tugs me by the hand, and in an instant, I find myself in his lap.

"You are crazy, you know that?" I say, trying to stifle a little laugh that rises up in my throat.

As Caleb's dark eyes scan my back in the mirror, a flicker of satisfaction lights them up. "Now we both are."

"Your evil plan is working pretty great." I can't keep a straight face. "I love it."

"I love *you*."

An abrupt chuckle bubbles up in my throat as I'm overcome by the whirlwind of emotions flooding over me. "What?"

But Caleb looks serious. "I love you, Lilith." He tucks a strand of my hair behind my ear. "Since the day I saw you."

The smile slowly disappears from my face, and I just stare at his obsidian eyes, detecting something new in them, something I've never seen before.

Is this what real love looks like?

I suddenly shiver as a surge of strange sensations builds at the base of my spine in response to his words, causing my body to react in an unexpected way.

"Caleb, I—"

"It's okay. I don't expect you to say it back yet," he interrupts, a small smile tugging his lips. "I can wait till you are sure about your feelings."

My heart stutters out of rhythm as if it's sending the biggest warning signal I've ever felt. As I exhale sharply, the aftermath of getting the first, biggest, and most beautiful tattoo of my life mixes with confusion and a strange feeling from the unexpected words he spoke to me, making me dizzy.

"Okay."

"I'm not going anywhere."

Blake

My mother always told me that we aren't appreciative enough of little things in our lives, not until we lose everything. I told her she was ridiculous. It even sounded so corny – a typical be grateful, but for what? We lived pretty poorly, and I always was hungry. How could I be appreciative of something like that?

But now I get it. Except it's too fucking late.

I don't even know why I am writing this. Maybe some naïve part of me hopes that she will find this. That she will know how grateful I am, how I love her.

But it is ridiculous. I know I am never going to get out of here, and even more, be able to give her this letter.

I guess I am writing it out for selfish reasons. I am going to die pretty fucking soon, and I want to at least try to change something. As if this scribbled note can change something.

But it makes me feel a bit relieved, realizing that now I do understand what my mom had been trying to tell my stupid ass this whole time.

I never even told her how much I love her.

I'm sorry, Mom. I know you are probably driving yourself crazy, wondering where I am. I wish I could call you and just say how sorry I am for everything.

I guess, I see you on the other side.

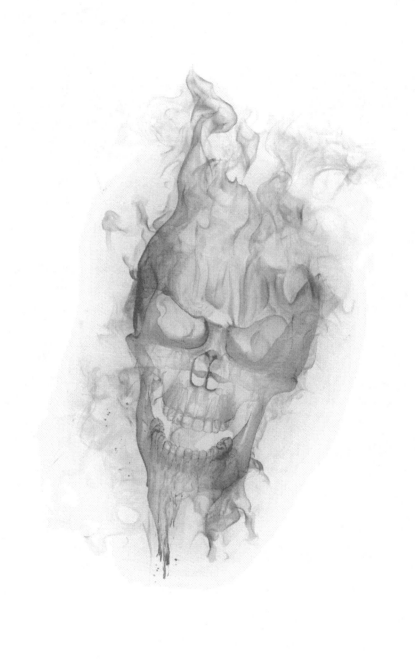

CHAPTER

TWENTY—SIX

Caleb

"I feel weird in this," Lilith says softly, smoothing the creases on her new dress. "I think I'm not going to touch anything because if something happens to this dress—"

I quiet her with a kiss, my fingers threading through her hair. After a fleeting moment, I reluctantly pull away, knowing we'll be late if I don't. "My Lilith, it's just a dress. I don't care if something happens to it, and you shouldn't either. Besides, I'll buy you thousands like it in the future."

We are attending a charity event that Grayson and his friends are hosting. He organizes these quite often, and I, unfortunately, always get invited. Well, *invited* isn't the right word—I'm forced to attend.

There's nothing I hate more than putting on a fake personality around Grayson's arrogant friends who joke about the weather, their idiotic kids, and their poor wives they regularly cheat on. But I can't be the CEO who doesn't socialize. I wish I could be completely shielded from all this, but that's not how things work in this field.

No matter how much I hate Grayson, he helped me build the foundation for my company. I often wonder why he was so interested in me specifically. He simply said he saw a lot of potential in me and would be disappointed if I wasted it. He and a bunch of his friends helped me find the right connections to pursue what I'm good at. So, I guess, that's what stops me from bashing his brains in—the little feeling that I may still owe him something.

On one hand, I wish I could shut off all my feelings and become an emotionless robot, indifferent to others and free from any sense of obligation. However, if I were a robot, I wouldn't be capable of falling in love.

As cliché and foolish as it may sound, the emotions I have for Lilith make me feel truly alive. They fill the void in my soul; it feels like I've discovered my life's purpose.

"One more thing," Lilith murmurs, bumping her chin into my chest. "What's this event called again? I don't want to seem stupid there."

I can't hold in my laughter. "We'll discuss how technology supports humanitarian aid and disaster relief, highlighting its role in crisis management, disaster response, and community resilience."

Her eyebrows shoot up. "Jesus Christ. I feel so stupid because I didn't understand a single word you just said."

My fingers slowly run through her soft hair, separating the honey-colored strands. "Don't worry. I won't let them put you in an awkward position. Just stay right beside me and everything will be okay."

She nods hesitantly. "Okay."

THE EVENT IS TAKING PLACE ON THE FIFTEENTH FLOOR OF THE OLD building.

Lilith doesn't say a word when we enter the elevator, obediently following me with her head bowed down. I attempt to read her emotions from her face, but she seems to be concealing them. Overall, she appears to be scared, hesitant to make any sudden movements in this box.

I push the button and as soon as it starts to move, she closes her eyes, her little hands gripping the fabric of the silk beige dress I bought her.

I know you can't just get away from your trauma all of a sudden, I haven't got away from mine—sometimes catching myself on echoes of uncomfortable feelings—but I can't just stand here and watch her getting back inside her little shell.

As we reach the sixth floor, I come to the panel and press the emergency stop button, forcing the elevator to stand still.

Lilith immediately opens her eyes, running them across me. "What are you doing?"

I close the distance between us in one big step, lift her up, and place her ass on a handrail. "Healing you."

Before she can answer, I crush my lips to hers, stealing protests she was ready to throw at me, my tongue prying her mouth open. Lilith hesitates for a moment, trying to push me away with her hands, but I don't plan on stopping.

My hand circles her neck like a collar as I squeeze it just a little, sensing an immediate reaction from her body—she tenses and releases a moan right into my mouth. I can't restrain a smile through the kiss. Watching how she slowly crosses her boundaries and becomes more open about her feelings makes me feel nothing but proud.

While one hand remains on her throat, my other hand reaches under her dress. I pause for a moment, gently pulling away from her, and teasing her with slow movements of my fingers across the fabric of her already-drenched panties.

Her head kicks back, bumping into the wall. "My God, Caleb—"

"Pray, little devil," I murmur roughly, enjoying her reaction. "And maybe your god will give you what you want."

"I want you," she breathes weakly, a deep crimson flashing across her cheeks, sending a thrilling jolt through my chest. "*Please.*"

My hand moves the cloth to the side and I dive two of my fingers inside her, meeting a whole waterfall that impatiently awaits me there. "Look here, baby." Holding her neck, I direct her gaze to the corner of the elevator where the camera hangs, its red light clearly visible.

When she notices it, she keeps eye contact with it, shamelessly grinding against my hand, appearing to not give a single fuck about the fact that security could watch us now.

I turn my face to the camera too, and a little smirk appears on my face as I keep thrusting two fingers inside her pussy, while my thumb circles her clit. "Do you like it, baby?" I ask, keeping the pace that drives her crazy. "Do you like being exposed while I'm fucking you?"

When I look back at her, she arches her back, causing the little diamond necklace I bought her to catch the light and shine brightly under the lamp above us. "Yes," she whimpers, her voice on the verge of breaking.

"I love seeing the *real* you," I say, shamelessly shoving one more finger inside her, earning a loud gasp that slips past her lips. "Little devil isn't as innocent as she seems."

When her lips part, signaling her readiness to let out another moan, I collide my lips with hers, capturing and silencing the sweet sound she was about to release. Her pussy tenses around my fingers and she stops responding to my kisses, ready to come, but that's not how I want it.

I get my fingers out of her and break the kiss, instantly hearing a disappointed little whimper. "No—"

I take off my belt and slide my pants along with my underwear down, then slam myself inside her with one rigid movement. "The only way you are going to come is right on my cock, Lilith."

I begin thrusting in her without giving her time to catch a breath as she is only able to wrap her hands around my neck and hold on to me for dear life. The pleasure sends her eyes to the back of her head as her moans turn into desperate screams.

"Look around, my love," I murmur, slowing my pace a little, just to give her a chance to see what I want her to see. "Fourteen years ago, you started to believe this is the scariest place to be in." I lightly brush my lips along her collarbones as they move toward her neck, eliciting a rush of goosebumps grazing her tender skin. "From today, you are going to only remember how I fucked that fear out of you, do you hear me?"

Her hands move into my hair as she grasps it. "Yes," she murmurs weakly as a tear rolls down her red cheek, leaving a streak of mascara in its wake.

I wipe it off, grabbing her by the back of her neck as I begin to accelerate again. "And about how you came all over my cock right here," I say, lightly nibbling her upper lip. "Come, Lilith. Right fucking now."

I tighten my grip on her as she complies, and an indescribable force of orgasm rips her apart, tarnishing the last bits and pieces of her innocence. Her body shakes violently, and I have to hold her tightly so she won't fall.

I break right with her, burying my face in her neck, emitting a loud groan of pleasure, surrounded by nothing but enveloping darkness as euphoria courses through my veins.

My body trembles as I struggle to remember to take a breath. The mere act of inhaling sends shockwaves through my system, causing my vision to be filled with a dizzying array of flashing stars. At this moment, it feels as though death is imminent.

"Oh my God," Lilith whispers, running her hand through my hair. "I can't move."

I cherish being the only one to see her true vulnerability and pleasure, beyond her facade of innocence. It's intoxicating, coursing through my veins like the finest drug, as I revel in the novelty of experiencing everything with her for the first time.

Despite my belief that I was incapable of loving someone, this woman proved me wrong.

I don't know how, but I find enough strength to let out a little laugh. "Just take a moment, baby."

We pause to collect ourselves before I assist her in composing herself. Gently wiping away her tears to preserve her makeup, I help adjust her dress as she regains her composure. "You good?" I ask, now focusing on my appearance and adjusting my clothes.

She nods so faintly as if her head is too heavy to keep steady. "I will be."

I run my hand through my hair, attempting to restore it to its rightful place, but I can't do much without a mirror. Lilith observes my struggle and approaches me, softly taking my hands and fixing everything herself.

I let her do whatever she planned to, enjoying the feeling of her hands. "Is it bad?"

She smiles but keeps her eyes on my hair. "Well, you are always walking around with a nest like this." She backs away, taking one last look at me. "Nothing too much to raise suspicions."

"I pretend that you didn't just hurt my feelings."

Lilith kisses my nose and walks to the panel, pressing the number of the floor we need to get up to. "We are probably late already."

I couldn't care less, though. If it were my choice, I would lift her up and rush back to my car, driving us to my apartment.

But she is the main reason why today isn't as unbearable as usual for me. Sensing her presence and feeling the soft touch of her fingers across my skin is the main thing that keeps me in a good mood. Maybe today I'll even restrain myself from mocking Grayson and his friends.

As the door opens and a glimpse of the place comes into our sight, Lilith slams her hand to her mouth, silencing a sudden gasp of awe. I suppress my own little chuckle because of how cute she looks when she is surprised by something. I knew that this place would affect her.

I find myself thinking that I want to take her to visit more places like this if it means making her happy.

Shit, how did we get here? All of my principles and usual beliefs become meaningless when Lilith appears. Nothing matters as long as I have her by my side.

"Fuck," she whispers, then immediately slaps her hand back on her mouth. "Shit, can I curse here?"

I can no longer contain my laughter. "Yes, little devil. You can do anything you want."

As we walk further hand in hand, Lilith's eyes round even in more shock seeing the full picture of the place.

Dozens of people in expensive suits and dresses, all blabbering loudly about something you can easily guess. Like I said before, here, the conversations are usually rotating around the same crocked topics.

The room is grand and opulent, with high ceilings and ornate moldings that are painted in gold leaf. The walls are covered in richly patterned damask wallpaper, with large oil paintings hanging in gilt frames. The floor is made of polished marble, with an intricate pattern of black and white tiles. The lighting is provided by several large chandeliers, each one dripping with crystal prisms that cast a dazzling array of light around the room. The windows are narrow, which isn't enough to spill much light in here, but with such chandeliers, it isn't a priority.

"Too many people," she mumbles, tightening her grip on my arm like a frightened child in a crowd. "Don't leave me, okay? Or I won't be able to find you, and then I'll start to panic, and then I'll probably die."

I press her closer. "I can't leave such a pretty woman on her own."

"Walker! You've finally made it," Mateo says—one of Grayson's little friends. The most annoying one, if so. "We've been worrying you won't come." He closes the distance between us—steps even closer than he should. "And this beautiful lady is that writer you've been talking about, right?"

My jaw clenches at the way he calls my Lilith and the way he looks at her. You don't have to be a genius to realize what he is thinking about. Mateo is a typical spoiled brat who has no fucking boundaries. He is the type of guy who thinks he can do anything he wants.

Just like all of the people in here.

"Lilith, this is Mateo, one of the hosts of tonight's little party," I inform. "Mateo, this is my woman, Lilith, the talented writer who published the article everyone loved."

"Oh, it isn't like that," Lilith shrugs off, delivering an awkward smile to him. "It wasn't something mind-blowing. But I've tried my best."

Mateo grins smugly. "So humble. I can see why Caleb loves you. You know, we haven't seen him with a woman, not once. It's good to see he find himself such a pretty girl."

"She is a *woman*," I snap, trying to switch the fucker's attention to me because the way he looks at Lilith makes my stomach sick. "My woman, Mateo. Behave yourself."

Lilith tightens her grip around my arm. "Caleb—"

"No, no, it's okay," he answers, letting out a laugh past his lips as if this is funny. "Caleb always had such strong boundaries. I apologize if I mislead you."

Oh, no doubt he is apologizing. As if he didn't just undress my Lilith with his eyes right fucking here.

"It's okay," Lilith answers in a soft, gentle tone. "I'm sorry, I think we're going to head out. We need to say hi to others."

Mateo takes a step to the side, demonstratively allowing us to go. "It was nice seeing you both."

I pay no attention to his gaze as we pass by him and continue into the crowd.

"Caleb, what is it with you?" Lilith asks with a worried look directed at my side. "Didn't we come here to have a little fun? Or do you want us to end up in a police station after you beat up one of the hosts?"

I take a deep breath in an attempt to calm myself down. "Lilith, these men are unhinged. Mateo was the only one whom we just met, and he already undressed you with his eyes. Do you think I'll allow myself to stand still and watch it?"

She comes to a halt, causing me to stop as well. Then she cups my face in her hands, running her thumbs along my jawline. "Haven't you always said that I am yours?"

"What does that have to do with this?"

"I am *yours* and I am not going anywhere. Even if they want something, they won't get it from me. The best you can do is raise your chin high along with me and show everyone that we don't give a fuck about them. Let them live in their fantasies."

I exhale, letting her words sink in. She is right, and I know that. I also know that being jealous of every single man in her life is pretty fucking stupid—something a fifteen-year-old boy would do—but my brain doesn't ask me if I want to be jealous. It just sends this feeling and it spreads across my whole body, heating my insides as if a virus itself. But I have to try for her. It isn't going to be fun if I'll beat someone's ass up to death tonight.

"Okay. Sorry," I answer, placing a kiss on her forehead. "Let's go catch up with others."

AFTER SEVERAL HOURS OF ENGAGING IN SMALL TALK WITH DOZENS OF idiots, my cheekbones ache from the forced smiles, and my tongue hurts from the plethora of words I've exchanged in mostly pointless discussions. Fortunately, it seems like we're finally prepared to leave this place.

I wait for Lilith by the bathroom, and when I check my watch, I can't help but think that she's been in there longer than expected. I'm fighting the urge to go inside and check if everything's okay because that would mean I don't give her the space she needs, and blah blah blah. In such a big place surrounded by so many people, I should be sure that she's safe. There are cameras all around, and dozens of witnesses.

But for some reason, an unease crawls down the back of my neck the whole time I wait for her. I hadn't felt anything while I was alone at these events—every time surrounded by all these people—but with Lilith, somehow, I have a gut feeling signaling upcoming danger. Maybe I'm just overreacting because for the first time in my life, I've found a woman I've fallen in love with, and my instincts scream with an urge to protect her wherever she goes, always staying sharp for her safety.

But she has lived in the most dysfunctional neighborhood, surrounded by junkies, criminals, and other trash without a drop of fear. She even made friends with an alcoholic next door who has a pretty interesting story of robbery and domestic assault.

The woman is the definition of fearless.

After all, that's what had drawn my attention the most. With one hand, Lilith opens the door, while the other hand presses the phone to her ear, concluding her conversation with someone.

"Okay. Stop. Just stop it. I said I'll call you later." Then, she hangs up. "Hey. Sorry it took me so long."

I wrap my arm around her shoulders. "Who was that?"

Shaking her head, she unzips her purse and tosses her phone inside. "Kevin."

Kevin Ross. I forgot about him already. "Are you okay?" I ask, noticing a hint of discomfort on her lovely face. "Did he upset you?"

She purses her lips into a thin line. "No. He's just become very...a little rude after I told him I found someone."

Of course, he did. I can't even understand how a smart woman like Lilith could make friends with such an immature, insecure little boy. When I was stalking her, each time I read their conversations made me roll my eyes so hard that it was painful. The boy was always annoying. "Let me talk to him."

She shakes her head in denial. "No, it's fine. He sometimes acts like that. He will calm down after a few days and then apologize. It's not a big deal."

"Walker! Stay right there!" We both turn around, our eyes darting across the crowded space to find a man who just shouted. Grayson comes out, his fat ass shamelessly bumping into people as he rushes to us. "Leaving already?"

Lilith knows how much I hate talking to him, so she takes the conversation into her own hands. "We had a really good time here, but I feel a little sick, so we're heading home," she explains softly. "Thank you so much for inviting us, Mr. Grayson."

He throws his hand up, and a satisfied scowl darts across his face. "Oh, darling. No need to thank me! We all would like to see Caleb and you more often at our little gatherings." He lowers his head. "You better not be pregnant, you know?"

He starts to laugh at his own joke—this fucking idiot—and after a few seconds, Lilith bursts into the fakest laugh she ever made, jabbing an elbow into my side so I could do the same.

But all I can do is crack a tiny smile. "Your sense of humor is always on top, Moore," I say unemotionally.

He straightens up, running a hand through his hair. "Nothing has ever made you laugh, Caleb. I am not surprised now." His expression rearranges into a serious one. "Though, I mean it. We need to keep working, and if she's pregnant, that would complicate everything."

Slowly, my neutral mood evolves into escalating aggression. "That is none of your concern. We will deal with it ourselves."

A flash of dissatisfaction crosses his face, but he quickly gathers himself. "That is fair. I won't allow myself to keep you any longer. Drive safe."

When we finally reach the elevator, Lilith asks, "What's going on with you two? The tension between him and you is so palpable and thick, I can taste it in the air."

"He is just a pain in the ass, that's all. He is the type of person who won't shut up even if what he says is total bullshit," I explain, pressing the button on the panel. "Because he knows most people won't dare to shut him up due to the position he's in. A typical rich prick."

"You are rich too," she says, leaning her back against the wall with a challenging gleam in her eyes. "And a prick, sometimes."

"Feeling brave enough, huh?" I take a step toward her, trapping her in an invisible cage as I press my palms above her head. "Ready for another round in my car?"

"God, please, no," she scoots away, closing her eyes. "I still can't feel half of my body."

Last time she couldn't feel her whole body, so, I guess, she's slowly getting used to me.

CHAPTER
TWENTY–SEVEN

Lilith

As I attempt to type while holding my phone tightly against my cheek, talking to him, I soon realize it's a bad idea when I read the sentence I just wrote. The words don't make any sense. I release a loud sigh, shut my laptop, and clench my fist as I feel the first sparks of aggression heating up my insides and churning in my stomach.

"I don't understand what you want me to say. I never stopped talking to you, right? So what's your problem, Kevin?" My words stun him, of course, but I just can't endure this anymore.

Kevin has become incorrigible—every time I tell him about hanging out with Caleb, he starts to act aggressive and demanding. I don't know what in the hell happened to him. But all of this makes me realize that he wasn't the person I pictured. I thought he was a calm, shy, a little awkward guy—a peculiar little mirror of me. Now he has shown his other side—rude and unpleasant, soaked with unjustified jealousy.

"Why don't you tell me how you met this guy, huh? Is there something you're hiding, Lily?" he asks, his voice growing slightly more aggressive if that's even possible.

I've never told him the truth about how Caleb and I met. He wouldn't understand. He would just judge us and call me all kinds of names when he's angry. I don't want that. I'm tired of his whining and negativity about Caleb and me.

"I'm not hiding anything," I answer through clenched teeth. "I'm afraid to tell you anything because you simply don't listen. You become aggressive and skeptical about everything I say, so I don't want to bother trying."

"I *care* about you, Lily. How can't you realize that? Don't you remember how many times you've been fooled?"

I stop breathing for a moment. "What's that supposed to mean?"

He sighs as if he's the only one tired of this pointless conversation. "It means—" He stops briefly. "Never mind."

"No. Finish what you started, Kevin. Stop beating around the bush and just tell me what your problem is."

He snaps—I hear the crash of glass on the other side of the phone. "It means that you are very naïve, Lily. Naïve and sometimes stupid to an unbelievable point. I feel how this guy has already changed you," he explains. "You never cursed so much before. You were humbler. You aimed to be at the top of your class, to finish writing your books, and to start a career. And tell me, what are your plans now?"

My jaw drops. He couldn't have just said that. Not Kevin. "Are you serious? He was the one who pulled me out of a dead end and inspired me. I'm finishing my second book now, Kevin. If you were focused on my work rather than my relationship, you'd notice how everything has become better for me."

"In what way?"

"What the hell do you mean by asking me that?"

"Maybe it became better. Maybe he gave you a huge amount of inspiration, but in what way? You were writing a story that reflected your personality, Lily. That's why it was so good. Because it was the real you. But whatever he inspired you to do, I'm sure won't feel the same, because it's not you. None of this is you."

"Fuck you, Kevin. You don't even know me," I release a chuckle. "You don't even know my real name. I wasn't sure I could trust you even with that, so how would you know me, huh?"

I hang up before he can even process what I've just said. Then, I block his number and every account he has on social media. I'm so done with him. And frankly, now I get why most people think that making friends online is a waste of time. I wasn't honest with Kevin, too, but I would never say such things to him.

I would be happy if he found someone.

I don't realize that I'm crying until my room becomes a blurry vision. I take my glasses off and cover my eyes with my hands, allowing myself to burst into tears. His words sting like the sharpest razor, slicing my skin. They hurt even worse than my mother's words because I always knew who my mother truly was, while Kevin was my only friend. He was my backup, my support. And what has he turned into, eventually?

The gentle touch on my shoulder makes me flinch as I realize I'm not alone. I look up at the blurry silhouette, and it doesn't take long to realize that it's Caleb. I'd recognize him even if I were surrounded by imposters. Though sometimes I still can't get used to the fact that he has a key and can visit me whenever he wants.

"Baby, what happened?" he asks, sitting beside me and wrapping his arms around my shoulders. "Who made you sad?"

I fist the fabric of his hoodie, burying my face in his chest. "It's Kevin. But I blocked him."

He pats my back and kisses the top of my head. "What did he say?"

I shake my head, wipe my eyes, and reach for my glasses. "I don't want to talk about it. I just want to switch my mind to something else."

Once I can see clearly, I meet his obsidian eyes, noting a hint of worry in them. "Do you want me to *kill* him?"

I stare at him for a moment, then a sudden chuckle escapes me. "Stop it. I just want a distraction."

He kisses my cheek. "Do you want something sweet?"

A thoughtful expression crosses my face, although I already know the answer. "I want a cherry donut and a large cup of coffee."

"Then I better get going and grab you a cherry donut and a large cup of coffee, although I still can't accept the fact that you like cherry-flavored things. Gross."

A watery laugh rises in my throat. "*You* are gross. Stop humiliating me for my sophisticated taste."

Caleb gives me one last kiss on the forehead before getting up and walking to the front door. "Are you sure you don't want to come with me?"

"I'm fine. I don't want to flash my red face on the street."

"Red, gorgeous face. You're right. Sit at home. I don't want others to look at you."

I give him what is supposed to be an annoyed look, and he smirks before closing the door behind him. I take a deep breath, trying to gather my thoughts. I open my laptop and delete the few incoherent sentences I wrote while talking to Kevin because they don't make any sense. Before his call, I was peacefully working, minding my own business, and feeling creatively inspired.

But he ruined everything. Now, I can't remember where I started or what idea I wanted to convey.

I grab my phone and delete every single chat I have with him, intending to completely erase him from my life. He doesn't deserve my time, not after treating me like I am nothing but trash and convincing me that people don't actually want anything to do with me.

It's ironic that Kevin accuses Caleb. He never tried to alter my personality; instead, he helped me discover my true self-worth. He opened the door to my authentic self and showed me how valuable I truly am. He has a unique ability to listen and show affection that makes me feel valued. Unlike anyone else, he truly understands who I am and doesn't try to change me.

His unconditional care and acceptance of me as I am is un-paralleled. I don't need to hide and lie to him. I can be myself without feeling ashamed and embarrassed.

The sound of a doorbell makes me flinch, ripping me out of my thoughts. I glance at today's date and silently curse myself for forgetting that today is the day to pay my rent. I rush to the front door, and upon opening it, I am met with a disheveled Randall. His clothes are wrinkled, his pupils dilated as if he is high, and he reeks of alcohol.

"Randall?" I ask hesitantly, unable to squash my surprise. "Are you okay?"

He places his hand on my chest and pushes me inside my apartment. "No, dolly. I am not okay."

I almost fall to the floor from how hard he pushes me. "What are—" Randall presses his lips to mine before I can even process what is happening, forcing himself on me while pushing my body onto the couch and getting on top. With all the force I possess, I knee him in the balls and press my hands into his chest, pushing him away.

He groans in pain and bends in half. "You fucking bitch."

I get up from the couch and wipe my mouth, desperate to erase his disgusting taste from my lips. "What the fuck is wrong with you?" I ask, feeling anger surging in my blood as my heart begins to pound in my ears.

When he recovers from my punch and straightens up, a psychotic smile tugs on his lips. "You know, Lilith, I waited. I waited for you to notice me, to finally understand everything, but apparently, you don't have much brains for that."

He takes a small step closer, and my body jolts away as a zing of fear courses through my whole being. "I thought I just needed to give you more time because you were always so shy and awkward, hiding from everyone in your little hole that I gave you the chance to live in."

An abrupt laugh escapes him. "But I keep hearing you and Caleb almost every fucking night, and as much as it pisses me off, it made me realize that you aren't as innocent and shy as I thought you were. You are a whore, Lilith, and I came here to take what I want, so you're going to give it to me."

My eyes quickly dart to the knives in the kitchen as I contemplate how quickly I could reach and grab one. "You are sick, Randall. I won't give you anything you're dreaming about."

"I don't think so."

Before he can reach me, I run toward the kitchen. As my hand grips the knife handle, he wraps his hands around my waist and lifts me up. I hold on to it, swinging the sharp end at his body, but my attempts are laughable. He is stronger than me, and given my skills, I am more likely to stab myself than him. He tosses me on the floor and slaps my hand, causing the knife to fly somewhere to the side.

"Were you going to kill me, dolly?"

Randall slaps my face, causing blinding pain to shoot through my cheeks. I stop fighting for a moment, only able to hear the sound of him unzipping his pants.

"Don't do this," I beg, my voice breaking as I feel on the verge of a mental breakdown. "Randall, please, stop."

But he doesn't hear me. Blinded by rage, jealousy, and animal desire, he leans to my ear, whispering, "You're going to scream for me just the way you did for him."

Breathless and choking on my tears, I feel liquid dripping from my lip. I can't determine if it's blood, my tears, or both. Despite this, I continue to fight him. He doesn't relent, eventually pinning my hands above my head and pressing himself so tightly against me that I can't move.

Out of nowhere, someone grabs Randall by the collar of his shirt with one hand and throws him away from me, giving me a chance to catch my breath. Feeling relieved as he's no longer on top of me, I attempt to get up because lying on the floor makes me feel sick to my stomach. My eyes immediately land on Caleb, who is now on top of Randall. A single blow from his fist is enough to stop him from moving completely.

"You wanted to rape her, Randall?" he asks, his hands tightly grasping the collar of Randall's shirt, shaking him with such force that it seems like his head is going to fall off any minute. "You fucking piece of shit that doesn't even deserve to breathe the same air as her."

Then, his fist flies into his face again.

And again.

And again.

And *again*.

After a moment, he begins to use both of his hands, slamming them against Randall's skin so hard and fast that I can only watch with my mouth open. Just a few punches are more than enough to turn his face into a bloody mess. The sound of bones crunching makes me flinch, but it doesn't stop Caleb. He continues to hit him, and I can't even see the distinct parts of his face anymore—just a bloody mess. Eventually, Randall stops moving, only his head reclining with each punch.

Blood splashes on Caleb's clothes, painting them a shade darker. "Caleb, stop!" I scream, but he doesn't hear me. It's as if the person I talked to around twenty minutes ago is gone, replaced with a man consumed by animal rage. He is going to fucking kill him.

Crawling to him, I catch his hand before it lands on Randall's face, and that's when he finally notices me. The metallic scent surrounding Randall makes my stomach sick as I inch closer to him. I survey his clothes and the lower part of his face that is dotted with drops of blood. When our eyes meet, I see a flicker that I've never seen before.

Something terrifying.

As I take his face in my trembling hands, his gaze softens, and I force him to focus on me and only me.

"Stop it, please," I beg, my voice nearly a whisper. "You're going to kill him."

He brushes his fingers across my hands before shrugging me off. "Pack your bags."

"What?"

"You will not ever fucking stay in this apartment, Lilith," he growls, getting up and grabbing Randall by the collar of his shirt like a bag of trash. He whips his eyes to me as I stand there, frozen. "What did I just tell you?"

His tone sends shivers down my spine, and I give him a quick nod before disappearing into my bedroom. I try not to think about how many broken bones Randall has as I get my suitcase, place it on the bed, and unzip it. I take all my clothes, then throw all my makeup products into my little cosmetic bag, and shove them into the suitcase.

I don't even realize what I'm doing until I get all of my stuff and my room becomes empty. I never had much in here, but for some reason, it feels like I need more than one suitcase.

"Do you need help?" Caleb's voice makes me flinch as he magically appears behind my back, wrapping his arms around my waist and inhaling my scent. I glance at his hands, realizing that he washed all the blood off them.

"No, I'm—" I swallow. "I'm fine."

WHEN WE'RE ALREADY IN HIS CAR, I TAKE A SIP OF MY HALF-FROZEN coffee, my stare glued to the empty street through the windshield. Caleb loads my suitcase into the trunk, then slams it shut before getting inside the car and closing the door. I feel his stare, but I avoid looking at him. He cups my chin and forces me to look into his eyes.

"Baby. Are you *okay*?"

Am I okay? I almost got raped, and then my boyfriend beat the living shit out of that man so hard that he blacked out. I don't know what I feel.

"Where did you—" I pause, swallowing another ball of anxiety. "Where is he?"

Caleb lets out a heavy sigh. "Not in the trunk, don't worry." As my eyes snap to him and he sees my concern, he adds, "The door to his apartment was open. I threw him inside, so he's chilling at his place right now."

A part of me feels relieved that Caleb didn't throw him in a dumpster or something like that.

"I think we should call an ambulance for him."

He tears his gaze away from me, shaking his head. "Don't say you feel sorry for the fucker. He tried to rape you, Lilith," he says, his eyes closing at the last words as if he's considering going back and finishing him.

"I don't feel sorry for him, I just—" I pinch the bridge of my nose, thinking. "He might die, Caleb. I don't want you to carry that baggage for the rest of your life."

He emits a chuckle that makes me feel uneasy. "He won't die, little devil. Now, would you do me a favor and stop thinking about him?"

I twirl my fingers. "Okay."

He plants a gentle kiss on my temple. "Prepare yourself for living with me."

I offer him a tight smile to let him know that I'm not worried anymore.

But why does what he just said feel like a threat?

CHAPTER
TWENTY—EIGHT

Caleb

"They're going to need you here, Caleb," Grayson pushes, his tone so serious that a surprised frown never disappears from my face—this fucker isn't serious most of the time. "I'm not fucking around now."

Leaning back in my chair, I let out an annoyed sigh. Moore has been acting out of character for the past few days. His constant display of worry and anticipation of something negative happening is becoming bothersome. He tries to overload me with work—projects that don't make any sense.

My team and I have been working as usual, but he insists on piling on dozens of new projects as if we're fucking robots. We can't stay here until night, working on something we never planned for.

Maybe if I were alone, I'd take the opportunity. I've always loved keeping myself busy. But now I have Lilith. She moved into my penthouse a week ago, and a couple of times, I've even left the office earlier than usual just because I miss her. Having her right under my wing—safe in my apartment—is supposed to make everything easier for me, but instead, my thirst is growing.

It's a struggle to sit in the office when I know she's alone in my bed, working or studying.

I now understand why everyone makes such a big deal about love. While being alone and independent was nice, having someone to come home to at the end of the day makes everything better.

"I've already said it once, Moore, and I'll repeat it, in case you're having trouble with your hearing," I say in my most patronizing voice. "I'm *not* interested. We're already busy enough as it is. I don't need zombies walking around me. Everything is going just the way it's supposed to. Now, if you'll excuse me, I need to work."

Ignoring the disapproving scowl on his face, I focus straight ahead on my usual tasks.

HER FRAGILE SHOULDERS BEAR A TATTOO THAT I TRACE WITH MY FINgers, marveling at how it has already healed. In the moonlight, her wings take on new shades of blue. Her beauty leaves me in awe— she is a masterpiece coming to life. Sometimes, I still can't believe that she's completely mine. A part of me will always think that she is too good for me, though. But maybe, with time, this feeling will become nothing more than background noise. I can live with that.

Lilith turns her face to me. "Caleb."

I run my hand through her hair—this has become my peculiar form of therapy. Every time I touch it, gently stroking it, I feel a sense of calm and improvement.

"Yes, little devil?"

"I love you too," she whispers, brushing her finger across my jawline.

I squash the satisfied smile that desperately tries to make its way across my face because I shouldn't react like a fifteen-year-old idiot.

All the emotions I experience toward Lilith are atypical. I think it's the influence of first love—something pure and slightly naive—a sensation I've never experienced before. It's that indescribable feeling that gives people butterflies, or whatever they like to call the swirling sensation in their stomach. A love like this only comes once in a lifetime, and I am committed to embracing it as my first and last.

I don't want anyone but her.

I CAN'T SLEEP, NOT EVEN HOURS AFTER LILITH SAID SHE LOVES ME back. I don't even want to, despite today—or yesterday—being one of the toughest days at work. I keep stroking her hair, replaying her words in my mind like a broken record because nothing else has ever made me feel as good as she does. However, I need at least an hour of sleep to function at the office. Gently, I move her body from mine, carefully placing her head on the pillow. Then, I walk to the kitchen to search for some sleeping pills.

Her phone rests on the kitchen table, its screen flashing with new messages—the sensor must have detected my presence and connected to Wi-Fi. I pick it up and take a look—dozens, no, thousands of messages and calls from furious Kevin. She has blocked him, but he persists by creating fake accounts. I open the messages to see what he sent.

UNKNOWN:

It's Kev. Can we talk, Lily???

Hello?

Why are you ignoring me?

So all this time our relationship didn't matter to you?

I stifle a laugh. Kevin is one of those people who will feel their crush breathe in their direction and assume the feeling is mutual.

UNKNOWN:

You know what?

Fuck you. You're just a typical whore.

I hope the way he fucks you is worth dumping our relationship for.

My jaw clenches as I read further; my brain already hurts from all the junk I'm consuming. Kevin is very brave when it comes to accusing and hurting a woman he's never met, desperately seeking her attention. He's an immature boy upset because she found someone who truly loves her. Of course, he's mad. The only way men like him can get attention from women is by paying for it.

I've noticed how he terrorizes Lilith, but I didn't interfere before. I waited for her to tell me about it, but every time I cautiously asked if he was bothering her, she shrugged me off. I guess I need to take matters into my own hands now. Evan has learned his lesson. It's time for Kevin to do the same.

IN ONE SWIFT MOTION, I REMOVE THE BAG FROM HIS HEAD AND THEN rip the tape off his mouth.

"Fuck!" he screams, desperately trying to loosen the ropes on his body. "What the fuck? Who the fuck are you?"

I love this question. "Do you have guesses, Kev?"

He appears smaller than he did online—shorter than Lilith, with black hair plastered to his forehead, soaked with sweat and blood from the wound I inflicted. Not so brave to keep up with the insults.

"What guesses?" he spits—literally—his blue eyes bug out with shock. "You are a sick fuck!"

Recalling the memory of Evan, I enjoyed playing with him much more than with Kevin. I bet the fucker still thinks he was hurt because of his daddy's muddy business.

But with this piece of shit is different. He doesn't have anything other than Lilith, and getting him out of his apartment was way easier, not to mention dragging him here.

Too boring.

I disregard his muttered curses, heading toward the bag containing my supplies. I take out the hammer, the very same one I used on Evan's knuckles.

Now his eyes are ready to pop out from his sockets as he looks at me like a scared deer, afraid for his little pathetic life. "Woah! Woah! Chill man, let's talk!"

But I don't listen. When I look at his hands, all I see is how he holds his phone and types insults to my woman, throwing threats at her and accusing her of things that are definitely not her fault.

I take his right hand and bring the hammer up. "From now on, you're going to think twice before insulting someone."

I swing the hammer, shattering his thumb and hearing the crunch of the bone amidst his loud screams and cries.

"Man! Please, stop!" he pleads, twitching in his chair like I'm electrocuting him. "I'm begging you, don't do this! Let's just talk, PLEASE!"

The last word leaves his mouth with such volume that it sounds unpleasantly revibrates in my chest, awakening an urge to cover my ears.

It was easier with Evan also because I cut off his tongue before he started to squeal like a pig. But with Kevin, I didn't plan to cut it off because he mostly was brave in his little texts.

As I prepare to strike his forefinger with the hammer, something clicks inside me—a flash of Lilith's face comes to mind, and the thought of her finding out what I've done to him gives me pause.

I try to shrug it off, but it's impossible. I still can't forget how she looked at me when I turned Randall's face into nothing but a bloody mess. Those green eyes flickered with pure fear and it seemed as if she didn't recognize me.

I take a deep breath, trying to grasp what my next move should be.

The whole point of me flying to Canada was to kidnap the fucker and teach him a lesson by smashing all his ten fingers. Then, I would've flown back and everything would be okay again.

But for some reason, I can't keep torturing him. I just *can't*.

I walk back to my bag, toss the hammer inside, and zip it up.

"Man, what are you doing?" Kevin squirms and fidgets in his chair, once again resembling a worm. "Where are you going?"

I look down at my hands and all I can see is blood. Maybe it's not even real, because Kevin could not bleed out so much from just one of his fingers. But technically, I guess, it is real. I've taken so many lives without a slight feeling of guilt for it, their blood could possibly soak in my skin, imprinting inside me.

Kevin's screams and cries are muffled now, I am too distracted to pay attention to any of that. Why can't I finish the plan? And why the fuck am I thinking about things that shouldn't bother me?

As I approach the bound fucker, I grab the bag and squat down, locking eyes with him. "Here's what is going to happen, Kevin," I begin. "I'm going to leave now. You'll get away with a broken finger which isn't something I actually planned to do because a scum like you deserves more brutal punishment." I come to a momentary stop. "But when I leave, I want you to forget everything about Lily."

A frown takes over his sweaty face at the sound of her fake name. "Lily? The girl that I met online?"

"Yes. You are going to delete all of your fake accounts and stop bothering her, do you hear me?"

He nods, but when I stay silent, waiting for his answer, he mutters, "Yes."

I let out a frustrated sigh. Dealing with this idiot takes so much of my time. So much of the time I could spend with Lilith. "Repeat everything you've understood, Kevin. Loud and clear."

He chokes back a lump in his throat. "I'm going to delete all of my fake accounts and stop bothering Lily."

"And?"

Various emotions pass over his face, the one that is more vivid than the others—frustration. Lilith is a woman not easily forgotten, and it will undoubtedly be tough for poor Kevin.

But she is mine. And I've been very patient on this part, but everything has its fucking limits.

"And I will forget everything about her," he croaks, his voice barely audible. I take the knife out of my pocket and brandish it in front of him, his eyes following the tip of the blade.

"Because if you keep bothering her, I'm going to come back and finish what I've started. Even if you decide to move to another fucking hemisphere, I'll find you, Kevin. So don't even think about anything stupid, do you understand me?"

"You can't get away with this," he says calmly as if he wasn't screaming like a bitch just a minute ago.

"Are you thinking about going to the police, Kevin?" I let out a low laugh. "Of course, you can do that. I won't stop you. But what are you going to tell them, huh? Do you think a police officer will care about a little boy who probably got too drunk and lost a fight?"

He bows his head down, now speechless. After cutting the ropes with my knife, I turn around and leave the area.

"You can't own her, you know," he throws when I'm already near the exit. When I glance at him over my shoulder, he adds, "She is not an object to possess."

A small smile plays on my lips. "That's the thing, Kevin. I have no desire to possess her. There is no need for it, as she has chosen me just as I have chosen her. Our love is based on something much deeper and more meaningful than just an obsession."

He never answers to that, though he doesn't need to. My words already hit the mark.

Cecilia

I just hope that you will find this letter before he gets to you.

My name is Cecilia Skylark, by this time you should know who I am if you watch the news.

I was kidnapped by Caleb Walker on September 5th at around ten p.m. from my apartment.

I remember a sharp pain at the back of my head and everything went black. I woke up in the raw basement alone. There is nothing here except a toilet at the corner and a small window that opens nothing but a glimpse of the backyard of the house.

He visits me once a day, bringing me food and water, not even talking to me. I don't know what he planned to do. But I am sure that I am not going to make it out alive.

If there is a slight chance of you finding this before he gets to you, I am begging you, do **NOT** trust Caleb. He is not who you think he is. It may sound absurd, but please, try to understand. Try to analyze.

I thought he was going to rape me. Or torture me. But he does nothing. He doesn't even talk to me. And it hurts more than anything I thought he planned to do.

I know my family is looking for me. But I don't think they'll get me before he kills me.

He IS the **Black Widow**.

I am the ninth on his list. But if this letter can help you in some way, help you to not become his tenth, eleventh, or so on, please, listen to me.

The best you can do is run away from him. Just **RUN**.

CHAPTER
TWENTY—NINE

Lilith

Caleb will return home in twenty minutes after being away on a work trip all day. I've been alone in this huge penthouse, and I still can't get used to its size. I've always lived in small places, from my mother's tiny house to my new apartment in Pinewood. And I thought I was okay with that. Even when thinking about my future, I never imagined myself in a bigger place. There's something about small apartments—you know all the corners, all the secret places. I'm used to cozy and compact spaces, so this big penthouse is a bit overwhelming for me.

Knowing Caleb's wealth, I anticipated that he lived in something like this—modern style with high ceilings, marble floors adorned with luxurious carpets, furniture in neutral colors, and expansive windows so large that the space doesn't need interior lighting. The penthouse has two floors. On the upper level, he even has his own personal gym. When I first saw it during the tour of his residence, it left me in awe. While I knew some people have treadmills or weights at home, having an entire fully equipped gym room in a residence was surprising.

Despite the luxurious furnishings, there are no photos—neither paintings nor personal ones. Lately, I found myself remembering how genuinely thrilled Caleb was to see my childhood pictures. It's melancholic to think he has none of his own. My mother was always a bitch, but she enjoyed capturing moments of me occasionally. This recollection triggered one thought—Caleb and I have never discussed our future, mainly because we've only just begun and prefer living in the present moment.

Yet, despite this, I've considered the idea of us starting a family. I never aspired to a traditional family life or saw myself as a wife or mother, as it didn't interest me. But being with Caleb has expanded my perspective. I'm unsure how to acquire the skills of a good wife or mother or if there are defined rules for those roles. Maybe all you need is the right person for support.

Picturing us as a family brings me immense joy. Each time I imagine creating our own haven and capturing moments with our future child, showering them with love, it feels like a dream.

It would contrast our experiences with our own parents. Despite our broken pasts and shattered minds, happiness isn't impossible for us. But it's just a dream. It's strange because I never considered this before, but it's now a fantasy of mine. Meeting Caleb has sparked so many new perspectives within me.

He's shown me a brighter, more optimistic side of life where anything is possible for *both* of us.

For now, I'm slowly adjusting to my new life, which is proving more challenging than expected. It's nice to live in comfort, where my needs are met, but I wrestle with guilt and the desire to leave my studies for work to share in covering rent. Every time I bring this up, Caleb waves it off.

Don't even think about that, Lilith. Just keep doing what you love, he always says when I start to bring it up again.

I keep glancing at the clock on my laptop, checking the time for the fifth time in the past couple of minutes. I decide to go downstairs because Caleb will be here any minute. Even though it's only been one day,

I've missed him terribly.

I rise from the bed and exit the bedroom. On my way to the stairs, I pause by the entrance to his office. I refrained from entering when he was absent and never purposefully searched through his belongings out of respect for his privacy, despite his repeated encouragement for me to feel at home and shed my shyness.

I could have explored more earlier, but I was preoccupied with writing. Caleb's penthouse is undeniably stunning overall, but his office is exceptional. The room features rich, brown walls and creamy floors, with an asymmetrical wooden desk standing in the middle. To the right, a few shelves are illuminated by soft, yellow lamps affixed to the wall. The large window is now covered with blinds, making the room almost dark. Honestly, at this moment, the space feels somewhat ominous. Nevertheless, I venture further inside, running my fingers over cabinets containing documents and other significant items.

I inhale deeply; even without Caleb's presence, everything in this place smells like him. The room is so quiet that I can hear my own breathing as I take in my surroundings. Reaching his desk, I sink into the leather chair, allowing myself to relax. I inspect every nook, yet find nothing that piques my interest.

Before getting up to check the lockers, I place my phone on his table in case he decides to call. Carefully, I open the shelves and find nothing but piles of papers and books. Just as I am preparing to leave, something catches my attention. One sideboard, filled with papers, appears different from the others. It's smaller, and the paint is peeling off from one side.

I remove all the papers from the sideboard and practically immerse myself, burying my face in it, reaching for the spot where the paint is peeling. With it now empty, I notice a glimpse at the top, as if there's something behind. Every sideboard here is anchored to a wall, so there should be nothing behind it.

Upon touching the peeling paint, it yields to my touch, and I realize it's a small door.

Why would there be a door inside a sideboard?

Opening it and peeking inside, my attention is drawn to a couple of papers. Taking them out, I settle in as I begin to examine the papers. Half of them are wrinkled, as if they were meant for the trash rather than being stowed away here.

These are unlike the other papers—handwritten letters. I start to scan the first paper, then another. With each word, my heartbeat quickens, and my chest feels heavier.

A frown creeps onto my face as I continue to read—the more I read, the more bewildered I become.

Some letters are stained with dried blood, while others are moist as if soaked with tears or water. This only adds to the mounting panic rising in my chest, constricting my airways, because I *don't* understand.

Nine letters, each from different girls who were confined in a basement, detailing the horrors they endured. My hands begin to tremble, and I only realize it when I reach the last letter from Cecilia. Her final sentence urges to run, the words stained with blood.

Now, it's not just my hands shaking; my entire being is overwhelmed by an eerie sensation, spreading numbness throughout my bones. A loud sob breaks free, and my ears ring. I instinctively cover my mouth with my hand as tears stream down my face onto her letter, making the paper even messier. The realization hits me now, as if the first written message wasn't enough, as if I didn't want to accept what I was reading.

Ava, Eloise, Jade, Piper, Reese, Lia, Rowan, Blake, Cecilia.

All the girls who went missing.

Victims of the Black Widow.

Something makes me believe each of the girls wrote numerous letters, but he retained only those that captured the moments when they reached their breaking point, as if it empowered him— giving him a sense of control over their emotions once more.

"Lilith?"

I turn my face to him, incapable of uttering a single word. Somehow, I gather the strength to rise slowly, clutching the letters in my hands. As Caleb's gaze falls upon them, a flicker of pure fear flashes in his eyes. It's the first time I see Caleb afraid.

"Lilith." His voice is shakier than before.

Tears fill my eyes as I struggle to speak, looking at him. "It's you." My voice is barely above a whisper, and I feel my knees beginning to buckle under the weight of fear. "You are the Black Widow."

Caleb's bag thuds to the floor as he strides menacingly toward me. I instinctively flinch, my back colliding with the window with a resounding thud. He notices my reaction and halts in his tracks, throwing his hands up in a peaceful gesture.

"Lilith, I *can* explain."

My breath quickens the moment he pronounces those words. Some part of me had anticipated his denial, hoping to catch that little spark in his eyes signaling this was all a mistake—a falsehood. But as I gaze at him, the truth dawns on me like a symphony building to a crescendo—it has been him all along.

I believed I understood Caleb, but in truth, I couldn't have been more wrong.

Just a few minutes earlier, I'd been yearning for his return, eager for us to share that precious time together. I had been dreaming about embracing and kissing him, longing for the sensation of his fingers in my hair, relishing the tenderness of his touch. But the man standing before me is no longer the Caleb I once knew. That was all the girls had been writing about—the kind, caring Caleb who is no longer here.

He was never there.

He is the Devil. A walking evil.

And he is scaring me.

"Please, let me explain," he begs, taking a tentative step toward me.

I shrink into the corner of the room like a scared mouse. "Stay the fuck back."

"No, no," he mumbles, grabbing his head and shaking it. *"Fuck, no, no, no."*

Suddenly, he drops to his knees in front of me, and upon meeting his glistening eyes, I realize he is in tears. "Baby, *please* don't do this to me."

"Don't do this to you?" I ask, my voice teetering on the edge of breaking. "You are a serial killer, Caleb. That was your plan all along, wasn't it?"

I release a pathetic sob, my hands reaching out to wipe my eyes, but it's pointless—the tears flood too fast.

I can't stop crying.

"When did you plan to kill me?"

"No, no, Lilith. I didn't plan on killing you. Not anymore."

I choke back a lump in my throat. "Not anymore?"

"I don't want to kill anymore, my love. You've changed me, Lilith. You are the first woman I fell in love with. I never lied about what I feel toward you!"

I feel sick in my stomach. I want to throw up. "Then let me go, Caleb."

As he slowly rises to his feet, I scramble to move away, but I find myself cornered in this small room. Desperate for a way out, I snatch the thick book from his shelf and hurl it at his head. "You'll stay where you are or I swear I'm going to fight you!"

He effortlessly deflects my attack, and the book never reaches his face. "I'm not going to hurt you, Lilith, can't you understand that? I never will."

I want to believe him. I do. But how can a serial killer be trusted? He has taken nine lives, but I'm sure there are more. Much more. Now I understand what I've felt when I just met him. He is dangerous. Truly fucking dangerous.

"Caleb," I cry out, my whole being shaking. "*Please let me go.*"

His face rearranges into a pitiful expression as his tears fall from his eyes. "I can't do that, Lilith."

All of a sudden, my phone begins to ring. It feels like a ray of hope, causing my hysterics to momentarily cease as I take a deep breath and turn my eyes toward it. I calculate how fast I can reach it—if I try, I can make it. He is bigger and taller, but I have more agility. I just need to run as fast as I can and press the green button before he gets me.

Caleb raises his arms in the air as if warning me not to do this. "Lilith. Please."

In a sudden burst of energy, I glance at him and bolt toward the ringing phone as if the numbness that had enveloped me moments ago had never existed. I run. I reach the desk, but his arm wraps around my waist, pulling me away in one swift movement.

"No!" I scream, trying to slap his hand off and kick him in the balls, but he dodges all my attacks. "Caleb, please! Please, LET ME GO!"

My hand tries to reach the phone, but I can't even touch it as he pulls me into him, locking me in his arms.

"Stop it, baby," he says, tightening his grip around my body. "It's pointless to try."

"You're hurting me," I lie, hoping to win some time, trying to kick harder. He doesn't physically hurt me; his grip isn't painful. Let's say I talk about the ache in my heart that won't stop bothering me since I've found out the truth.

VALERIIA MILLER

We both drop to our knees, and he buries his face in my neck. "Calm down, Lilith. Just calm down, please."

But I can't. And I don't want to. So, I keep trying to break free from his grip. I keep crying and screaming. My throat aches, and it seems like I'm on the verge of losing my voice. "You are scaring me, Caleb. *You are scaring me so much.*"

Sobbing in a pathetic manner, his body trembles with each convulsion. "I will never hurt you, do you hear me? I will never do that, baby, *I will never.*"

I don't even realize how he carries me to the living room, unlocks his safe, and retrieves something from within.

"Caleb, please."

"It's okay," he reassures, kissing my temple. "It's going to be okay, little devil."

I feel a slight discomfort in my neck, and then, I am suddenly overcome by a sense of calm as if none of this has occurred. It feels like a bad dream from which I am now awakening. As my head becomes heavier and my eyelids droop, I whisper softly, feeling as light as a flying cloud, "What did you do?"

"Everything is okay, Lilith," he reassures, but his voice is barely audible now. "You're *safe.*"

His words echo in my mind as the last thing I hear him say before everything goes dark.

Part 2

THE TRUTH

CHAPTER
THIRTY

Lilith

N umbness consumes me, my body a weightless shell amidst swirling thoughts. I blink, trying to focus, but my head refuses to cooperate, forcing me back onto the bed. A shadow looms, his voice calm as he reaches out, offering to help me up. Hatred boils within me—I want to lash out, to strike him—but the drug renders me powerless, and his touch, warm and familiar, ignites conflicting emotions.

Safety? No. He's trapped me, just as he did those poor girls. Am I his tenth victim, destined for a more horrific fate?

When I muster the strength to push him away, surprisingly, he retreats. Caleb steps back, watching as I struggle to sit up. "How are you feeling?" he asks, his tone unsettlingly composed.

"How am I feeling?" Anger begins to replace the drug's haze, emotions flooding back. "What did you do to me, Caleb?"

"I needed you to calm down," he explains evenly, his calmness almost lethal. "You never let me explain."

I glare at him, my forehead pounding with an impending headache. "Where am I?"

"In my basement," he admits, and despair threatens to drown out my rage. I glance around—it's nothing like the dungeon described in those letters. This basement is a pseudo-home, with comfort and care, a cruel mockery of normalcy. "I made it comfortable," he adds, seeing my disbelief. "You have everything you need here."

A bitter laugh escapes me. "What do you mean by this?"

Caleb sits beside me, his weight sinking the mattress. "I was afraid you'd run if you knew the truth. I can't let you go, but I won't condemn you to the dungeon. You don't deserve that, Lilith."

"And what do I deserve?" I choke out weakly. "Being haunted by a fucking serial killer, sedated, and trapped in a basement that looks like a separate house? Does this mean that you're being nicer to me than to those girls, and I should be grateful for that?"

Caleb rubs his hands together. "I wanted to kill you, Lilith. I *did*." His gaze softens. "But when I started to learn about you and when I realized that I fucking fell in love with you, everything changed. You made me better, can't you understand it?"

"If you do love me, you'll let me go, Caleb. Because that's what I want."

He lets out a frustrated sigh, although the expression on his face is telling me that he predicted my answer. "That's not what you want, my love."

I hug my knees and take a pause before saying, "Aren't you the one who knows everything about me? Because if you think I want anything other than to get out of here and never see you again, then you don't know anything about me."

He gives a disapproving shake of his head. "And where would you go? Hm?" he asks, lowering his head as though addressing a child. "What will your plans be if I let you go?"

I open my mouth to answer but nothing comes to mind. Shit. This isn't the moment where it's best to say nothing. He caught me off guard with this question—a part of me is still in denial, and the other part is half-clouded because of the sedative he gave me.

But I have to think about...God, fucking anything. Maybe I'd love to move back in with my mom, find a job at a local café, or just continue studying—anything to show him that I have goals in my life.

"I'd go back to the university and graduate like I planned," I begin, injecting a fake pep of confidence into my voice. "And I'd write more books. And I'd do more stuff that doesn't fucking concern you, Caleb. What kind of question is that?" I snap, not even realizing how my tone becomes nothing but a shaky, inconvenient one. "You have no right to trap me in here like an animal in a cage without a chance to choose."

He purses his lips and his features rearrange from neutral to... offended? This motherfucker feels offended, doesn't he? "How many times do I have to repeat that you are not a prisoner, little devil? Not an animal, nor any other thing you're trying to compare yourself with."

A devilish smirk stretches across his face. "Listen to yourself, Lilith. You can't even fake that you want all of what you've just counted."

"I don't give a fuck what you think," I blurt out impulsively. "I have my goals and I don't want to just sit here and entertain your sick ass."

"I never said I would take anything from you. You'll still have the resources that you need so you can write."

When I swallow, my throat hurts with a bitter lump of upcoming tears as I realize that it's pointless. I can't convince him, nor can I escape him. I am trapped for as long as he wishes me to, and I can't do anything but accept it.

"Why are you crying?" he asks softly, reaching for me, but I recoil, retreating to the other end of the bed.

"You're sick, Caleb. You don't understand what you're doing."

"I do," he protests, anguish flickering in his eyes. "Do you think I enjoy this?"

His words cut deep, and I recall the faces of those other girls, the ones who never saw his love. "Was any of it real? Even a little?"

Caleb moves closer, grasping my hands, kissing them gently. "Everything was real, Lilith. I'd cross any line for you."

Hysterical tears overtake me, torn between believing him and hating myself for it. His presence still feels real, his love, once genuine, now a twisted paradox. As I avoid his gaze, memories flood—his warmth, his affirmations, the belief I was worth something more. My heart aches, betraying me with each beat, whispering I'm not alone anymore.

How can I still feel a glimmer of hope, knowing what he really is?

A liar. A serial killer. A man who plays god with lives.

He should repulse me, incite nothing but anger. Yet, I still love him. I cling to the hope that I'll wake from this nightmare in his arms, that everything will be okay again in the morning.

"Look at me," he insists.

I turn away, but he gently grasps my face, forcing me to meet his gaze. "No. I don't want you near me. Just leave."

Instead, he peppers my face with kisses, just as I once comforted him through trauma. His warmth now feels dangerous, deceptive—like he's distracting me before plunging a knife into my heart. Eyes closed, I brace for the pain, but all I feel is the warmth of his body against mine, the softness of his lips on my skin.

"Leave me alone," I plead, tears streaming down. I try to pull away from his touch. "Please, Caleb. I don't want this anymore. Just leave me."

He pauses after a final kiss on my jawline, his warm breath lingering on my skin, sending shivers down my spine. He's warm and alive, unlike those girls. Their families shattered, their lives cut short. I should focus on their pain, their suffering. How he held them captive, broke them down, and ultimately ended their lives, discarding them like trash.

He can't keep getting away with this. It's unjust. A man like him deserves nothing less than the death penalty. Maybe if I repeat this enough, I can finally start to hate him. Maybe hate can consume me, fill every crevice of my soul until he becomes nothing more than a vile memory.

But as he rises and walks away, locking the door behind him, I lie there motionless, curled into a ball on the bed. My eyes fixate on the pillow, now stained with mascara. I'm left alone with a shattered soul, wondering if it can ever be whole again.

Just as I feared it would be.

CHAPTER

THIRTY-ONE

Lilith

C aleb comes a couple of times a day, bringing me food and checking if everything is okay. He keeps trying to start a conversation, but I give him nothing but a blank face; my mouth is sewed shut.

"You aren't going to even eat anything?" he asks when I push away another plate he brought me. "It isn't poisoned if that's what you're worrying about."

"I would prefer it to be," I say, immediately feeling discomfort in my mouth because it's the first time I speak in a few days.

Caleb sighs, plopping down on the bed beside the chair where I'm seated. In response, I deliberately lift myself and grasp the chair with both hands, relocating it to another corner of the basement before settling into it.

He emits a little chuckle as if it's funny, lighting a sparkle of anger inside of me. "It would be easier for you if you cooperated with me," he says casually.

"Okay. Maybe we'd go on hunting together? I'll help you to kill a couple more girls," I ridicule scornfully.

The muscle in his jaw clenches. "I told you I'm not interested in killing anyone anymore."

I can't keep a straight face. Every time he repeats that, re-minding me that I, allegedly, changed his psychotic mind and he doesn't want to kill anymore, he expects me to what? To forgive him and jump in his arms maybe? To forget everything and live happily ever after?

"You are a psychopathic fuck," I bite, not even scared if he snaps and bashes my brains out right fucking here. "Do you even hear yourself?"

"What can I do for you to forgive me?"

I think I've stayed silent for too long because now the only emotion that occupies my being is pure rage.

I can't stand him anymore. I can't keep looking at his face, recalling every single sweet memory of ours and admitting that some part of me wants to forgive him.

I jump off the chair. "Are you kidding me, Caleb? Is this fuck-ing funny to you?"

He gets up from the bed right after me. "Just tell me what to do, Lilith, I—"

"NOTHING!" I scream so loud that my whole being shakes. "You can't do fucking NOTHING. YOU RUINED EVERY FUCKING BIT OF US!"

He doesn't react to my aggression, just offers me a barely de-tectable nod.

And that makes me even more pissed as I grab the book he brought me yesterday and throw it into him—it hits his chest and falls on the floor with a thud—but the fucker doesn't even flinch.

If he fought me back, it would be a lot easier. Like I said before, the chance of him accidentally hitting me too hard in a fit of anger is likely possible.

I want to count on that, and I want that to happen because it's better than living in a basement that feels like a normal home, waiting for him to decide my fate.

"She ate her fucking skin, Caleb," I nearly whisper, an upcoming wave of tears stings my eyes. "Jade was so hungry that she peeled off the skin of—"

"I know." That's all he says, his head bowed down.

Nausea comes up to my throat as I remember the last few sentences she wrote. Jade ended up here, just at the spot where I am standing right now, alone, cold, and broken. She was the only one who believed that she could get out.

"You are nothing but a fucking monster. I wish you would just kill me so I wouldn't have to see your fucking face anymore."

He gets up as if he's ready to go—apparently, hearing such hurtful words is painful for this maniac. Who would've thought?

"Oh, poor Caleb can't hear the bitter truth?" At the door, he comes to a halt, never meeting my gaze. Hastily, I move toward him, grasping his arm to turn him to me. "You aren't going anywhere until I tell you everything I think about you."

He looks at me, his eyes narrowed into thin slits. "Okay."

He catches me off guard with this response. I expect cursing, slapping my face or pushing me away. But his calm tone and steady posture tell me that he is prepared to listen to whatever I am going to say to him.

Caleb is impossibly close to me right now, I feel the heat of his body along with his heartbeat. It's calm and steady as if he is a fucking robot whom my words don't affect. I am the one who closed the distance and broke the possibility of not paying him any attention so he would finally get bored and kill me, and now I am paying the consequences.

I keep telling myself that it's my body that's still attracted to him in some kind of way. Not my mind. Subconsciously, I understand that he is nothing but a trash that doesn't deserve anything but jail—or the death penalty—but my body pulls to him like a fucking magnet.

The fucker is illegally perfect in every sense, and I keep telling myself that if he was ugly or short, I wouldn't even bother dealing with him.

But he has to be the most dangerous, disgusting person alive enveloped in a beautiful, shiny wrapper which makes my stupid body want to cling to him and remember every night we've spent together.

It's reckless to stand so close to him right now because he is smart, and he reads my emotions better than I do. And if he manages to do that, whatever I am going to say isn't going to make any sense.

"Every morning I wake up I think about how perfect my life would be if I never met you," I begin, trying to keep away the shakiness in my voice. "I just want you to know that I regret every single second shared with you. Every night. Every kiss. Fucking everything. And if I knew what you were from the very beginning, I would never give you a chance of even breathing near me, Caleb."

He flashes me a self-satisfied smirk as if he enjoyed everything I just told him. "After all this time you still haven't learned how to be a good liar, little devil."

He leans his face closer to me, causing the numbness to spread across my body. I blink at him, paralyzed to the toes, as he continues, "Remember what you've said to me? About how you want me to stay? Even when I warned you that you don't know what you're signing up to."

"Do you even hear yourself? I never thought you were a serial killer. I was attracted to the version of you that doesn't exist, to the one that you've shown me," I answer through gritted teeth. "You were always a liar."

"I never lied to you. If you'd asked me if I was a killer, I'd have given you the honest answer, Lilith." He runs his fingers through my hair, and I am forced to turn my head away. "You knew I was a bad man, little devil. I cut off the man's tongue, do you remember that?"

"I—" I begin, but then stop, realizing that I have nothing to say.

He nods as if he finally sees the confirmation of everything he said before. "We're both broken, my love. Both have the darkness inside our souls that only those like us can see and understand, can tame our inner demons."

"I'm *nothing* like you."

"You're wrong again. I never ruined you, Lilith. I never changed you. I just opened your eyes to the real you, just gave you the little push you needed. I just showed you how gorgeous you are."

I feel his piercing stare, but my eyes are closed and I don't want to open them. I don't want to face him, don't want to give him the satisfaction he desperately needs while telling me all of this.

"We don't have family. We don't have friends. We're miserable, weird to others," he continues. "And they all keep putting on the same old record for us, don't they? *Something is wrong with you,* they keep saying. And they are right."

Despite my denial, his words pierce through me like daggers, deflating my invisible balloon of lies. I shake my head in disagreement, but deep down I know that every single word he says is true. The only thing that sets us apart is that I never acted on my desire to kill. But the truth is, I wanted to.

As I reflect on my past, I remember how I was forced to confront the dark thoughts that have always lingered in the back of my mind. Even as a child, I considered the idea of harm coming to those who angered or frustrated me.

I remember vividly the time when my mother was accusing me of something I didn't do, and I imagined how satisfying it would be if something happened to her. I remember her taking her prescribed pills regularly. One day, I couldn't resist the urge that lurked inside my soul for a quite long as I blended them into a smoothie and watched as she drank it unsuspectingly. When she began to feel ill, I was gripped with fear, not because of the possibility of her death, but because I knew that if the police questioned me, I would have to confess to my crime and face the consequences.

Similarly, when Evan wronged me and Caleb took matters into his own hands, I felt a sense of relief. Even when I visited Evan at the hospital, it wasn't out of pity or remorse. It was merely a way to avoid raising suspicions from others. And just seeing his crippled form through the window was enough for me.

Enough to feel relieved.

As I delve deeper into my past, I am confronted with numerous instances where my twisted thoughts and desires are coming to the forefront. Despite my efforts to appear normal, my true self manages to reveal its ugly head.

I am tainted and depraved, much like Caleb. It is only a matter of time before I act on my impulses and cause harm to others. The incident with my mother is just one example of my corrupted nature.

If I were to continue down this path of self-reflection, there would be countless more pages dedicated to my messed-up psyche. It's a daunting realization, but one that I cannot ignore.

Not when he forces me to embrace it.

His fingertips brush across my cheeks, wiping away the tears that betray my inner turmoil. "Don't cry, my Lilith," he whispers, pressing a tender kiss to the tip of my nose. "We are two fallen angels, rejected by God and weak alone. But together, we are indestructible. We can either live in this world or burn it to the ground and create our own. The choice is yours."

After wiping away the remaining tears, he retreats from me. A hollow, desolate sensation consumes me as he departs and secures the door behind him, leaving me with a myriad of thoughts.

The most prominent one terrifies me as I come to the realization that Caleb has been correct about me all along.

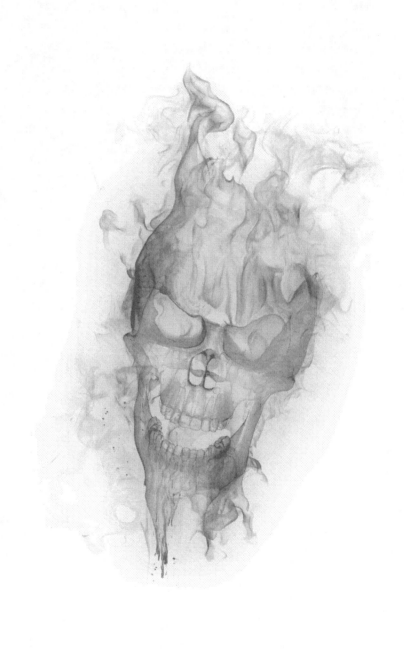

CHAPTER
THIRTY—TWO

Caleb

I fucked up. As you can already tell.

Leaving Lilith by herself in the basement makes me feel like a genuine shit. Things have just started to be normal with us, but the universe, or God, or whatever the fuck above us decided to dilate our happy days with shitty ones.

I collected the letters from my victims like a trophy. The same way I never washed off the hoodie I'd been in while cutting Evan's tongue off—the cloth stained in his blood regained the sense of control over and over again while I watched at it. I enjoyed the feeling of possessing control over and over again as I held the items that once belonged to my victims, it nurtured me.

If only I had let go of my possessions when I first met her and recognized that I was falling in love. If only I had understood that

I no longer needed any of this shit. I no longer felt the insatiable desire to possess someone else's vulnerabilities.

But it's too late to think about what if anyway.

I barely sleep—her scared face haunts me in my dreams, reminding me of what have I done to her.

To us.

I should've been more thoughtful. Especially when she moved out to my house. But I was too fucking distracted by her, by new feelings that she caused within me, my mind was too cloudy and distracted for any conscious decisions.

It truly hurts me to watch her ignore me and glance at me with disgust. My biggest fear was that she would discover my true nature and try to run away from me.

I didn't enjoy any second I spent sedating her and dragging her in my car, then locking her in the basement. I'm glad I've finished it, though. For her, it's like a little house decorated in the colors and shapes she likes.

I was glad that she at least started to talk to me, even if it was pure anger evaporating from her—I'd welcome anything rather than deathly silence. But after our conversation about our true nature, she shut down again. Every time I come in, she lies on her bed with her face turned to the wall. She never reacts when I call her name or when I'm trying to make a conversation with her.

It's evident that she requires time to comprehend all that has happened between us, but each time I observe her avoiding eye contact and shutting me out, I am afraid that I am losing her.

Today, I have something that might just bring her back to me. I've just returned from a meeting with a friend of a friend who helped me to meet with a writer whose books Lilith loves more than anything. I have fresh manuscripts in hand, ready to present to her.

Despite the fact that his two upcoming books were not set to be released for another six months, I was able to convince him to give me both manuscripts ahead of schedule through a conversation we had.

Talking about the benefits of being a respected CEO.

As I turn the key and push open the door, my eyes immediately fall on Lilith. She's perched on the edge of the bed, her hands wrapped tightly around her knees.

"Hey," I greet, stepping inside and closing the door behind me. "What are you doing?"

She looks at me like I'm an idiot. "What can I do here?"

I shrug my shoulders. "You have dozens of your favorite books here along with your laptop—"

"Without the Wi-Fi and signal," she interrupts, frustration evident in her voice. "Caleb, who is impossible to scare, is suddenly afraid that I might call the police?"

A smile plays on my lips. "So eager to get me in handcuffs?"

She huffs in irritation. "Better on the chopping block right away."

"Old school much? Nowadays they use electric chairs or drugs."

She rolls her eyes at my sarcasm. "Why did you come?"

As I unzip the bag and pull out two fresh manuscripts, I hold them up in the air and wave them slightly. However, Lilith's expression remains blank, and her eyes fail to light up with any sort of excitement or interest. "Brought you something you will definitely like."

"I want nothing from you."

Yeah, that was predictable. I ignore her little statement, sitting right next to her and placing each of the books on the bed. "Wesley Kim, one of your favorites. These are the books that will be available for reading only six months after."

She eyes me skeptically, but eventually switches her gaze to the books in front of her and picks them both, examining their insides. "You beat this out of him?"

I let out a laugh which I desperately try to turn into a cough. "No. A friend of a friend of mine helped. It's not a big deal."

Her lips curve into a warm smile. "Well, if you brought me exclusive manuscripts—"

As my head jerks to the side, a burning pain immediately envelops my right cheek.

She just slapped me with two books at once.

I rub a hand over my cheek, trying to ease the pain. "I am a very patient man, little devil, but your attempts to hurt me are starting to annoy the living shit out of me." Her emerald eyes beam with a flicker of pure anger as I meet her gaze. "Eager to get punished?"

She swings the books again, but I catch her hands and take the manuscripts out of her grip. In one movement, I pin her hands above her head as I get on top of her. "Want to start the power play, huh?"

She fidgets like a worm, desperate to shrug me off her. "Fuck you."

I can't help but smirk, relishing in her anger. While I did mention her laughable attempts to hurt me were a bit annoying, there's a part of me that's turned on by her rage. It's like witnessing a transformation—the timid Lilith I once knew now becomes a fierce lioness.

Despite her attempts to scoot away from me, I refuse to let her move even an inch. I press my body against hers, inhaling the scent of her neck before brushing my lips from one side to the other.

"Fucking creep. What the hell are you doing?" she asks, irritation evident in her voice.

"Calculating the proper size of the collar I'm planning to buy you."

Lilith exhales wearily. "In your dreams. I will never let you do anything to me anymore."

"Maybe I need to bring that ribbon from the first present I ever bought you so we can tie your little hands as I planned?"

"The only thing we are going to tie are *your* hands and legs," she answers, her voice filled with such bitterness that I can almost feel the way her anger seeps from within. "Then I'll bring the cops, and they will put you away for good, fucker."

I grab her by the cheeks, squeezing them tightly. "Insult me one more time and you're not going to be able to sit for weeks, do you hear me?" Lilith tries to break free from my grip, but I only hold her tighter. "Do you hear me?"

She eventually nods, and I release her face, letting my hand move down to her pants. She can only observe my actions, her eyes fixated on my fingers. "What the fuck? Don't—"

She never finishes her sentence as I dive my hand inside her panties, meeting a thick, warm pool of wetness between her legs. "You'll never learn how to lie, my little devil," I tease, gathering her juices on my fingers as I watch her reaction—she tries to keep an angry face, but her eyes roll and she shivers beneath my touch. "So fucking wet, and I didn't even do anything. Sure you don't want me to continue?"

"I will never want anything from you anymore."

"Mm. That's not an answer to my question."

"Fuck you."

I release her hands and withdraw my hand from her underwear, grabbing her by the waist and rolling her onto her stomach. Before she can process anything, I slap her ass so hard that her pathetic little sob revibrates from the walls.

"Say that again?"

"Motherf—"

Another slap at the same spot—now she cries harder, burying her face in bed sheets. "Your record is stuck, my love. Anything else?"

"I—"

I slap her ass again.

And again.

And again.

And again.

I lean my ear to hear another curse, but the only sound that emanates from her is her quiet sobs. I begin to massage the spot, easing the pain.

But she doesn't stop crying.

Eventually, I let go of her. She collapses on the side, burying her face in her hands and moving into an embryo posture. In this state, she appears incredibly vulncrable, so fucking much that it brings tears to my eyes as well. One part of me acknowledges that my actions toward her are unfair and egocentric, and she doesn't deserve that. However, the selfish side of me desires to retain her, even if it means confining her here until she eventually forgives me.

Feeling unable to continue doing nothing, I find myself moving my hand onto her knee, beginning to gently caress it, even though I'm uncertain of my motivations. Maybe I am just trying to make it a little easier for her if that's possible.

"I hate you," she murmurs in a trembling voice. "So fucking much."

My fingers don't stop brushing across her knee. "I love you, too."

CHAPTER
THIRTY–THREE

Lilith

My right ass cheek burns like hell.

I never had my ass whooped by anybody. Until yesterday.

I started to cry right after it, but not because I was in physical pain. The reason for my breakdown is the fact that I, somehow, found it enjoyable.

The sensation of his hands' imprints on my skin is not just pleasant, but far beyond it.

Every fucking day I work on how to develop disgust and hate toward Caleb when in reality, I am ending up feeling all these emotions only toward myself.

I keep convincing myself that it's my body, not my mind who still craves for his touch. Basic animal instincts—that's what it is supposed to be. Because I can't allow myself to feel anything warm toward a serial killer. A guy who kidnapped nine documented girls, and I'm sure there are more about which police don't even know.

Especially when he did this to me, too. He acts with me like he owns me. As if I'm some kind of toy, not a living human being. He limited my freedom, and he plans to do it for I have no idea how much time.

But why does a part of me feel like it's somehow better than my previous life? How the hell a person who was kidnapped and trapped in the basement can think that way?

My stupid brain keeps recalling the conversation that we had around a week ago, about us being the same. Caleb shamelessly got into my brain and peeled off all of my layers, leaving me naked and vulnerable in front of him. He uncovered the darkness that lurked in my soul and forced me to look it in the eyes and accept it.

Even when I understand that all of this is wrong, his words somehow convince me of the opposite. I started to think wider. As if the world can't be all about white and fluffy things. As if the darkness inside of us needs to exist at least to keep a balance.

I don't understand what is right and wrong anymore. The thin line between those two concepts is irrevocably destroyed, and I don't think I can get it back.

Caleb shifted my tectonic plates and showed me my other side, but instead of making me feel afraid and ashamed for it, he wanted me to feel nothing but proud of myself. Maybe it was really meant to be.

Maybe we are the only people who can understand and accept each other, and therefore, share love and support.

I was never afraid of Caleb. Even when he was just my stalker—something that should've fucking concerned me, make me feel terrified, instead made me feel thrilled and excited.

I wanted to see him. To touch him. To talk to him.

Every thought ends up with the I *could've* and *should've* done and think like *this* or *that*.

Of course, my basic instincts told me that it was wrong and I shouldn't do what I did, but it was more like background noise. All the time Caleb made me feel nothing but seen and important.

And then, he showed me his *love*.

Love in sincerity of which I don't know if I believe anymore.

This is the thing with people like me—people, who never received even a tiny bit of love. We jump at every opportunity beaming at the horizon, clinging to the first person who shows us a tiny bit of attention.

Because we don't know what real love looks like. So every time we see something that looks like it, we embrace that without even thinking twice.

Pathetic, I know. But it is true.

Most of the people end up with broken hearts at maximum. But I, the girl who was always more like a fucking shadow at the side—a grey mouse whom nobody has ever noticed—didn't get away that easily. I am kidnapped and trapped in the basement by the man whom I still love, no matter how fucked-up he is.

And no matter how fucked-up he made me.

"If you're not going to eat, I will feed you from the spoon," he says when he returns thirty minutes after bringing me my food, which I never even touched.

"I'm not hungry," I cut unemotionally.

When Caleb closes the distance between us and sits next to me, I don't scoot away like I usually do. Maybe I am too feeble to do that. Or maybe I am used to him, and I know he doesn't want to hurt me.

At least yet.

"Lilith," he says, and I am forced to close my eyes and bow my head down because the way he says my name brings back old, pleasant memories that I shouldn't fucking have. "Look at me."

"You've done your job. I'll eat later. Just go already."

"Talk to me," he says, his voice a shade lighter than usual. "Tell me what you're thinking about."

I bite the inside of my cheek till I taste copper in my mouth. "I am locked in a fucking basement for weeks, Caleb. What can I possibly think about?"

"You've started reading them," he states, pointing his chin at Wesley Kim's unreleased books he managed to get me. "Are they good?"

I understand that he tries to cajole me. He brings me my favorite food, gets the books I've been dying to read, and tries to talk to me. If not bringing up the fact that he is a fucking psychopath, and closing my eyes on what he's done, Caleb would seem like nothing but a man who puts my comfort first and cares about me.

So cute. He expects me to melt and give him everything he wants—my little approval after which we will live happily ever after.

And it hurts to admit that it fucking works. I am aware of what he is, but every time I see those obsidian eyes flickering with nothing but warmness and concern toward me, and hear his voice that sounds cold and bottomless for others, but for me, he makes it softer and loving, I feel guilty for calling him names and trying to slap him.

What he does is pure manipulation—he literally throws dust in my eyes, forcing my mind to replay all the sweet memories we had together as if giving me hope that nothing changed.

And it gets worse when I remember what he has done to other girls. They wrote about how he laughed at them, behaved with them as if they were trash and starved them.

But his behavior toward me is quite the contrary.

That makes me feel emotions I shouldn't be feeling. It's as if I'm special and he genuinely cares about me. It's as if I'm the *only* woman capable of taming the beast. And it's as if I'm the first one who doesn't trigger an urge to kill within him.

I find it absurd and reckless that I'm experiencing warmth and love for a psychopath who kidnapped me. I never imagined I could end up in this situation. I want to laugh at myself for feeling this way.

Maybe it's just a Stockholm syndrome? It has to be. Because I don't have another explanation for my stupid fucking brain.

"What about my university?" I ask, although my education is my last concern right now. I guess I just wonder if anyone called to check why I am not attending the classes.

If anyone noticed that I am fucking gone.

"I solved the problem right away. They won't bother you."

I let out a sigh of frustration. While there was a moment when I longed for someone to solve my problems for me, now the thought of it makes me feel nauseous. I don't want him to solve fucking anything for me.

"It's not an answer to my question," I say through clenched teeth.

He nods as if he predicted my desire for more explanation. "You took an academic leave."

"For how long?"

"A year."

I inhale a deep breath in an attempt to gather myself. "And nobody asked anything? No suspicions?"

Caleb purses his lips in a thin line. "No, little devil."

I can't stifle my laughter. "Because they spoke to one of the most respectable men in New York, huh?" I edge myself closer to him. "You have everything, Caleb. Why did you become a serial killer?"

He swallows a ball of emotion lodged in his throat. "I experienced a sense of power when I ended their lives. The feeling of being able to determine their destinies was empowering. It was incredible for me, beyond enjoyable, and nothing could compare to it."

The realization washes over me like a deluge. An urge to wield power, to dictate the fate of others. The way he held them in a basement. "You were acting toward them just the way your mother did toward you, huh?"

The muscle in his jaw clenches as he looks away from me. Caleb broke the eye contact first? That means I hit the nerve.

I realize I play with fire, but I have nothing to lose, so I push, "You wanted to replace those feelings your mommy made you feel?" He still doesn't look at me, nor does he give me an answer. "Poor little Caleb who never grew up, still offended that his mommy was hurting him?"

A smile creeps into his face, making me feel a little uneasy. "You got me, Lilith. Solved the puzzle no one could."

A grimace takes over my features. "You need a fucking therapist."

"And you don't?"

My eyebrows shoot to my hairline at his response. "After I was kidnapped and locked in a basement? I do, too."

He wets his lips and I am forced to look away. "No. I am talking about the way you almost killed your mother, Lilith." His stern voice slices through me, causing my chest to constrict, and heat floods my face when I'm caught off guard.

"How do you know that?"

"Searched through the old local medical records. She almost had a lethal overdose, didn't she?"

I force down a lump in my throat. "I don't know what are you talking about."

"Remember, I will never accuse you of anything. I don't bother with what you did, little devil. But stop denying me and thinking that we are different."

As I am stunned, he takes hold of my hand. With a gentle squeeze, his words penetrate the deepest recesses of my being, blending with my anger toward him, "We are bonded, my girl. Our connection goes beyond mere obsession or love. Neither of us will ever encounter anyone similar. We are truly alone in this world."

I tightly shut my eyes, allowing the tears to stream freely down my face. They trickle over my cheeks, carrying with them a mix of heat and saltiness, and flow into my mouth. A queasiness churns in my stomach as his words sink in, the realization hitting me that I'm still drawn to the serial killer who believes we're kindred spirits and might have spared me only because he saw our similarities.

I pause before opening my eyes. "When can I get out of here?" I inquire, swiftly redirecting my gaze toward his chest. I just can't bring myself to meet his eyes.

"Where do you want to go?"

I can't contain my sudden laughter. "As if you'll let me go wherever I want?"

"I own the huge area we're in right now. This house and acres of woods surrounding it—the territory is all mine. We can take a walk around here if you want to."

"With me on the chain behind you?" I scorn with contempt.

"Do you want to be chained, baby?"

"Stop being an idiot. Okay. I want to get out of here."

I've never seen the house he's keeping me in, not to mention the woods he's talking about. And as much as I hate the fact that he is going to walk around by my side, controlling my every move, I can't resist such an opportunity. Because no matter how much of an introvert I am, I can't keep fucking rotting in this basement no matter how cozy and pleasant it looks.

I need a fresh air.

"Okay. Get up." After saying that, he walks to the door and half-opens it, waiting for me.

I eye him skeptically, unsure if he's really letting me out just because I asked. However, I'm not going to sit here and wait for him to change his mind, so I comply, getting up and walking toward him.

Once we're out of the basement, he places his hand on my shoulder, then shuts and locks the door. I glance at the keys in his hand, attempting to think of something I could do with it, but nothing comes to mind.

Caleb shoves them into the pocket of his sweatpants and turns his face to me. "Planning on knocking me out and stealing the keys, little devil?"

Fuck him. "I am not going to just knock you out. I am going to bash your brains, and get out of here only when I'll be sure that you're dead."

He bites his bottom lip and slightly nods as if what I've just said has turned him on. "No doubts you'll do that."

I want to throw something hurtful at him, but I can't think of anything. I used all of the possible curse words on him a couple of times, and if I'll call him *motherfucker* or *fucker* or something like that again, no doubt that he's going to whoop my ass again.

I don't want to feel embarrassed again. Besides, it gets old. I need to think of something new.

His possessive hand remains on my shoulder as we climb up the stairs and he opens another door.

The corners of my eyes round in shock from the picture I see.

A glass house. It doesn't have a single wall—everywhere I glance, I see nothing but large windows surrounding it, opening the view on the dark woods around the place.

So many girls died in here, and the fucker doesn't even try to hide. He surrounded himself with nothing but a translucent glass as if he were sure that he'd never be punished.

This is fucked-up. So, so fucked-up.

"Impressed?" His calm tone sends shivers down my spine as I recoil, bowing my head down.

"That your torture house looks like a normal one? Yeah, a little impressed."

"I've never tortured anyone," he states coldly. "Except Evan."

Ignoring what he said, I take a few steps further. I expect him to grab my hand, blocking my freedom because I am nothing but a puppy he takes on a walk, but he doesn't stop me when I keep walking.

He probably hid all the knives and took care of an emergency exit in here, so I don't feel any better. Caleb isn't planning on letting me go, and this little glimpse of freedom is nothing but an illusion.

I should remember that.

I take a look around the house, and I'll admit, all the pictures I had in my mind while trapped in the basement aren't meeting my expectations right now. I thought we were in the middle of nowhere in a small box that looked more like a bunker rather than a place where people could live. But this house is the total opposite.

A lot of wood and warm lighting. One floor, but the area is large, with a huge bedroom, a living room with a tremendous plasma TV and a bathroom with a fucking jacuzzi instead of a regular shower.

It boggles my mind that he killed people in this place because on the outside it looks like nothing but a luxury house with as much comfort as you can possibly imagine. Makes me wonder how many pretty places like this are actually murder houses.

"We can spend our time here instead of in the basement," he begins in a calm voice. "More space here, plus the TV, if you like it."

I stop and meet his gaze. He radiates with calmness and confidence as if I am the girlfriend who just moved in with him, and he casually shows me my surroundings, deep down afraid that I may not like something.

That's what bothers me the most—his calmness transfers to me, enveloping me from head to toe. I don't know how he does that, and I don't know if I can prevent him from getting into my brain like this.

I leave him without an answer. The last place we're entering is the kitchen, and my eyes automatically scan the tables for the knives. And despite my thoughts about that he did hide all of them, here they are—stuck inside the holder, shape and size on every taste.

"See, I didn't hide anything because I trust you," he says, noticing how my eyes scan the knives.

Fuck, I can't be so obvious. "That's your mistake, Caleb."

A smirk stretches across his face that pisses me off. I can't give him the satisfaction. He loves my anger and denial, it empowers him.

I need to be smarter. He set his own rules for this sick game he started, and due to the fact that I can't escape—not now anyway—I need to think wider.

The best thing I can do now is pretend that I'm in. I need to give him the false hope that I can forgive him. That we have a future.

Caleb says he trusts me, but in reality, he knows I am capable of tricking him, throwing something ridiculously stupid to hurt him.

As much as I want to strangle him right now, I need to be patient. I can't just snap because it would only make everything worse for me—I am going to be trapped in the basement again, forced to look at the ceiling and make up a new plan, which is, no doubt going to be harder to think of than the one I can make up right now.

Caleb hands me his jacket before opening the front door. "It's cold outside."

Certainly, it is. If he hadn't given me my laptop, I wouldn't even know the date. Time moves differently when you're trapped in a basement. And I still can't bring myself to accept the fact that it's already the end of winter.

I take his jacket and pull it on, ignoring how pleasant his clothes still feel on my body. It reeks of his perfume, and I find myself wishing I could catch a cold and have a runny nose just so I wouldn't have to smell anything. But he won't let me get sick, so I swallow all of my emotions and soften my gaze as he shifts the glass door to the side and lets me out.

The air immediately hits my nose—so fresh and clean that it hurts. I inhale deeply, refilling my lungs and giving them what they craved for the past few weeks. After a moment, I take a few tentative steps further, as if I'm afraid that something is going to pop out at me like those mechanical monsters in haunted houses on Halloween.

But I become braver with each step as the realization washes over me—nothing here that could hurt me. Except the shadow that follows me right behind like a predator hunting his naïve little prey—slowly, but confidently—scanning each of my moves, giving me a false sense of freedom, an illusion.

"If you're thinking about running into the woods, I feel like I need to warn you that there are big and scary animals that will eat you without chewing," he explains calmly. "I wouldn't like you to take risks."

"Gators?" I ask, my question pulls an abrupt laugh out of him. "I am sure that your psychopathic rich ass could buy one or two in here in case the poor girls manage to knock you out and run away."

"I am not that cruel, little devil," he answers. "Your brain is so creative, though."

"Learning from my psycho boyfriend."

A surprised grimace takes over his face. "You still consider me as your boyfriend?"

Fuck. The words had left my mouth so easily that I never even stopped to consider how they sounded. That's not what I meant. "An old habit. But you're working hard on helping me to get rid of it."

"Because boyfriend sounds corny. The next name you'll be calling me is *husband*."

I sneer disdainfully. "In your dreams maybe."

Thank God he shuts up as we keep walking. His arrogance makes me want to punch him, which would be stupid, but restraining this need is impossible when he keeps getting on my nerves like a pebble in my shoe.

His murder house is located on the hill, which is pretty fucking disappointing because if I am going to run, the chance of me wrongly calculating the speed, stumbling against my own legs and rolling off the fucking hill is pretty high.

I have no idea how far the woods stretch, but something tells me it's going to take hours and hours of getting out of them if I decide to run through. Besides, I doubt Caleb was joking about animals. If not gators, then bears or a fucking lynx. New York woods are filled with different animals that aren't friendly by any means, and I don't want to test my luck.

Somehow, this area reminds me of the place where my mother lives. It would be ironic if she'd actually a block over from here, peacefully drinking her tea, having no clue that her daughter was kidnapped by a maniac and trapped in the basement.

Though I highly doubt if she knew, she would worry. I think she would be happy to see me suffer.

"What are you thinking about?" Caleb's voice behind me brings me back as I realize I just stare at the tree for I have no idea how long.

"Mother," I cut shortly.

"What about her?"

I shake my head, having no idea how to gather my thoughts into something coherent. "You forced me to remember about how I wished her bad, and now I can't unthink about it. Are you satisfied?" I turn my head and look at him from under my lashes. "Funny how I didn't remember anything before you started talking about demons in our souls and shit."

"Would you like that better, Lilith?" he asks. "Keeping your secrets deep down when in reality you know you can't escape the truth?"

"I don't know."

"You *do* know. You're just afraid that you can't live with that. That's what I am trying to tell you, little devil. It isn't something you should be afraid or ashamed of."

"And how should I feel? How are you feeling knowing that you killed innocent people, Caleb?"

He tilts his head, his piercing gaze darting across me from head to toe as if he is trying to detect the thing I doubt I can get used to. That I ask this mechanically, when in reality, when I say *innocents*, I sense very little.

I should care more. These thoughts should be all I have to think about. But I don't. The feeling isn't strong enough to cloud my love for Caleb.

"The only thing I care about is your condition, Lilith. I care about what will we do next. About our future. I have no desire to waste time on the thoughts about my past and on regrets of my previous choices," he explains. "I enjoyed killing people. Until I met you and realized that I could feel something besides anger and desire to take power over them. I love you, and I don't give a fuck about your little attempts to convince yourself that you don't love me back and that you don't need me."

277

I give a disapproving shake of my head. "You don't love me, Caleb. You are *obsessed* with me and with the darkness inside of me that you forced me to embrace."

"I possess every demon in your soul the same way you possess them in mine. And one day you'll understand that running from me is no different than running from your true self, my Lilith."

CHAPTER

THIRTY–FOUR

Lilith

I moved out to the upper floor and I now spend all my time in a glass house, alone, surrounded only by luxury pieces of furniture.

Mostly I read, write, or surf through TV reality shows or movies. The illusion of my freedom pops like a balloon as soon as I glance once again at the cameras all around the house—white balls shining red in every corner of every damn room.

Ah, and all doors and windows are locked from the outside, so I can't go out even if I want to just catch some fresh air. Caleb works almost the whole day and gets home around seven p.m., always in the same cheerful mood as if he doesn't hold me as a prisoner in here.

As I finish watching a silly romantic comedy I only put on to keep me company, the doors unlock, and I hear the weight of his footsteps on the wooden floor. I don't bother looking at him when he enters the living room.

"Hey," he greets.

"Hey," I answer mechanically. My legs are crisscrossed on the coffee table, and he takes them in his hands, raises them to clear the way, and then sets them back down as he plops down in the seat next to me.

"A rom-com? Seriously?"

"Just to keep me company," I blurt out while attempting to hold my breath as the pleasant scent of his perfume tickles my nose, knowing deep down that I could never bring myself to feel repulsed by his scent no matter how hard I try.

"I saved thousands of good thrillers in here just for you." He takes the remote from my hands, pressing the buttons to rid us of this terrible movie and find something else to watch. "Here."

He did, in fact, save thousands of movies in my favorite genre. I just never noticed.

"Cool. Thanks."

"If you want something else, you can tell me."

"I don't."

"Maybe a horror movie?" he pushes. "I've never seen you watching any movie in this genre."

"Because I don't like horror."

"Have you ever watched any?"

A frown takes over my face as I try to remember. "I didn't," I lie. I watched one when I was a kid, but that was more like an accident, so it doesn't count, I guess.

"Then how do you know that you don't like it?"

"I live in a horror," I taunt insultingly. "I don't need more of that in my life."

But Caleb never listens. He scrolls through the library of movies on the TV, the sound of him clicking his fingers on the remote fills the room as the awkward silence envelops the space between us.

My stupid fucking brain sends me a little signal, and I focus my stare on his hands. On his fingers, to be precise, recalling the memory of them being inside of me. And now, even when he does something simple—presses the damn buttons on the remote, forcing the blue veins across his skin to bulge with every movement—I can't take my eyes off him.

The longer I stare, I detect a throbbing between my legs—a signal that with every single day, I am becoming more and more fucked-up, somehow even more than I used to think I was. I shouldn't be attracted to a man like Caleb. Though this thought was supposed to cross my mind way earlier, the moment he started to stalk me, not now, when he already locked me in the glass house.

I get my legs on the couch and hug my knees, trying to distract myself from the heat that now envelops my cheeks along with the unstoppable throbbing in my pussy.

"Let's make some popcorn," he offers as he gets up and stretches his hand to me. "We can't watch the movie without it."

I rise and disregard his outstretched hand as I quickly make my way past him and head toward the bedroom.

"I don't want to watch a movie with you."

With just two swift steps, he catches up to me, his arm enveloping my waist as he effortlessly lifts me up and carries me like a fucking mannequin.

"I never asked what you want, my love."

I struggle, trying to slap his hands away, but, as always, it's pointless. Upon entering the kitchen, Caleb releases me, and I proceed to straighten out my rumpled clothes, attempting to undo the mess he created. I observe as he retrieves the popcorn from the shelf, opens the microwave, and inserts the bag of popcorn. With an annoyed expression, I press my palms onto the table, watching him.

"Make us some tea," he commands, and I almost snort at his tone, surprised at how he still manages to think that I'll obey him without hesitation.

"Your idea, so you are the one who will make it."

Caleb gets every single tea box that he has—seven different flavors—and demonstratively shoves them to my side.

"Even if the flavor is an ass, somehow, you still manage to make the tea good. I don't have that power." Then, he clicks the button on his electric kettle, starting the inevitable process of boiling the water.

I roll my eyes at his little attempt to trick me. "That's because you need to read the instructions. If it says you need to remove the tea bag after two minutes, you have to stick to it. So when you're always off in the clouds, forgetting that you even have the tea in the kitchen, and then come back after ten minutes when it already tastes like bitter ass, no tea will taste good."

A warm smile makes its way across his perfect features. "See how smart you are? Make us tea, Lilith."

I don't want to keep arguing with him because it's fucking pointless. This conversation has already drained me. And made me thirsty. So, I guess I'll make the damn tea. I don't bother looking at him, I just grab the cups and choose the box with herbal tea.

I need to calm myself down, and as for him, there's a slight chance that he will relax too, and, therefore, stop talking for good. Maybe forcing me to make tea is not a bad thing after all.

As I open the box, a delightful aroma of herbs wafts out, greeting me. I lift it to my nose, inhaling deeply before carefully measuring the appropriate amount of herbs onto the teaspoon and filling the bags.

"You look so cute when you're concentrated," he states, reminding me of his presence. Though he doesn't need to talk to remind me that he's here. It's hard to ignore a 6'8 mammoth who watches you closely, shadowing more than half of your world with his silhouette.

I flip him the bird and he laughs. I maintain a blank expression, concealing the urge to fucking slap him.

Once the popcorn and tea are ready, we bring them to the living room, instantly filling the space with the delightful blend of herbal scents and caramel popcorn. My stomach growls at that as I detect a sudden urge to eat. I didn't feel hungry at all, but now, I guess, I want to eat.

Caleb switches off the lights, leaving only the gentle glow of the large plasma screen to illuminate us.

"Why do you need to turn everything off?"

He takes the remote and presses the play button. "It's more romantic this way."

I shield my eyes with my hands and shake my head. "Caleb—"

"For a better effect," he interrupts, making himself comfortable near me—in fact, too close to me. "It will feel like we're in a cinema."

I scoot away from him, but as always, he doesn't care about my desires—his arm wraps around my waist and he pulls me back to him as I bump into his side. I take a few deep breaths as I try to calm myself down and accept the fact that I am going to need to sit like this for an hour and a half at minimum, if not longer. I want to ask him how long the movie is, but that would only show him how uncomfortable I am, and he would just laugh in my face.

So, I guess, I am keeping my mouth shut, only being able to make guesses.

The opening ten minutes already feel tense—the movie doesn't give a fuck about telling more about the characters or their motivations—it throws us right into the crater of unease. And frankly, for me, the girl who cares the most about the thoughtful build of the characters and their story, I already feel annoyed.

"I don't like it," I mumble in frustration. I feel how Caleb switched his eyes from the screen to me, but I don't bother looking back at him.

"Scared, little devil?"

"I'm not scared. It's just stupid."

"You don't even try to give it a chance," he complains. "Shut your pretty mouth and watch it."

Caleb begins to softly caress my waist, reminiscent of a lover's touch, but for some inexplicable reason, it makes me mad. Mad because of him ruining everything that could be between us. Mad for him telling me the truth only under pressure. Revealing his true nature right at the moment when I said I love him back.

Right after I just began to understand what it feels like to be loved and cared for by someone. He tries to make everything normal, to pretend like nothing bad happened and we are just a lovely couple that watches a movie on Friday evening in an embrace. He forces me to believe in all of this, forces me to accept us. But I doubt that I can do that.

I don't know *what* I am anymore. I don't know what I feel or what I want. I am only able to realize that I am in a fucked-up situation, and by this moment I should start thinking about what to do next, whether it be staying and accepting, or planning on running away.

A loud scream brings me back from my thoughts—one of the main characters has already been killed. I try to understand what killed him, analyzing the creature on the screen. I guess I missed an explanation as to what that was because I was thinking about me and Caleb. But I agreed to watch this, and the best way to make the time fly faster is to dive deep into the film, and at least pretend like I am interested.

"What do you think it is?" Caleb breaks the silence, attempting to hear my thoughts about the mysterious force that keeps killing everyone. I never missed anything; this movie just didn't bother to explain, which is not surprising. The laziness of the writers and directors is justified as this is how it's supposed to be, therefore, we can keep doing this, confusing the audience even more, passing it off as our tricks.

"The guy who owns this cabin feels odd," I answer, grabbing a handful of popcorn and shoving a couple of pieces into my mouth. "I think he will be alive at the end."

He repeats after me, grabbing more popcorn for himself. "And how is that?"

"The creature, or whatever the fuck it's called, attacks everyone with a bigger force. He got off with a little scratch on his head while half of his friends were strangled, beheaded, or gutted. Doesn't it tell you something already?"

"Maybe he is just lucky?"

I shake my head in denial. "It was his idea all along, wasn't it? I mean, to get in the cabin. I believe he trapped his friends here and now he kills them one by one."

Caleb's eyes are glued to the side of my face this whole time, and I doubt he's even blinking. "Why are you smiling?"

"Because I hate how corny this movie is. Everything happens in the damn cabin in the woods, and it's a fucking cliché," I explain, waving my hands in the air to show the scale of my frustration. "That's why I hate horror movies. Their ideas end at demonic possession, a laughably invisible human killer, or a fantastic idiotic creature. It isn't even close to reality, which makes this genre pointless."

"You're saying you hate the genre when you never watched any?" he asks, skepticism evident in his voice.

"I don't need to watch it. I already know the outcome for all of them."

Caleb presses me closer to him, his scent occupying my nose once again, and I squint, trying to focus on something else. "I love it when you're being a smart-ass, my love."

"I'm not being a smart-ass, Caleb. It's just my opinion."

"Most people watch horrors to catch up with the feeling of fear," he explains, leaning closer to my ear. "They want to awaken their adrenaline, triggering the chemicals in their brains so that they contemplate what they would do when their lives are threatened."

As his hand glides from my waist to my shoulder, a gentle brush of his finger sends a shiver down my spine. Inwardly, I curse myself for not draping some sort of cape around me. "There are different types of horrors, Lilith. Not every movie is a cliché such as a massacre in a deserted cabin. Some of the ideas are more about the psychology of humans."

"And what can this genre possibly offer in a psychological aspect, huh?" I ask in a mocking voice, whipping my gaze toward him for the first time since the movie began. "A story about a mentally ill person who butchered his family and friends?"

"It's not always about gore and blood, little devil. For the person who enjoyed watching horror films since I was a kid, I can easily tell you about some good plots."

"Name one."

He graces me with a warm smile, perhaps delighted that I am displaying interest, even if only in this one thing. "A movie where the main character deals with grief."

Regardless of my skeptical stance, he launches into it anyway. "Let's say it's a girl who lost her mother. The feeling of grief is a superior idea in this movie, but the second one, not less important than that, is spirits. The girl tries to talk to her mother through the session, desperate and consumed by her grief, but she goes too far, in the end, calling some demons instead of the spirit of her mother. It kills her friends, the rest of her family, and maybe her, too. It's not just a slasher because the foundation for the gore and blood in this one is the power of grief and what it could do to humans. How far they can go to reach out to their loved ones."

I was ready to throw something at him, like another skeptical look or an idiotic grin. Instead, my teeth clicked shut, and my expression shifted from one of boredom to one of genuine interest before I even realized it.

Now I find myself in a stupid position because of how narrowly I actually thought about the genre. I don't even know where the hate came from, especially when I never bothered to watch something besides a teen slasher I accidentally watched when I was a kid. I was driven by an urge to do something that I shouldn't—a typical reckless child behavior—and I surfed the TV, eventually finding a 90s cheap slasher.

I was never the same after seeing so many guts, brains, and blood.

The subject suddenly captivates me, igniting a deep desire to delve deeper into it. "What else?"

A tiny smirk touches the corner of his lips. "Guilt. The same concept here, the main character could be a guy who saw how his family was butchered by a masked killer when he was a child. He could be the only one who escaped him, and then for years trying to find him, eventually stumbling on something more than just a butcher psychopath. The killer could be possessed during the time he was murdering the guy's family, and eventually, the main protagonist would deal with something more powerful, eventually dying from its hands."

Caleb lowers his head, seemingly enveloped in his own thoughts. "Or maybe he would go not alone, inviting all of his friends so they could help, and eventually everyone would be dead except him, therefore, the feeling of guilt of not doing anything to save his family would change to the feeling of guilt of inviting his friends and losing them in the process of the restoration of justice."

His words make me think. If you dig deeper, most movies actually have a lot more to them than meets the eye. I've never bothered to think wider about any of this because I simply wasn't even interested, yet now, I find myself invigorated and compelled to explore further within this genre.

"That…makes sense," I answer in a hushed tone.

"Well, not every single horror movie has much depth, my love. Some of them are as narrow as you think they are, showing nothing but guts and blood. But even this concept has its own fans."

"And what idea do you prefer?"

He takes a moment to think. "Depends on the mood. When I am tired and all I want is to relax, I may turn on a movie about a group of stupid teens being butchered by an indescribable force in the woods."

Shockingly, my eyes widen. "A nice picture to loosen to."

He beams. "Everyone has their own way."

I guess he is right. We watch the rest of the movie in silence, both immersed in it, never stopping guessing what the fuck is actually happening in it, because with every single second, it just gets more and more confusing, leaving us with dozens of questions.

But when the last ten minutes confirm my guesses from the start, I can't help but jump from the couch, almost flipping off the empty bowl of popcorn, screaming, "I TOLD YOU SO."

So, the person who set everything up was the guy who invited everyone in the first place. He made everything look like there was some creature—an indescribable force—that killed everybody when in reality, it was him and his other fucked-in-the-head friends. Their motivation was to have some fun, and, of-fucking-course, to get famous by recording everything and eventually uploading it online.

"This one was not that impressive," I state, proud of myself. I predicted everything during the first thirty minutes of the movie. We could just scroll through it and save our time.

"Are you sure that it is everything?" Caleb asks calmly.

A frown touches my face. "What do you mean?"

He doesn't say anything, just points his chin at the TV. Sinking back onto the couch, I await the end of the credits, eager to uncover the post-credit scene promising a revelation beyond what I've just witnessed. And when I see what Caleb is talking about, everything drops down inside me and my lips part in surprise as I am only able to stare at the screen, admitting my defeat.

The movie was made based on true events. This damn cliché movie is a real fucking story.

"What? That can't be possible," I protest desperately.

"You want to Google it?"

I shoot him an exasperated glance, and he reaches for his phone, typing away. As he hands it to me, I skim through the article detailing the deranged individual central to the movie.

"Real life can be a boring cliché, too," he says, his pride palpable.

I check a few more articles, then hand him the phone back. "Shut up."

As I am staying upstairs now, I am forced to share my bed with Caleb. Every time before going to sleep, I try to convince him to unlock my basement so I can sleep there, but he, of course, never agrees. We spend more time together now, and he wants us to sleep in one bed. Pressed against each other, he never attempts to encroach beyond respectful boundaries, his hands and lips never venturing where they shouldn't. Thanks for that alone, I guess.

About thirty minutes ago, Caleb drifted into slumber, the weariness of the day causing him to almost black out, his murmurs referencing the day's toil. Now, he rests soundly, one hand gently cradling my waist while the other rests above my head on the pillow, resembling the peaceful sleep of a contented baby. Right now, I envy him for how effortlessly he's able to recline and fall asleep.

Meanwhile, my mind brims with a swarm of thoughts, rendering it impossible to keep my eyes closed, even for a fleeting moment.

As I roll over, Caleb's hand rests heavily on my waist, almost as if it is a chain itself. It takes me three attempts to roll over completely, finally facing him. In the tranquil lunar glow seeping through the curtains, his countenance boasts impeccably flawless features, reminding me of an ethereal being at rest. The sight of him so innocent makes me want to touch his skin and kiss his peaceful face.

Which is so fucking wrong.

I still can't believe that this man is a serial killer. I picture how he got rid of the bodies, then returned here, and went to the same bed we're lying in right now—calm and unbothered—as if taking someone's life is nothing serious.

A tear slips past my cheek, staining the white sheets as I can't rip my eyes off him. I hate this man. I hate how he forced himself into my life, how he showed kindness and made me feel beautiful, rousing a tumult of unfamiliar emotions within me.

Emotions so consuming that I can't fucking stop them, not even in the face of his monstrous nature.

But maybe it's my fault that I can't stop myself from feeling toward him. Maybe I am not doing enough, just blindly hoping that it will come naturally. Maybe I need to finally fucking do something.

But what options do I have? The only impulse gripping my mind right now is the urge to hurt him. I can't simply fall out of love with him, yet he possesses that ability. He can stop loving me. Or he can stop feeling anything at all, both mental and physical.

Right?

As my mind sifts through potential solutions, I realize that my words hold no sway over him. It's my actions that might make a difference. I'm not referring to mere slaps or other attempts at physical retribution—actions so utterly laughable that they're a stark reflection of my own foolishness. When I look at him now, he doesn't seem so tough and strong. He seems vulnerable. Caleb's trust in me is evident—enough to share a bed without concern that I might deceive him while he sleeps.

I warned him that this was his biggest mistake. He never stashes the kitchen knives away. What if I could filch one and hide it under my pillow? It doesn't seem overly complex. His routine is familiar to me; I can calculate the brief moments when he won't review the camera footage—perhaps during his return home, it's achievable.

I just have to be brave.

And I need to aim for the throat. Or somewhere where it can slow him down. There won't be a second chance. He kept convincing me to embrace my demons and stop feeling scared of them. Here comes the time when I'll finally do that.

VIOLENT TREMORS COURSE THROUGH MY ENTIRE BODY, WHILE MY palms persist in their clammy state no matter how often I attempt to wipe them against my thighs. Today was another movie night, but I couldn't concentrate on the screen at all. I kept acting normal (at least trying to), and I don't think Caleb had noticed anything. Once more, he was utterly exhausted today, so much so that he dozed off halfway through the movie.

I find myself darting my eyes back and forth between him and the flickering pictures on the screen, battling my inner turmoil as I attempt to summon the will to slide out from under him, snatch the knife, and act on my plan.

Never before have I felt as overwhelmed as I am at this moment. Strangely, it's as if half of my body has succumbed to paralysis. Perhaps it's because Caleb has dozed off, his arms embracing my waist like a tender cocoon, bathing me in his comfort. It becomes increasingly challenging to reaffirm to myself that he is a walking evil and deserves to be punished when he consistently exhibits care and tenderness toward me.

I draw in a deep breath and begin disentangling myself from his firm embrace. With measured movements, I carefully lift both of his hands and set them aside before I finally release myself, slip out, and lower to the floor. As I exhale, the quivering of my breath reverberates through my entire body. Rising to my feet, I steal one final glance at him—clearly too large for the couch—he lies with his face nestled into the pillow, his chest undulating in a tranquil, steady rhythm. He has no idea about everything I've prepared for him.

Without giving myself time to reconsider, I wrench my gaze away from him and make my way to the kitchen. Though I stashed a knife under the bedroom pillow, he's drifted off on the couch to-night, and the kitchen's proximity to the living room works to my advantage—I can expedite the process of getting the weapon.

I extract the knife from its holder, moving as quietly as I can. It shimmers under the bright light of the kitchen lamp—the blade glistens with a flawless sheen. Touching the tip with my forefinger, I assess its sharpness. With a hiss, I swiftly retract my finger as a jolt of pain courses through my body. It's sharp enough to cut through anything, even the seemingly invincible skin of Caleb.

As I walk back to him, the weight on my shoulders seems to intensify with each step. Anxiety churns in my stomach, and no matter how many times I swallow, my throat remains dry—an un-relenting surge of emotions steadily multiplies with every passing second, refusing to be contained.

But I will be fine. Cold-blooded murder isn't in my nature at all, but under these circumstances, I can force myself to do it.

I won't have to do anything like this again.

It's just one time.

I narrow the gap between us, and force myself to look at his face. Yet, I refuse to see the man I once believed him to be; instead,

I conjure the image of a brutal serial killer. I steel myself to visualize his callous indifference toward others and the unwavering certainty with which he took innocent lives.

Raising the knife, I suddenly notice the tremble in my hands. I can't afford to let go of the knife. I tighten my grip, collecting every ounce of strength within me. I steady the knife, targeting the side of his throat, inhaling a deep breath, and trying to disregard the unexpected flood of tears.

I meet his half-closed, drowsy, but now alert dark eyes.

He woke the fuck up. And he is staring at me.

I'm stunned, and my eyes nearly fall from their sockets, but I don't wait—I stab him with all the remaining force I have inside me. In the shoulder. He caught me off guard. I accidentally stabbed him in the place I never intended to stab. Caleb lets out a pained groan as I thrust the knife in as deeply as possible, then snatch the keys from his pocket before making a dash for the front door without a glance backward.

"God fucking DAMN IT!" His screams jolt me, the rage in his voice causing me to flinch. In my haste, I drop the keys, but I seize them again without delay. "I'll *kill* you for this, Lilith!"

Jesus Christ. I fucked up. So, so fucking much. If he catches me, he kills me right away, I know he isn't fucking around.

Sliding the glass door to the side, I hurriedly step outside, briefly catching a glimpse of his silhouette in the corner of my eye.

He chases after me.

The moment I glance outside, the biting cold wind slices through my entire body and snowflakes settle on my skin, causing me to shiver uncontrollably.

As I attempt to escape a fucking maniac, the timing couldn't be worse for it to start snowing. However, catching a cold is the least of my concerns right now.

Inhaling the sharp, frigid air, I fill my lungs.

And I run.

I run barefoot in my thin pajamas at night, pushing myself to do it as fast as I can. The adrenaline courses through my veins like a dose of the best drug that ever exists as I pick up the speed and race down the hill.

The rustling of the grass and leaves not far behind me tells me that he is catching up with me. He is much taller and faster, and I am fucked if I don't move my ass quicker.

Caleb chases me like a skilled predator stalking his little prey, and my body is already weary. The chill outside is seeping into my feet, and I feel the impending numbness, as well as the discomfort in my throat from gulping down the freezing air.

I acted like an idiot when I didn't prepare myself for a plan B. I recklessly thought I was going to be brave enough to stab him in the throat and then leave this place with no rush.

As my body begins to shut down from the cold, I can't help but blame myself for the situation. However, a glimmer of hope appears as I spot blinding lights in the distance down the road.

A car.

A smile creeps onto my face before I realize it as I sense a rush of strength across my body and the wind that was my burden a minute ago, is now nothing more than a helping jolt into my back that forces me to run even faster.

"Hey! I'm here!" I scream, waving my hands at the car. "HELP!"

Just when it feels like the car slows down, aware of my voice, something knocks me off my feet as I fall on my stomach, my face almost dips into the dirt. A body presses into my back, one arm circling my waist when the other one slaps on my mouth, silencing my screams.

No. It can't end like this. I am too fucking close.

I keep trying to scoot away from under him when he leans to my ear. "Don't make a fucking sound."

I want to protest, to bite his hand and scream for help, but I can't. I feel even more fragile under the pressure of his weight, and the effects of everything I was afraid of, start to slightly occupy my body. I feel weaker with every second. My whole being feels sticky and dirty with sweat and mud from the ground, my hair is wet from the snow, my throat hurts—I probably already caught a cold—and my face feels swollen from all the tears I am spilling right now.

I keep whimpering and sobbing under him—the heat of his body is the only thing that warms me up right now—as I am only able to watch how the car drives past, not seeing us among the night darkness, appearing more far and far away.

I had a chance to escape Caleb. But now it's over for me.

After ensuring that the car has vanished, he hoists me onto his shoulder like a sack of potatoes and carries me back to the house. "Let me fucking go, you psychopath!" I try to scream, but it comes out as a raspy plead.

"You made me really upset, little devil," he says, delivering a loud, painful slap on my ass that pulls another raspy sound from me. "You act like a bad, bad girl. And bad girls need to be taught a good lesson."

Oh, God. He is going to do something horrible to me, I know that. I wish I'd rather fall off and hit my head against the stone or something like that. I don't want him to torture me. I don't think I will be able to live after that.

"Caleb, don't hurt me," I mumble through the tears while he gets us back in the house. "Please don't do anything."

But he doesn't answer. Instead, he carries me back to the living room and throws me on the floor—my back welcomes the fluffy carpet as it tickles my half-numb back. He backs away just for a second, but when he returns, he hovers over my being, this time with his face to mine. He keeps eye contact when he brings the bloody knife I stabbed him with to my face.

"Oh, God," I gasp, not prepared for whatever he is going to do right now. "Please, Caleb—"

"You stabbed me with my own knife, Lilith," he interrupts, his breathing still erratic from the chase. "Don't you realize how *impolite* that was?" He shifts the knife's tip toward my lips. "Open your mouth."

I try to move my face away. "Please, Caleb—"

A sinister sneer plays across his face as he growls, "Don't make me repeat myself."

I comply because the last thing I want to do is make him angrier if that's even possible. He carefully brings the knife to my tongue. "Lick it."

What the fuck is he planned to do? It could be even worse than I already pictured myself.

I do as he says, slowly touching the place where his blood ends with my tongue. "For fuck's sake, don't just touch it, lick it," he barks, and I shut my eyes in an attempt to alleviate the shame of his coercion.

I run my tongue from bottom to top, feeling the coppery taste of his blood. "That's my good girl," he praises after I circle the knife, his words sending indescribable sensations coursing through my body.

Then, without even realizing it—probably still in shock from everything that has happened for the past ten minutes—I wrap my lips around the tip of the knife and suck it, carefully swirling my tongue across the edge of the blade. "Oh, fuck me," he breathes, I feel his stare boring into me. "This is fucking beautiful."

When I'm done, I open my eyes and he takes the knife out of my mouth and brings it to my top. The blade touches the middle of my pajama, right at the recess of my breasts.

He slightly presses the knife to the cloth and draws the line down, slicing the thin fabric in one slow movement. "Don't move," he warns, sucking the air out of my lungs with his sick enjoyment from my fear as I anticipate his next move. "I don't want to slice up this tender skin of yours."

This is fucked-up. In so many ways. But I can't do anything than just allow him to do what he intended to. When Caleb is done with my top, he moves to my shorts, doing the same thing with them. He cuts them apart, and moves the pieces of cloth to the side, leaving me completely naked in front of him. His free hand travels down to my pussy as he shamelessly digs his fingers inside me, the pool of my wetness envelopes him right away.

"Punishing you feels more pleasant than I thought it would, my love."

"Please, stop it," I beg, releasing a pathetic sob from my lips. "Caleb—"

"I should stop? I haven't stabbed you in the shoulder, have I? Although I have to admit that you impressed me." Pride colors his voice as an inferno of vexation and lust blazes in his dark eyes.

I shake my head, but he doesn't back away from me. I watch how he moves the knife right between my legs and turns it in a way its handle is right in front of my slit. "*Oh, God*—"

When he pushes the tip of the knife handle inside me, a loud gasp slips past my lips. My eyes widen as I feel something unusual inside me, causing discomfort. "Spread your legs wider," he commands, tapping his fingers on my leg, but I shake my head. "Lilith."

Tears won't stop flooding through my eyes as I comply, and he pushes the handle further, forcing my head to kick back at the sensation. We haven't had sex for some time, and I forgot how it is—to feel anything inside me.

"See how easily it slides inside you, little devil?" he asks, his voice thick with sick lust. "So fucking wet that I don't even need to prepare you."

I am, in fact, wet. Even too much. I don't even remember how I got to this point, but now when I feel everything closer, it forces shame to spread across my body, consuming every inch of my consciousness. I feel how a deep crimson flush suffuses my cheeks.

Caleb begins to move the handle faster in and out, giving me zero time to process what the fuck is even happening, as I am only able to cry and gasp for air with my head kicked back. His thumb circles my clit at the same pace while the knife handle digs deeper inside me, hitting that spot over and over again.

"What have you learned, my love?" he asks, teetering between gentle and rapid motion, forcing me to experience something beyond pain, something profoundly captivating.

Lust, anger, and despair overwhelm my mind. Heat coils within, spreading from my womb and propelling me into a desired oblivion. "I'm sorry I stabbed you," I utter with a squeal, my eyes tightly closed.

"I never told you to apologize. I asked what have you learned."

"Don't stab you," I answer, my voice grows shakier with every minute. "I've learned that I am not allowed to stab you."

"Not until I ask you to," he corrects, bringing his mouth closer to mine. "Can I be sure you've learned the lesson?"

Pleasure surges in fierce waves, causing my legs to buckle beneath me. "Yes," I whisper and he crushes his lips to mine, savoring the remaining taste of his blood mixed with my tears.

He kisses me like a man starving, and only now do I realize how I missed feeling his lips on mine. He always gave me kisses that made my head spin, whether they would be quick ones or something hungry like this one now.

I hate myself for how much I love it. I am a weak person, a person who goes along with her animal instincts and listens to her body more than her mind. Caleb's presence clouds my thoughts, especially when his touch ignites a fire within me, doing things to me that no one else ever could.

I want to tell my body to stop feeling this good, I want to prevent the orgasm before it hits me, but he keeps the right pace on my clit along with the handle that slides in and out of me, stretching my walls to impossible levels, and continues to deliver waves of pure pleasure through me as I realize I am seconds away from breaking apart.

His actions toward me are both twisted and toxic. Although he insists that he hasn't changed me and that I have always been as dark-minded as him, I cannot deny that he has had an impact on me. Now he is attempting to claim me and corrupt my soul, forcing me to suffer the consequences of my past actions toward him.

At the moment I am almost done, Caleb moves his finger away from my clit, keeping only the handle in its place. "Touch yourself, Lilith."

I know what he wants to do. He wants me to make me come myself so it would look like I've enjoyed this whole thing from the beginning. "No."

"Why do you keep denying your feelings, little devil?" he asks, capturing my whimper with his kiss. "Just admit that you love everything I do to you."

Before I can stop it, a moan escapes my lips, my body too powerless and inundated to resist the delightful sensations spreading throughout. "I'm not."

He shakes his head, then guides my hand to place two of my fingers on my clit. "You're going to come with my mouth devouring you and my knife fucking your pussy one way or another, Lilith. It's up to you whether I am giving you the pleasure of providing you the final bliss or you do it yourself."

I attempt to turn my head away from him, but his lips persistently pursue mine as he consumes me, nipping my tender skin and consuming every ounce of awareness and rationality remaining inside me, aiding him in leading me to the euphoria that only he can evoke. Stimulating myself to the brink with my own fingers is the least I can do to regain a semblance of control at this moment.

I begin to circle my clit at the precise rhythm, while he continues to penetrate me with a handle and passionately kisses my lips as if he cannot get enough of me. I cease to react to his mouth as my lips part and my eyes roll back. I succumb to euphoria before I even comprehend it, emitting a scream so intense that my own ears begin to ring, and my lungs feel starved of oxygen. My body trembles, and he enfolds me in his arms, offering the comfort and warmth of his own body as I teeter on the edge of the unknown.

With my eyes shut, I sense the brush of his lips against my cheek, and then a gentle peck, as if signaling the time to cuddle. When the gravity of everything that transpired descends upon me, I burst into tears once more, but this time with greater intensity and desperation. His body atop mine is the sole covering for my naked form, leaving me feeling exposed, more vulnerable than I've ever been before.

It doesn't even matter if I liked what he did to me because one way or another, I am officially corrupted and blemished without turning back.

Whatever Caleb aimed to prove to me, he achieved it. Perhaps he manipulated my thinking, or maybe he simply provided the push he claimed he would, but at this point, it no longer holds significance.

What matters is that I am already broken and I would not ever be the same anymore.

CHAPTER

THIRTY—FIVE

Caleb

"God fucking damn it," I hiss as another attempt to bandage my shoulder proves unsuccessful.

I neglected my wound yesterday, too caught up in chasing Lilith and punishing her. After a shower, we went straight to bed, ignoring the blood that stained the once-white sheets. Now, just an hour before work, I finally decide to take care of my wound, which has been bleeding throughout the night.

I am not mad at her, though.

When I opened my eyes, I was caught off guard by the sight of her hovering over me with a massive sharp object in her trembling hands. Her eyes were wide, almost popping out of her head. Her stab was more uncomfortable and unusual than painful, although she cut me deep. Not deep enough to stop me from running after her, but still, deep enough to feel discomfort.

For some fucked up reason, it makes me feel proud of her. Like a parent who watches their kid grow bigger and stronger, realizing they've learned all the lessons given to them and no longer need to be taken care of. However, in this case, the last one is impossible.

I will *always* take care of my little devil.

"Let me help you." My attention is diverted by a gentle voice as I turn my eyes toward her. Lilith's old pajamas are no longer an option—the dirty pieces of them are in the trash can—so I gave her my clothes. Now, she is wearing a pair of sweatpants and a T-shirt—garments that appear too big for her as if at any moment she is going to drown in them.

It's not the first time I've seen her wearing something of mine, but fuck me, now she looks hotter than ever. Maybe the main reason for my feelings is what happened last night when I fucked her with the same knife she stabbed me with, forcing her to come on it.

I'm still enthralled by the sight of her so disheveled—so opposite to her previous self, the version she pursued throughout her whole life. It's intoxicating and addicting to realize that I am the one and only who made her this way—peeled away all her fake layers, revealing that her sanity is rotten from the inside just like mine.

"If you're not planning on stabbing me again, then go ahead." When she wets her lips, a jolt of electricity shoots through my body, and she takes a few hesitant steps closer. Shamelessly, I allow my eyes to roam over her from head to toe, reliving the sweet memories of the previous night.

As I pursued her through the darkness, my desire for her intensified with every passing moment. It was an overwhelming feeling that consumed me, and I couldn't wait to finally catch up to her and deliver the punishment. But among all the sweet adrenaline and arousal, a slight beam of fear coursed through me, too.

Only a tiny thought about the possibility of her slipping away from my hands, escaping from me for good, had me fucking terrified.

I have no idea how I got from *she would be my tenth* to *I don't want to kill anymore and I am in love with her* point, but I can't deny that she changed me forever.

I don't think I will ever be the same.

Beneath Lilith's weight, the mattress sinks as she sits right beside me on the bed. "Does it hurt?"

Funny how she asks this only now. "It doesn't. But I am proud of you."

Her emerald eyes whip to mine, flashing all emotions at once. "You are proud of me for stabbing you?"

I nonchalantly lift my shoulders—the slight burning pain in my left one reminds me that I have to do something with this before work. "I am proud of you for finally seeing what you're capable of."

Her eyebrows pinch together. "Are you trying to make me a killer on purpose, Caleb?"

"You're far from becoming one," I answer. "Yet."

Lilith lets out a defeated sigh before grabbing the bandage from the nightstand. She starts wrapping it around my wound, her gaze fixated on the spot where she had stabbed me. Despite the intensity of her stare, there's no hint of fear or regret in her eyes. It's more like an *I need to try harder next time.* I observe her attentively, noting every single graceful movement, captivated by her beauty and the realization that she belongs to me.

"Done," she says after a brief moment.

I glance at my perfectly wrapped wound, and a warm feeling invades my stomach—a fucked-up thing to feel—something about the picture of her hurting me and then taking care of what she's done is turning me on. I imagine her doing something more to me, and my cock twitches in my pants at the tiny glimpse of the possibility of fucking her after she harms me in a fit of her intoxicating anger. Or letting her fuck me, taking all the control right after that, dominating me in the way she wants.

"Are you going to be late today?"

I shake my head, trying to get rid of the thoughts I definitely shouldn't have at the moment. "I'm going to try to come earlier." A smile emerges on my face. "Thinking about new ways of stabbing me?"

She adjusts her glasses, her gaze pierces into me. "What's that with your new schedule?" she asks, curiosity woven into her gentle voice as she completely ignores my little joke. "You've been coming home bone-tired."

The way she says *home* causes my stomach to flutter pleasantly. "Grayson's fault. He overloads us with new projects as if we don't have enough money and work already."

Her eyes flicker with something when I bring up his name, yet she remains silent. "Is everything okay?"

Her features soften. "Define okay."

I suppress a chuckle with a bite of my lip. "Though, really. I can take a vacation if you miss me."

"Stop being an idiot. I am perfectly fine."

"Ouch. Careful with the words you choose, my love."

Rolling her eyes, she expresses a nonchalant gesture. "Okay, if you're back to your idiot self, I am not participating."

She turns around to leave, but I grab her hand and pull her back toward me. She falls onto my lap as I try to distract her from her thoughts by nuzzling my face into her neck and inhaling her scent. The sweetness of her skin overwhelms me, making my head spin.

"I'm serious, little devil. If you need anything, tell me."

She reacts with a scoff. "You are funny."

I softly grasp her chin, tilting her pretty face toward me. "What about the books? Have you finished them already?"

Just for a fleeting moment, her eyes linger on my lips before locking onto my stare. "I did. They're better than I thought they would be. Thank you."

My eyebrows shoot to my hairline as I am taken aback by surprise. "Wow. Not a single *fuck you, psychopath*?"

Her head tilts, accompanied by a contemplative nod. "If you want to."

I gently sweep a strand of her hair behind her ear. "And what about your new book? Did you write anything?"

"I did. Almost finished it."

I must confess, there's a sense of excitement that I catch myself feeling when it comes to her upcoming second book. No secret that I am a fan of her work. "Can I read it?"

"No," she cuts shortly.

"What if I say please?"

She expresses disapproval with a shake of her head. "Nah."

"What if I beg on my knees?"

"Immediate no." She shrugs me off. "When I'm sure it doesn't suck ass, I will give it to you."

"It can't suck. Your writing is brilliant."

"Don't suck up to me."

"I am not. I'm just pointing out the facts."

Skepticism colors her gaze as she looks at me. "You are telling me this because you're obsessed with me. Your judgment is cloudy. You can't be trusted."

"Silly. I became obsessed with you *because* of how incredibly smart you are," I respond with complete honesty. "Smart, unique." I stop momentarily to think. "And pretty, of course." A tender kiss is placed on her temple. "So stop seeking flaws inside yourself, or I will think about a new punishment for your little stubborn ass."

Crimson blush paints her cheeks. "Aren't you supposed to go to work already?"

As I get up from the bed, I gently move her onto the pillows and recoil. I grab my sweatshirt and pull it over my bare chest, feeling the warmth and comfort of the fabric. "Choose a movie for tonight. Whatever you'd be interested in."

She remains unresponsive, lost in her thoughts, probably torn apart by the confusing feelings cascading down her insides. I thought that I ruined everything after she found out the truth about me, but with time passing, I realized that was a good outcome for us. Not the best, of course. I would prefer to tell her everything in a…softer manner, not just throw her into the crater of my darkness.

But maybe it was indeed the best way for her because she had no choice but to accept everything. She had plenty of time to think about every detail, to think about us. And now, after numerous attempts to resist me, she finally started not only to accept me but also to embrace me. Even if I ruined anything, that is her phony facade, the one she attempted to project to everyone, including me.

I don't feel like I did something wrong.

CHAPTER
THIRTY—SIX

Lilith

I stopped fighting back. Any thoughts that swirled in my mind, leaving me with nothing but countless flooding questions, are not even the background noise. They are just gone. And I don't think they're coming back.

My whole life, all I've been doing was hiding in the shadows. Countless times, I've tried to change my life so I would simply fit in. I tried to act differently, to dress differently, and to say words I would not ever say even if a gun was pressed to my temple. Despite all my attempts, the shadow that has defined me throughout my life has become deeply ingrained in my skin and seeped into my being without any hope of erasing it. I was nothing but a blank canvas—a person whom nobody ever noticed, let alone heard or understood. Trapped in my own shell without hope of escape.

Forever the unnoticed girl, the silent mouse with her lips stitched closed.

I never thought my life could change. I never even hoped for it—it was more like an unachievable dream of mine, hidden deep in the corners of my mind. I was nothing but an empty vessel until I found Caleb.

Well, he found me. The man of my dreams, the man who made me feel beautiful inside and out, who made me feel seen and important. Who showed me the other side of life and proved to me that I can live and not just survive or exist. He didn't just take my soul, he retained it for himself and has been, is, and will continue to protect it without giving me a chance to discard it.

When I found out more about this man, about what he has been doing for the past few years of his life, I felt as though everything had shifted. My instincts surged as I was forcefully confronted with every demon residing within his soul, unable to escape him.

He killed people, and if we had never met, no doubt he would still be doing that without a single thought of remorse. Or I could have become his tenth documented victim if I had never hooked him with something I never thought I had until he showed it to me.

Caleb and I share many similarities, and while I once believed I could never be more than a mere shadow, he proved me wrong. He forced himself into my life just as he compelled me to face each of my demons, and I have been resisting. For a long time. But now, I don't think I can keep doing it.

I don't think I want to.

Because no matter how sick and twisted the darkness lurking inside of my defiled soul is, with it, I feel whole. I feel like it's the most beautiful thing that could exist inside of me, mainly because it makes me feel like myself. I don't need to pretend when I am accepting it.

I don't need to run from it.

I don't feel tired anymore.

It feels like the thing I needed to do a long time ago, and finally, after so many years of resistance, I'm embracing it. Naturally, not without shame, fear, and confusion, but ultimately, encircling it fully.

My whole life, I fought with intrusive, not by any means sane, thoughts that kept stretching their claws into my head, attempting to consume me whole. And finally, I am able to let it go. Label me as insane, but I don't feel remorse.

It's because, for the first time in my life, I feel completely free. I don't want to run anymore. But it's not so fucking simple. Now, I feel angrier. As if my true personality contains not just unholy thoughts, but anger as well. In all aspects, from my mother to Caleb, all at once.

I glance at the side of his face as he works on his laptop, sipping the hot tea I made him. My gaze travels over his flawless features—a jawline so sharp it could carve marble more precisely than a sculptor, with a hint of stubble; his hair, as disheveled and wavy as ever; obsidian eyes fixed on the letters on the screen, so focused and serene that I want to break his concentration.

I want to *provoke* him.

To show him that it isn't okay to fucking gut me from the inside out, unraveling the darkness I wasn't quite prepared to embrace.

My gaze whips to his hands—long fingers clicking on the keyboard, the blue veins popping out with each movement he makes—forcing the heat to spike through my middle. The reaction is so familiar and laughably predictable that only adds fuel to the fire of building anger inside me.

While most men try too hard, he doesn't try at all. Every aspect of him pulls me in like a vortex, leaving me no opportunity to turn away.

And he sits here fully aware of what he is capable of. He knew I was his, he claimed me as soon as he saw me, already knowing that I couldn't resist him. It pisses me the fuck off because it shouldn't be like that.

I should have been smarter. Despite his perfect appearance, intelligence, and the way his touch feels on my skin. I shouldn't have been the stupid bitch who keeps listening to her heart or body or whatever the fuck I was listening to. Hell, I would like to say I needed to listen to my brain, but he is so deep down inside my head that even my cerebrum likes him.

Loves him.

"You don't even care, do you?" The words leave my mouth before I can process that I am talking.

Caleb rips his eyes off the laptop, meeting the flames of anger in mine. "What are you talking about?"

"I'm talking about the time when you started haunting me." As I clarify, a hint of childish indignation creeps into my voice. "You knew that I won't be prepared for any of this shit you forced into my life."

After a moment of staring, he shuts his laptop and slides it onto the coffee table. "Do I need to remind you that I've warned you I am not a good man, Lilith?" As he settles into the couch, a defiant glint appears in his eyes. "And what have you answered to that?"

I laugh scornfully. "You know what I am talking about, Caleb. Just admit that you are a selfish motherfucker who claimed me without even fucking asking me. That was only an illusion of a choice."

His eyes widen in surprise at the insult. He stays silent for a moment. "Okay. I admit it," he says, leaning his elbows on his knees. "You were mine before you had even realized that, it's true. And yes, I didn't give you a choice. And yes, I fucking claimed you despite the fucking shit of a person I am because when it comes to you, I am selfish. What else do you want me to say, Lilith?"

He raises his arms to the sides, waiting for me to speak, but I'm unable to. Speechless, I can only gaze at him wide-eyed, trying to anticipate what he will say next.

"I refuse to let you go because I fucking *love* you. Think whatever you want, but I truly love you. This is me," he contours himself with his hands, "and I am a fucked-up person who shows his love in a fucked-up way. You make me feel good in a way I've never felt before, and I want to do the same for you. I'm not going to let anything get in the way of us being together," he declares, his eyes fixed on mine.

"I don't want to lose you. No matter how many times you're angry at me, at the end of the day, you understand that we were always meant for each other. So yes, I am a fucking selfish, rotten-from-the-inside, horrible person who doesn't even deserve to be loved. But I'll keep taking what you give me, even though I know it's wrong and I don't deserve any of this. I'll keep trying to get *better* for you every day."

When Caleb stops talking, I am frozen in my seat. I blink up at him, still digesting everything he said. He doesn't take his dark eyes off me. I abruptly stand up from the couch, ready to storm into the bedroom, but I freeze halfway through my step.

I take a few seconds to compose myself before turning to him and slapping his face.

Hard.

His head jerks to the side, and he freezes in his stance. I wait for his reaction—whether he'll respond by striking me or hurling insults. But he does neither.

Therefore, I gather all the strength within me and deliver a firm slap to his chest. "Hit me," I challenge.

"No," he cuts, welcoming each of my punches as if it's a familiar action to him. My anger escalates with each punch he ignores—emotion intensifying—pressure spreading across my body with every reverberating slap against my bones. Hatred seeps from within me, the heat consumes me entirely as I persist without stopping.

"I said fucking hit me. You said you won't hurt me until I ask you to. So I am asking you now."

Caleb's stubborn nature is evident. His facial expression stays unmoved, not a flicker of a flinch. "You can beat me to death, I won't hit you back, Lilith."

Tears sting my eyes as I continue to slap and punch him, desperate to elicit the reaction I've longed for all this time.

Hatred.

With each passing second, I feel like I'm on the brink of bursting into hysterics. It's prompting me to do something unexpected—I clutch the collar of his hoodie and pull him toward me, pressing my lips against his. He immediately responds to the kiss as if he was waiting for this, his arms circling my waist and pulling me in his lap. I straddle him now, my hands still fisting the cloth as I hold on to it for dear life while he devours me.

The kiss isn't sensual and slow, it's the opposite—ravenous and untamed—as if we were famished for each other, each of us engaged in a battle to possess the long-awaited control.

He tightens his grip on my waist, his fingers skimming across it with a lover's touch. Without breaking the kiss, I seize his hands and guide them to my ass, urging him to hold me as tightly as he can.

"Fuck," he groans, disrupting our kiss, but I pull my lips back to him like a magnet because the last thing I want now is him talking.

I don't know what I've started, but I'd rather proceed in silence, with my mouth glued against his.

Within a moment, I can't even tell that we're kissing. It's more like we're both ravishing our mouths, exploring and feasting on each other. I rock my hips, sensing his firm erection against me. Fabric still divides us, but I can already envision the pleasure when he thrusts into me. I grab the edge of his hoodie and assist him in removing it, revealing his perfect abs. I run my hands along his chest, feeling each of his muscles tighten beneath my touch as my lips continue to kiss him. He tears my crop top apart—the sound of the fabric ripping fills the room, melding with my quiet gasp.

Without affording me a chance to act upon my desires, he envelops his lips around my nipple and sucks, causing my head to kick back, inviting his fondle. I bury my hand into his hair, gripping it as tightly as I can while holding him close, permitting him to continue only with what he initiated, without a chance for anything else.

He nibbles, kisses, and caresses me, prompting butterflies to erupt in my stomach—a blend of delightful feelings mingled with a nagging, pulsating ache between my legs. I allow him to transition to my other breast, keeping his head in the same position. A loud moan escapes me, while enjoyable sensations continue to wash over me like enveloping waves against my shores.

But what he's doing feels pleasurable—in fact, too pleasurable—and I don't want to climax yet. Not when I never carried out what I planned to.

I yank his head back forcefully before pressing my lips to his, but this time, I have no intention of giving him even an ounce of control. I start by biting his upper lip—so hard that I hear his skin tear between my teeth—inviting the metallic taste of his blood that fills my mouth. He groans from pain, but that doesn't stop me, in fact, it excites me to do the same with his lower lip. I do just that—I bite until I hear the split and taste his blood.

As I draw back and survey my handiwork, I feel a sense of relief. His hair is even more disheveled, with a few dark wavy strands cascading onto his forehead; his face is flushed from the impact of the slaps I delivered, and his lips are marred, both of them leaving a trail of blood.

A newfound energy crackles between us, thickening the air with something none of us has ever felt before. But I don't want to think about anything at this moment, so I trace my tongue over his mouth, encircling it over the blood, meaning to savor every single drop of it. He moans, pressing his hands harder into my ass, yet his grip never tightens too much, not even after I harm him.

I expect him to lose his composure, but he maintains his control. But I've just started. I want to push him on his back, but this couch is too fucking small and it pisses me off.

"Not on the fucking couch," I hiss, and he lifts me with his lips returning to mine as he carries me toward the bedroom, but that's not my desire, so I pull back. "Right here. On the floor."

He hesitates for a moment but eventually lowers both of us onto the plush carpet, and I assist him in removing the remainder of his garments, then repeat the same actions with mine—our clothes are undone in record time. I draw him closer as my lips move to his neck and I nibble, relishing the sound of his composure faltering.

It's the best sound I've ever heard, and I'm on the verge of wanting to tear every inch of his skin, drawing as much blood as I can. Caleb slides himself inside of me slowly, as if he's afraid to hurt me.

It's not what I want.

"Harder."

His warm breath pleasantly brushes across my face, and the groan he emits after burying almost his entire length inside me sends my eyes rolling back as I nearly scream from the intrusion. While he starts thrusting inside me, his lips press against mine, and I bite him again, wondering how much he can endure. I sense fire spreading throughout my entire body, an intense inferno searing my sensitive skin. My nails dig into his shoulders as I feel the tattoo resembling mine, evoking a nostalgic memory filled with anticipation and happiness from that day, almost compelling a few tears to escape from my eyes.

"I said harder," I demand through the kiss, and he obeys, but that still isn't enough for me. I shift our position—now his back is against the floor, and I am on top of him, just as I desired. I squint my eyes, sensing more pain than before—this angle feels more uncomfortable than the previous one. But I keep going, sitting my whole self on his cock, feeling with every inch of my body how he tears me apart, stretching my walls to impossible levels.

"Baby, take it slower," he says.

I shake my head as my breathing escalates. "Shut the fuck up." My eyes are closed as I ignore the pain, rolling my hips with the sensation of him buried even in my stomach, squashing every single butterfly that he freed previously.

Caleb raises up and wraps his hands around my waist, holding my position and readjusting himself in a way that allows me to take a breath. "You feel too fucking good, Lilith," he murmurs, placing a sensual kiss on my cheek. "So fucking tight. I love to feel how my cock rips you apart." His words send a surge of electricity through my entire body, warmth tingling in my lower stomach.

Just when I feel like I've finally grown accustomed to him, I place my palms on his chest and push him onto his back once more, unconcerned if it would feel too forceful for him. "And when did I allow you to get up?"

His bruised lips curve into a smile. "The dark side suits you so fucking good, little devil."

I feel like that, too. I arch my back as I keep rolling my hips, and his hands travel from my stomach to my breasts as he squeezes and starts to massage them.

"I wish you could see how gorgeous you are now," he says lovingly, his hands keeping the right pace that makes me melt beneath his touch. "While surrendering to my caress, allowing me to treat you like you deserve. Such a fucking goddess."

His words are more than enough to ignite a spark within me, and I'm not just referring to physical pleasure. Allowing him to see me in this state somehow makes me feel a little embarrassed. I am exposed, naked in every possible sense, letting him in to unravel me. But there's something more than mere embarrassment because permitting only him inside my body feels like real love.

I simply can't envision myself doing it with anyone else. I don't even want to picture someone else other than this psychopath.

I grab him by the cheeks, forcing my nails to dig into the skin of his face so deep that I draw blood. "Just shut up, Caleb."

I claw against his cheeks, watching his reaction, failing again at predicting his actions—he allows me to do whatever the fuck I want, even if it means physically hurting him numerous times.

I feel the softness of his skin and how I puncture it, leaving behind small red marks. It feels a little uncomfortable because I am not used to…doing something like this. But the pleasure covers up the discomfort, taking advantage of it and causing new sensations to spread across my body.

Caleb was right. I enjoy hurting people.

Our chests rise and fall in unison as we gaze at each other. He doesn't avert his eyes—his stare is saturated with desire, hunger, and something else that resembles pride. Of course, he is fucking proud of me. He is the one who wanted to unleash my darkness. And if before I had trouble with keeping eye contact, now it's the only thing I want to do.

To watch. To enjoy what I see.

When I remove my hand from his cheeks, the blood is pouring out of both of them. The wounds are deeper than I intended, but he doesn't seem to care about it.

So I don't care, too.

I keep the right pace that drives us both crazy, feeling my orgasm building and building uncontrollably, enveloping my whole being in pleasant warmness as I near my ecstasy.

"That's right," he croons, giving not an ounce of fuck of the fact that the blood pours nearly from every inch of his face. "Ride me, baby. Let me tear that pretty pussy apart."

I grasp Caleb by his shoulders and draw him close to me. My nipples graze against his warm chest, eliciting another wave of pleasure to engulf me, resulting in a moan escaping my lips. I continue to move on top of him, my hands press into his shoulders, my nails digging into his tattoo. He moans as I slash into the skin on his back with all the force within me, as if I aim to tear that fucking tattoo from his skin.

"I want to fucking *kill* you," I say, feeling how tears sting my eyes as I continue causing him pain while he brings me to the edge. But no matter how much physical pain I may inflict on him, it can never compare to the pain he caused me.

I desire him, I long for him, I love him, but it will never erase the scar he left on my soul.

The world falls silent around me as I can only hear the cries of my shattered heart and soul, acknowledging that I will never be the same.

He bumps his forehead into mine. *"I'm yours."*

These two words are tapping into the deepest part of me, being the last thing that I hear clearly before the ringing consumes me from head to toe as I break apart, feeling like my pussy clenches around his cock, caging him as if I'm afraid that he would leave me.

I allow myself to completely let him consume me because I don't know how to exist without Caleb.

Because I don't *want* to exist without him.

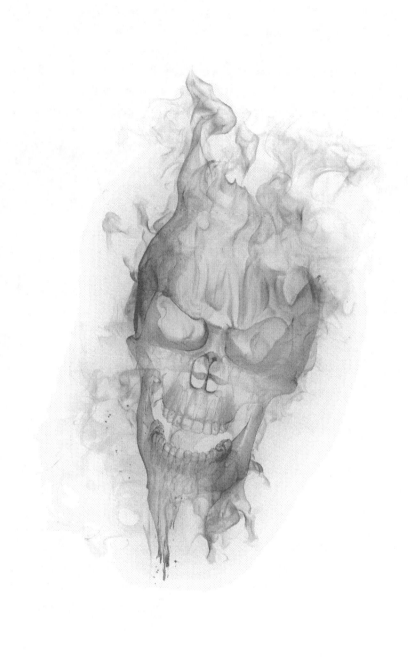

CHAPTER
THIRTY—SEVEN

Caleb

The air feels different today. Maybe it's what people usually call a *bad* feeling, as if something terrible is going to happen.

And it's not just because of last night, when Lilith fucked me like it was our last time, leaving her little marks all over my body as if she tried to cut me open and climb inside.

My entire body still hurts, reminding me of each bite, every scratch she left behind. To claim that it doesn't arouse me would be a lie. Witnessing her in this state—as an unleashed lioness ready to tear me apart and revel in it—sends a jolt of electricity through me, causing blood to rush to my cock as I yearn to experience that once again.

I've never had anything like this before. Every time I had sex with Lilith, it revolved around both of us—she was opening up, but slowly, without clawing against my skin like she wanted to peel it off me with her bare hands.

This seemed like a final step in her accepting her true self. The way her eyes surged with a multitude of emotions, where one stood out in vivid detail—love. She's the only person who has witnessed all of my facets, from the brighter to the darker ones, and she's the only one who stayed.

Who *chose* to stay.

For some reason, just when everything between us seems to be resolved, instead of waking up feeling content, I wake up with a sense of unease and paranoia. And for the record, I am not usually a paranoic.

Today is my day off, and I had hoped to think about the best way to spend it with Lilith, but the only thoughts that come to mind are these small, paranoid thoughts as if my gut instinct is attempting to ready me for something negative.

Everything started with the call I received from Grayson. It wasn't the first time he had called me during the weekend morning, but what struck me as unusual was that he had no apparent reason to call. We discussed some work stuff, but it wasn't something he already didn't know.

And the way his voice sounded—calm and unbothered—the total opposite of the Grayson I used to hear for the past couple of weeks.

"Who have you been talking to?" A tender voice flows through my ears, and while Lilith usually forces all negative emotions to evaporate without a trace, now she seems to amplify them instead. Because when I glance at her, something dreadful creeps inside my stomach as if signaling that she might be in danger.

"Grayson. I have no idea what the fucker wanted. He just called to blabber about the stuff he already knows." Something in her face changes as she looks down—the reaction I've seen before. "What was that?"

She looks to the side. "Uh, I just—"

I rise and close the space between us, placing my hands on her shoulders. "There's something I don't know?"

Her eyes whip to mine with a vivid worry flickering in them. "I didn't tell you that around a couple of months ago I met Grayson at the café when I was working."

My eyes narrow. "What café?"

"The one and only in Pinewood. I found it a bit strange because a man like him was visiting such a shitty neighborhood, you know," she explains. "And...well, he said that he wanted to grab a coffee, but he left without it."

The feeling of paranoia not only grows bigger—it takes over my insides, filling the cracks with unease and discomfort as my heartbeat immediately increases after her words. "Why didn't you tell me that, Lilith?"

A feeling of guilt takes over her features as she fixes her glasses before answering, "I'm sorry, I...I didn't know it was a big deal. I thought I was overreacting."

I draw her closer to me, my arms enveloping her delicate shoulders as I nestle my nose into her hair, breathing in her scent, seeking to absorb at least a hint of comfort from her. "It's fine, little devil," I reassure when it's anything but fucking fine.

I could never fully understand Grayson. I never even tried to. We were working together for a long time, and I took him for an annoying buzzing idiot, but nothing more. I let slide all the personal questions he was asking me, pushing it on the fact that he blindly believed that we were friends, and friends usually like to seek every detail in each other's life.

I feel like I've missed something. Underrated him.

I never paid attention to what he does for life, only caring about him being the main sponsor of my company. I provided him a seat on the board of directors, allowed him to be one of the main figures in my place, and for years I've been taking it for granted.

I let him be among my people because I needed him. No doubt he could use that to his advantage. Reflecting on the memory of his call, I try to understand what I've missed. Maybe there really isn't anything at all.

Maybe he was just playing for time.

"Pack a bag," I say before recoiling from Lilith and storming out of the bedroom.

"What?" she asks, a noticeable trace of confusion in her voice. "Why? What's going on?"

That's a good question because I honestly have no fucking idea. All I know is that we need to get out of here the sooner the better. Even if it's just my paranoia, it's always better to play it safe. "We need to get our asses out of here before something happens."

Lilith bumps into my back, trying to get my attention. "Caleb! Will you explain?"

I take hold of her hands and fix my gaze on her. "My love. Please. I'll answer all the questions later. Now we need to move out."

I feel like she wants to ask more questions, but thank God she just nods in agreement. "Okay."

Suddenly, our attention shifts as movement outside distracts both of us; the muffled voices are getting closer.

I guess there's no time for packing our bags.

"Who's there?" Lilith asks me in a hushed tone.

I wish I fucking knew. "Stay here." I give her a slight push into the bedroom and close the door, ignoring her frustrated sigh.

The loud banging on the door confirms my suspicions that whoever these people are, they're not here with friendly intentions. For the first time, I curse the fact that this house is nothing but fucking glass, making me visible wherever I go. But I don't waste any time. I peek into the living room and open the safe under the TV shelf, retrieving the gun stashed inside.

Glass explodes as the door is violently kicked in, and a clamor of footsteps floods the house. Swiftly, I tuck the gun behind my back, my expression steely as I take a few measured strides to confront the intruders. I emerge from the corner, my eyes locking on the three men in black who stand before me with unwavering intensity. "Invading my house, gentlemen?"

The tension in the air is palpable as we face off, each silently assessing the other's next move. The tallest man takes a step forward. His imposing figure is in stark contrast to his unexpectedly high-pitched, screechy voice as he says, "Get the girl."

I point the gun at the fucker who's already heading toward our bedroom. "Not so fast." I pull the trigger without thinking twice—one bullet flies straight into his forehead.

I shift my aim to the second one when something bumps into me from behind, the force causing me to fall and the gun to slip from my hands, flying somewhere to the side.

There are more of them, it seems.

My heart squeezes painfully as I watch the two men I had previously held at gunpoint storm into the bedroom in search of Lilith. A fierce protectiveness surges within me as I summon every ounce of strength, rising to my feet despite the weight of the two men still on my back, their bodies sliding down and colliding with each other.

Within seconds, I render each of them unconscious. Hearing the amid the mix of screams—one from Lilith and the other from one of the fuckers—I dash to the bedroom, picking up the gun I had dropped. They drag her out—the sight of it ignites a visceral rage within me. Blood trickles from the stomach of one of the fuckers as he grunts, struggling to maintain his grip on Lilith.

"Don't kill him!" he shouts to the tallest one who drops her when he sees me.

As I raise the gun, mere moments from pulling the trigger, something knocks me off balance. Another rat emerges from the corner of the house, and our bodies crash to the ground. Before I can fully process this sudden turn, both of their fists pummel my face. One, then a second time—accompanied by the sickening crack of bones, possibly my nose.

Despite the searing headache enveloping my head, I summon every iota of strength within me and deliver a forceful kick to one of them in the solar plexus, causing him to halt momentarily, giving me the opportunity to focus on the second fucker. I swiftly land a punch on his face—faster than he can react—and blood splatters across his features, dripping onto my face.

Something blurs my vision—whether it's my own blood, his, or a mixture of both—but I persist, landing blow after blow against his face, fracturing his bones much like he did to my nose.

The first fucker swiftly regains his strength, appearing to be a bit more powerful than any of his friends. In an instant, he dislodges me from his comrade and we begin to struggle for dominance, grappling and rolling back and forth on the floor.

"The boss ordered not to kill any of you, but I think he'll understand me when I bring him your head on the stick," he spits, and then I feel a sharp pain in my stomach that forces me to lose focus and to hold my breath.

He fucking stabbed me.

I grip his hands where he holds the knife and gather all of my force to prevent it from getting deeper, but I can't do much when the pain blinds me from head to toe, stealing my breaths. I observe his lips curl into a smirk just before the sound of a gunshot echoes.

One shot, then another.

The smirk vanishes from his face, replaced by a flow of blood pouring from his mouth as he begins to choke on it. I groan from pain when I roll his body off me, taking a look at the huge red stain on my hoodie along with the knife buried deeper than I thought.

"Caleb!" Lilith rushes to me, dropping to her knees in front of me, her gaze fixed on the knife lodged in my stomach. "Oh God. *Oh my God, Caleb.*"

I feel as though I'm teetering on the verge of blacking out. Every part of me is in agony—my face, my chest, my stomach, and my head. A burning pain courses through my skin, making every movement extremely difficult. "It's fine. I'm fine."

Her hands wrap around the knife handle and I scream before she does anything she'll regret later, "Don't pull it out!"

Lilith pulls her hands back. "Yeah, yeah. Sorry." She helps me to get up, holding me by my arm.

"Baby. Get the car keys."

Her breath quickens, bewildered eyes darting around the house, despite her efforts to keep a composed facade. "Where?"

"The shelf in the bedroom," I answer, biting my tongue to switch the pain, but compared to what I feel in my stomach and my face now, it's fucking flowers.

I lean against the wall as I watch her disappear into the bedroom. I quickly glance at the bodies on the floor, only now realizing that my Lilith had killed two men. Shot them in cold blood. A smile creeps into my features but I immediately cough—every muscle tightening—as the pain in the stomach grows more vivid with every second.

She returns within a second and wraps my hand around her shoulders. "Hold on to me. Let's go."

Every step is harder than a previous one for me, but I try to not show my pain because this is the last thing she needs to see.

"Take it slow baby, it's okay," she reassures. "We're going to get you to the hospital—"

"No," I interrupt—another wave of pain shoots through my whole body as I speak. "Not the hospital."

I have no doubts that Grayson has his people everywhere, including hospitals, and they would like to finish what they've started without thinking twice.

"Okay," she agrees, although her voice betrays her, telling me that she's not sure. "But where to?"

"We need to—"

Suddenly, I lose weight, collapsing on my knees, welcoming another zing of pain across my body from such an abrupt movement. The surroundings become nothing but a blurry vision as I realize that I am losing control.

Lilith's tender voice calling my name and begging me to hold on becomes more muffled with every second until I completely black out.

CHAPTER
THIRTY—EIGHT

Lilith

B lood coats my hands. I tremble violently as I grasp the collar of his hoodie, desperately attempting to keep him conscious.

"Caleb!" I call his name again, and again, obviously ineffective. "Baby, wake up! Just wake the fuck up!"

I keep shaking him, but he doesn't move. "Tell me what to do," I weep, my tears blending with the blood on his hoodie. "I don't know what to do. I don't know *what* to do, Caleb."

I have no clue what the fuck just happened and why Grayson sent his men to hunt us down. There was always something about him—the aura that frightened me, making my blood run cold. I guess, he is not a simple businessman.

A headache blossoms at my forehead as a myriad of thoughts inundate my mind, and one rises above the rest in its importance.

What do I do? I don't have anyone to ask for help. I don't even know anyone besides…my mother.

I promised myself that I wouldn't go back to that house.

Not now, not ever again.

But Caleb needs help. And if I don't provide it for him soon, he might die. And I doubt I can survive that. Grayson will pretty soon realize that his men are all dead—failed their mission, whatever it was. And then, he'll come for both of us.

I try to lift Caleb up, but how much I can do with a 6'8 massive pile of muscles? He is too big, and carrying his body and shoving it into the car seems like something impossible for me. Glancing at the garage, I realize it's not so far away. I'm wasting precious time standing here, succumbing to pointless hysteria.

It would be absurd to give up so easily.

The inhalation is a source of pain; the cold air stings my throat, the resultant discomfort spreading across my shivering form. With a surge of willpower, I lift his arm onto my shoulder and haul myself upright, dragging him along with me.

"Come on, you can do it," I talk to myself, trying to ignore how fucking heavy he is. "You can fucking do it, Lilith."

And I do it. After a third attempt, I successfully opened the garage and maneuvered him into the backseat.

As I lower myself into the driver's seat, incredulity washes over me at my success. A smile insidiously appears on my face as I transfer the gun—which I grabbed before we left the house—from my pants to the passenger seat. I then insert the key into the car with trembling hands, start the engine, and only then realize that I don't quite know how to drive such a modern vehicle. Panic begins to seep into my mind, but I shake my head.

I've achieved what once seemed impossible to me before, and succumbing to fear now would be a fucking absurd, especially just because I've never driven a Range Rover.

"God motherfucking damn it," I hiss. Trying to figure out which buttons I should and shouldn't press is really challenging. I place my hands on the steering wheel and press the gas pedal, letting out a loud gasp and immediately retracting my feet as the car lurches forward with indescribable force. "Relax."

This time I press my feet on the gas pedal more delicately. It's a miracle when I start driving. Sloppy and unprofessional, mainly because of fear, and the speed of the car that makes it easy to lose control and crash into a tree. But as I finally drive down the hill, and get onto a normal, straight road, I gain more confidence.

Now, allowing myself to turn on the map right in the car and find directions to my mother's place. When I had a feeling that the area looked similar to my mother's, it wasn't just a feeling. She literally lives fifteen minutes from here. I step on the gas pedal as hard as I can, the sense of urgency weighing heavily on my mind.

As I glance at the unmoving Caleb still with the knife deep in his stomach, I can't shake the feeling that I don't want him to die. I spent so much time hating and denying him, allowing myself to think that as soon as I had a chance, I'd kill him myself or give him into the hands of the police. But when I have a chance to let him die, it's the last thing I want.

Maybe because I've just accepted him. Allowed myself to be his forever.

What I do is probably stupid and unforgivable because a person like him deserves to die for how many lives he's taken. Saving him when my mind realizes the situation makes me his accomplice, a person that even worse than he is.

But I don't care.

It's a frightening sensation, just like all the other emotions he stirred up in me, but it's the one I choose to accept.

I ARRIVE AT MY MOTHER'S HOUSE IN LESS THAN FIVE MINUTES, NAR-rowly avoiding hitting her mailbox with the bumper. The lights are on inside, a sight that brings me relief. After parking, I step out of the car, open the backseat door, and lift Caleb out with care.

"We're almost there," I whisper, though I know he can't hear me. I just wish he could.

The doors click open before we even reach them.

"What is this? Lilith?" My mother's voice is as unfriendly as always, but I don't care at this moment.

"I need your help," I mumble, bypassing her and entering the house without permission. I make my way to the kitchen table and place his body on it, ignoring my mother's questions and gasps. I just need to move him, or my arms will fall off.

"God help us!" Mother screams, crossing herself. "Who is this man? What are you doing in my house with him?"

I don't know how this messed up thought crossed my mind, but without a doctor, there isn't much I can do. I head to the living room, my eyes immediately locking with the shocked expression of the woman on the couch, sitting there unmoving. I ignore her, kneeling in front of the shelf where my mother usually kept her sewing kit, recalling her frustrated sighs each time I failed at im-proving my sewing skills.

"Ayla, I'm so sorry," Mother sighs. "I have no idea what trou-ble she's gotten herself into."

Oh, Ayla. The neighbor with the precious child.

"Bring me the peroxide and ethanol," I mutter as I dig through the pile of unnecessary stuff my mother insists on keeping, grow-ing increasingly frustrated by the passing seconds.

"I said—"

"STOP!" My response is abrupt; every second of hearing her voice brings rising heat to my stomach. "Just bring me what I fucking asked for!"

It's the first time I've spoken to my mother like that. Major changes in just a few months.

"I'll get it," Ayla murmurs, her voice barely audible.

When I finally find the kit, I sigh in relief. Gathering all the supplies, I lay them out on the counter beside Caleb. With all my strength, I carefully remove the knife from his wound, trying to ignore the sickening sound of blood flowing, that is making me queasy.

With the scissors, I cut his hoodie in half, exposing the wound. Blood spills out, and I bite down on my cheek to steady myself and control the trembling, saving the panic for another time.

"We need to get him to the hospital," Ayla says, as if standing here and playing surgeon is my little fucking wish.

"Don't even think about that," I say with authority, my voice firm and filled with warning.

"Oh, God," Mother groans, slapping a hand against her forehead. "Is someone following you both?"

I select the thinnest needle from my mother's kit, carefully threading it—a task I had always struggled with in the past. Despite my trembling hands, I miraculously manage it on the first try, without much effort.

"They're not coming here, don't worry." I glance at both of them for a brief moment. "If you're going to keep asking questions I won't answer, leave."

"I won't watch this.' Mother sighs, taking Ayla's hand. "Let's go."

As they leave, I'm struck by the absurdity of the situation. It feels like only now am I realizing how we ended up here. Just when things were beginning to feel normal, Grayson had to come along and ruin it. I can't help but feel guilty, as if informing Caleb about

Grayson's visit earlier and sharing my concerns might have prevented all this.

But I can't turn back time, nor allow myself to stand here and tear myself apart with pointless guilt. Right now, Caleb needs me more than ever. Just like I need him.

I exhale deeply, steeling my nerves as I lean in close to the wound, carefully positioning the needle at the edge. With determined focus, I pierce the skin, pushing past my own apprehension. Stitch by stitch, I methodically bring the wound together, my movements growing more assured with each pass. Finally, as the last knot is secured, I step back. Relief floods through me, bringing a comforting sense of satisfaction.

As I start cleaning the wounds on his face, I methodically wash and disinfect each area, ensuring no part of his skin is overlooked. His chest rises and falls in steady breaths, reminding me he's still alive. I brush my fingers across his forehead, moving the falling strands of his soft hair to the side.

"You'll be fine," I whisper, placing a kiss on the corner of his lips.

Entering the living room, I find my mother and Ayla still wearing looks of shock.

"Do you have any antibiotics?" I ask, directing my question to my mother.

Her loud sigh fills the silence. "In the bathroom."

I hurry to the bathroom, searching through the shelves. I find a half-filled bottle of antibiotics, but nothing else of use, just an abundance of Xanax pills stashed in every nook and cranny, as if my mother feared they'd vanish by tomorrow, buying dozens just in case.

With urgency, I grab the needle and the antibiotics, swiftly returning to the kitchen. I inject it into Caleb's hand, hoping he'll awaken soon.

"Aren't you going to explain who the fuck he is?" I roll my eyes, though she can't see me. Mother doesn't care if I'm okay after stitching him up. She's just irritated I bothered her.

"My boyfriend," I reply shortly.

I feel her grin on my back. "Like I'd believe someone's actually interested in you."

For the first time, I feel nothing when she emphasizes the last word with obvious disgust. I've found someone ready to kill for me, and now her attempts to make me feel worthless have no effect.

"Help me move him to the couch," I say, ignoring her idiotic statement.

"No. I won't move this...stranger onto my favorite couch," she retorts.

"Better to have him on the kitchen table where the windows are bigger, Mom?"

Her teeth click shut. She comes closer to Caleb, and Ayla appears behind her.

Good. The more hands, the better.

They help me move Caleb to the couch, where I make him comfortable, adjusting the pillow and fetching the blanket I used to cherish during my time living here. Straightening up, I smooth the creases on my clothes.

"I'm going to get more medicine for him," I announce.

"You aren't going anywhere until I hear an explanation," my mother retorts.

I'm already at the front door, ignoring her, but my eyes quickly whip to Ayla. "I'm going to be back very soon. Please, don't do anything. Don't call the cops. Don't call an ambulance. You aren't the target, but if you make a call, no doubt you will be."

That sounded like a threat, but there's nothing I can do. They deserve to know this isn't a game, and I don't want all my efforts to be for nothing. Stepping outside, I freeze immediately.

"Do you have any cash?" I ask abruptly.

"I won't give you anything, not when you're bringing trouble into my house," Mother states firmly.

"Mom, please. I'll pay you back—"

"You're funny," she mocks derisively.

Ayla steps forward and stretches out her wallet. "Here."

My mother's smile evaporates. "Ayla? What the hell are you doing?"

I give Ayla a warm smile and mouth *thank you* before quickly leaving the house, avoiding my psychotic mother catching me and taking the wallet back.

When I get into the car, a newfound sense of confidence about driving settles over me. Starting the engine, I glance at the gun on the passenger seat, silently praying I won't have to use it again. As my mother's house fades into the distance, a realization hits me.

I had taken the lives of two men in Caleb's house. When they burst into the bedroom, I was prepared, with a knife hidden under my pillow. I fought back, managing to wound one of them, but they still dragged me out forcefully. The sight of the gun brought me a sense of relief, and I didn't hesitate to use it. I shot them without hesitation, saving both Caleb and myself from harm.

And I'm only realizing it now. Probably because I was in shock before. What do people usually feel after something like this? Because I don't feel anything. After all, those bastards invaded our house.

I won't have to travel far to reach the nearest pharmacy. I just need to get out of this isolated path and these woods, which I'm already tired of. Glancing in the rearview mirror, I notice a black truck right behind me. Muttering curses quietly to myself, I realize my recklessness. It would be better to use my mother's truck because Grayson's dogs are likely familiar with Caleb's vehicle. I've just put a target on my back by cluelessly getting into his car.

When I cast a quick glance at the gun, I mentally brace myself for the possibility of using it once more. If the truck closes in, I could attempt to target the tires or the gas tank inlet, though the second option could cause an explosion that might kill me in the immediate aftermath. So the tires are the best option.

As the truck accelerates, I step on the gas pedal, pushing the vehicle to its limits and grabbing the gun. In no time, it overtakes me and crashes into my side, nearly causing me to lose control.

"Fuck you!' I scream and execute the same maneuver, turning the steering wheel to collide with the truck, causing the driver to lose control and veer off the straight road. I'm so preoccupied that I fail to notice another truck approaching from the opposite direction. I only become aware of its presence when its shadow falls over me.

I turn my head just in time to see it collide with my car, shattering the glass and sending shards flying into my face. Blinded and disoriented, I struggle to maintain control as my car swerves erratically. Despite my efforts to steer, I can't discern my direction or surroundings.

Finally, as the car stops spinning, my heart sinks as I realize my glasses are gone, shattered and scattered somewhere amid the chaos. I can't feel much, only able to hear the pounding in my ears. The ceiling blurs into the floor, disorienting me further, but determination fuels my next move.

My hand fumbles across the debris-strewn ground until it lands on the familiar, chilling touch of cold steel. A glint of hope sparks inside me as I steady the grip, finding a small comfort in the weight of the gun amidst the turmoil.

When I shift, an excruciating pain shoots through my entire body, forcing a gasp to slip past my lips. Quick to silence myself with a hand over my mouth, I can't help but wonder if anyone outside heard. Fumbling about, I grope for a door handle, only to find it obstinately unyielding. However, the windows have been shattered, so I make a desperate attempt to extract myself from the car, ignoring the piercing shards of glass that tear into my chest and stomach.

Helpless without my glasses, I can't remain in the car, fearing it could explode at any moment.

The pain coursing through my body is overwhelming. If I was in shock a moment ago, I now feel every bit of it. It's pervasive—every part of my body hurts—and the pain intensifies with the biting cold of winter air. It feels like needles piercing me while I struggle to figure out where to crawl.

"I told you to take her unharmed, you fucking idiots!" The rough voice makes my blood run cold as I widen my eyes, sensing him close.

I continue to crawl, biting the inside of my cheeks to divert my attention from the agony coursing through my body. The gun remains tightly gripped in my palm.

In a matter of moments, he closes in—his heavy footsteps drawing near—and I am unable to react swiftly enough when he steps on my hand, compelling me to release my grip on the gun. The pain is overwhelming, and I sense I may have cut my hand too deeply in my attempt to escape.

As I release the gun, a whimper escapes my lips. Grayson kneels down, picks up my weapon, and tilts his head.

"Well, hello, darling."

FOR MY READERS

ANXIETY KICKS ME IN THE GUTS WHEN I REALIZE THAT YOU GOT TO this page. Thank you for taking the time to read this book. However this story has made you feel, I would greatly appreciate it if you left a review on Amazon or Goodreads. For you, it may seem like a small gesture, but for me as an author, every word is important.

Your attention means the world to me.

ABOUT THE
AUTHOR

Valeriia Miller is an author from Ukraine.

Her passion for dark romance novels and crime thrillers ignited a fire within her soul and encouraged her to create stories as soon as she started her second year of college.

She likes to explore the complexities of human relationships, diving into the themes of obsession and blurred lines between love and madness; creating complex characters with different issues.

Her biggest dream is to escape her small town and continue writing twisted stories somewhere in a big, noisy city.

Follow her on social media for updates and news: @valeriia-millerauthor

MORE BOOKS BY VALERIIA MILLER

Made in the USA
Middletown, DE
14 October 2024

62584765R00197